JOHN HENRY
THE REVELATOR

A Novel By

CONSTANTINE VON HOFFMAN

For more information, address:cvon@areporter.com.

First paperback edition December 2020

Book design by Priya Paulraj
Cover design by Charlene Mosley

ISBN 978-1-7363317-0-5 (paperback)
ISBN 978-1-7363317-1-2 (ebook)

www.curseyoukhan.com

**All proceeds from the sale of this book are donated to
the Equal Justice Initiative
www.EJI.org**

For Jennifer

You make it possible

Who's that writin'
John the Revelator
Who's that writin'
John the Revelator
Who's that writin'
John the Revelator
Wrote the book of the seven seals

> —Son House, *John theRevelator*

John Henry he could hammer
He could whistle, he could sing
He went to the mountains early in the morning
To make his hammer ring

> —*John Henry, Steel Driving Man (Trad.)*

1

What are you scared of when nothing can hurt you?

Everything.

The day we heard Uncle Roscoe was in jail I was 15 and mostly scared of what was usual for my age: Girls. Also, my father when he gave me a "don't push me" look, disappointing my mother, my voice cracking, Reverend Williams who'd send me to hell if he knew I had a crush on his daughter, Blanche, and afraid of her because of what she'd do if I told her. My regular fears, always there, but on that day, I was mostly scared of time running out.

Two hundred miles from us in Tuskegee to Hicksville, in Georgia where they had my uncle.

Didn't much care for Roscoe, momma's only brother. Fortunate he wasn't around much. Few times he was he'd slapped me for "sassing." I'm eight, smacks me on the face, said it never happened when momma asked him. I'm12, he did it again but had my powers then and he sprained his fingers bad. Major problem for Roscoe as it prevented him from playing guitar. He's a traveling man, getting money playing roadhouses and juke joints, so that cost. Surly when sober and mean when drunk but momma loved him no matter.

Not his first time in jail, no. Arrested for drunk and disorderly, vagrancy, stabbing a man, and beating a girl. Momma's love for Rosco didn't make her a fool, had no doubt he'd done all those. But this time it was rape. Or attempted rape – didn't make any difference because cops said was white woman involved. Even I knew he didn't do it. Was an asshole, not an idiot.

When daddy told momma, she dropped into a chair like she'd been shot. "Lord, please no," all she could say. Daddy and me traded looks. All of us knew me being only 15 didn't matter, I was only chance of Roscoe getting to live.

Least five hours drive. No highways like today, just back roads. Five hours at top speed and couldn't do that. Black and driving too fast means some cracker sheriff pulls you over. Be clear, we weren't black then. Colored or Negroes and only if we're lucky.

Drive slow or do the speed limit no guarantee of anything either. Cops want they get you driving, walking, or sitting still at your own house. What's the charge? Whatever they want. Sometimes it was not being from "around here," an area defined by a cop's mood. Maybe out of state, out of town, in town but wrong neighborhood, or right neighborhood and he doesn't know you. Being from around here didn't always make things better but not from around here always made it worse.

Didn't help my father's car was new. Rare enough anyone driving one during the Depression but one of us? It must be stolen and if it wasn't then we shouldn't have it anyway. Day my father brought it home Uncle Stanley, his brother, called it trouble. "Maybe forgive you for stealing a new car but never for owning one."

If we didn't get stopped too much we had about enough time to get there, maybe. If my parents' wishes were true. About six hours until sunset and they kept saying lynchers wouldn't come before then. Had to say it. Otherwise, nothing we could do at all.

Lynchings happened when they happened, night and noon and any other time. Whatever time it was was a wrong one. Mobs didn't make sense. Sometimes a few days all the whites to work themselves up for hanging or burning someone alive. Other times it faster than snap your fingers. How much sense is there in people wanting to watch someone twitch and struggle and beg for their life when running out of air or skin burning off?

Didn't only need the mob to wait until sundown so we could get there. Also needed night for a chance to get away. You can disappear in the night with a little work. I can do a lot but not everything. Can't fly or run so fast no one can see. Not me. Faster than any normal but mostly I'm strong and can't get hurt. So, driving there and back, hopefully with Roscoe, we'd need night for hiding.

Daddy drove. I wasn't old enough.

"Old enough to break Roscoe out of jail but can't drive?" I said and started laughing.

Grim little chuckle came from daddy. I kept laughing until it must have been too long. Pulled the car over, grabbed me, looking intense into my eyes.

"Moses? Mo?"

Finally got my attention. "Breathe. Breathe slow. Real slow." Kept saying until I was able to.

"I know this is scary. I'm scared, too. No one's ever done anything like this before because no one else could. That doesn't make it any easier. You've never been a fighter. Me either. Not in a knock-someone-down way, anyway. Imagine me hitting someone?"

Wasn't as impossible for me as he thought. Whipped me when I was younger, both of us crying the whole time.

Something changed hearing that. Until then he was my father, and I knew he could lick anyone. But now saw him as he was, not as I wanted. Short, not only compared to me. About six three then and he was likely eleven inches less. Pudgy, bald, thick glasses, thicker than the ones I used to wear. Still my father though and a way he'd always be bigger, better than me.

"Not unless they sassed you," I said with a small laugh, wiping some tears away because after laughter stopped crying started.

"We're going to do this thing. It's going to be OK. You're young but you know what you can do. I'll drive up, you go in and get him and we'll leave. Quick and simple." Held on to that like Gospel for the next few hours. Faith is whatever gets you through.

Pulled back on the road and that's when a red light started flashing.

What's a cop do all that time in his car? Likely nothing. Sit, check if buttons buttoned, hat straight, crumbs on the seat. Anything to make a wait longer, so you start to think and worry. Show who has power here.

Got nervous quick, started looking in the rear view over and over.

"Just sit. No matter what he said. Just sit. And be quiet."

Cop walked up to daddy's window and I took a quick look at him. Some whites all look alike. This was one of those: muddy brown hair, corpse-pale skin, and nothing particular about the face.

"Where y'all going?"

"Only a little ways into Georgia, suh. Visitin' family over ta Pine Manor." A smile in my father's voice, an eagerness to please, never heard before. "Did I do somethin' wrong, suh?"

"Well, I'll see about that. Lemme see your license and registration."

"Sure thing officer! Don't mean to keep you waitin'."

My father Tomming. Seen him talk to cops but he'd never done this.

"Nice car you got. New. Don't see many new cars."

"Yassuh, I got lucky. Cain't afford no nothing like this." Said like anyone would be surprised at him in a new car. "Won it at raffle."

"Raffle?"

"Yes, sir. Big church raffle. Baptist church in our town gots hit by lightnin' and folks was mighty generous helping out and buildin' it back. Pastor's brother runs a car store ta next town over."

"They let niggers buy a ticket?"

"No, sir, not alls of us. Jes my church. See we is National Baptist and ta other church, one hits by lightnin', dey American Baptist and so dey always nice for us." Daddy's smile got any wider top of his head would have fallen off. The tomming had me scared, like a world deciding to spin in another direction. Didn't even think of how I could crush that cop and nothing he could do to stop me. Afraid isn't about facts.

Cop nodded, then back to his car with papers. Waited. Cop knows time for a weapon.

"Daddy?"

"Don't say anything right now."

"But ..."

"Shut up." He was angry, almost to tears. "Damn you, Roscoe."

A minute dripped by, then another. In each I heard a hundred different sounds, imagined thousand more. Twig breaking or gun cocking? Car in the distance more police cars? Even birdsong made me jumpy. Didn't help I could hear things a mile away if I wanted.

"Breathe," my father said, and I did. Hadn't even noticed I wasn't.

Finally, a police car door opening and slow, even crunch of hob-nailed boots on gravel. Cop throws the license and a ticket through the window.

"Drive slow." Already walking away, not caring if we heard or not. Smashed a tail light with his nightstick. "Get that fixed!"

Waited until we pulled back on the road, followed us to the town line.

That happened sometimes, too. Never knowing if it was trouble or nothing makes it worse. Can't plan or do anything to avoid. Instead, always on a lookout, worrying, wondering. Do it all the time and still not enough. Something always gets by. Week before, buying something, white lady gives me too much change back. Give it back and she smiles and says, "Looky that, a honest nigger." Like a compliment. Could have torn the entire building down onto her. Instead I'm feeling like a little piece of shit she was going out of her way to be nice to. Her power, being white, somehow stronger than mine.

What she had, what they all have, what's behind them is the laws, money, being in charge. Could be a shit-brained street cleaner and he walks in the world with all that going for him. Not all lined up to help him, but at least not lined up to stop him. Go in to a bank about a loan and at least listened to, not already rejected because never to those people no matter anything. Maybe luckies his way into money. Maybe can't go everywhere he wants because stink of poor is on him so hard. Still, go more places than us with college, manners, money, and all. People don't cross the street to get away. Don't yell at him to cross the street. Go into a store, no one asks why. Police not always on, ready to beat, kill, or jail, on account of what they decide "isn't right" about him. Everyone's first think isn't 'he's a thug, his daughter a whore.' Don't go all day thinking about how to say, walk, look, so *they* won't be upset. Has the power of benefit of the doubt. That's a big, big power. Power of life itself.

Don't think?

Here's one: Means doctors don't automatically see a junkie or someone getting upset over nothing because you know how *they* are. Pays attention to what's going on in heart, lungs, or other parts, and treats him. Doubt it? Look much sooner the people die than anyone else. Benefit of the doubt gets you hired, promoted, warning not a ticket, ticket not an arrest, a smile not 'fuck you,' a school, a place to live, a seat at the table. Every word of this is fact, lived through every damn, stupid day. Not opinion, not self-pity, not something fixed by 'just work harder.' Because we're lazy, right? Weren't lazy we'd be doing better. What everyone knows, right? What everyone don't know, what everyone don't want to know because knowing it would shatter their world: We can't afford lazy. Know how many jobs the people have to have just to have be as bad off as they are? Takes so much work just to hold on by the fingertips. Benefit of the doubt means you don't have to work twice as much so someone thinks you're working at all. Ever see one of the people, a lady, who's a doctor? Sign up fast. Good couldn't get her all that, requires she's great.

That's power they have: Power always must be reckoned because can't be killed, can't be hurt, can destroy. Invisible to them but clear to everyone else. Not always invisible. See it clear they think any is going to someone else. Then they see clearly they're the victims. The people out to get them. Say treating anyone else equal means something stolen from them.

What the people need is a power like that. What they got was me.

Told my father about what that lady said to me. Both being scared freed us up to talk to each other like people, not so much like father and son. Told him about Blanche and being afraid of her and her father. Told me he'd felt same about my mother and her father.

"Your mother's father – Jordan – was big, like you. Well, not quite that big. And all those scars of his made him look even meaner." Let out a little laugh. "Nicest guy in the world if he liked you. And you weren't white."

Never met him but I'd seen his scars. My grandparents were all slaves but the other three were kids when it ended. Jordan about 20 when the war was over. Was a terror to his owners, just look what they did to his back. Escaped a couple of years into the war and came back in General Sherman's army, wearing the conqueror's uniform, and a sneer. Sherman only white Jordan ever liked. Only complaint was the general didn't burn, loot more. There's a photo of Jordan, shirt off, army hat on, looking over his shoulder. His back dirty with scars on top of scars on top of scars.

"I get frightened just looking at the photograph," I said.

"I don't blame you, but he'd have loved you had he met you. That man truly adored children. Nearly as much as he hated white people. Night riders killed him for it. At least 60 years old and still scared them so much they had to send a couple of dozen bastards to get him." Been hearing the story all my life and always ready to hear it again.

I looked out the window, trying not to think where we're going and why. Spring, Air thick and wet and green. Roads all two-lane blacktops, so narrow felt we might scrape anything driving the other way. Trees leaned in and over the road, so it was like an outdoor tunnel.

Not a lot of traffic in front of us but what was always seemed to be a farmer with a truck carrying too many chickens or pigs or hay piled so high and wide a wonder it didn't fall off. They'd go so slow almost didn't seem to be moving, then up hills went slower.

Any type of fast wouldn't have been enough, but we got stuck behind one of those trucks my father's knuckles went white holding the steering wheel so hard. Shoulders and head hunched up and leaning forward like he could make whatever was in front of us go faster. Wouldn't be any cars going the other way unless daddy started sneaking out to pass, then someone always came burning out of nowhere, riding their horn to scare the devil.

Sun all but down when we arrived. Looked for anything to show Roscoe's alive or dead. Don't know what I expected. Short of a body hanging from a street light no way to know if there'd been a lynching. Daddy pulled into an alley and we waited on more night to come. When it did, he pulled out and stopped about a block from the town hall.

"You know what you're going to do?"

"In the front door, find out where Roscoe is and bring him back. Somehow."

"Just like that."

Couldn't move. Couldn't lift my hand to open the door or turn my head. Staring at the dashboard but I wasn't seeing it.

"I can't," I whispered. All too much for me. Was saying "I can't" over and over, then crying. Felt dirty from shame. People depending on me and I'd gone coward. World gone huge in my head, making me nothing to it but small and afraid. No reason to this. I could pick an anvil up with one hand – but my mind didn't care. I was lost seeing how I couldn't do this. I'd do it wrong. All be my fault. It's impossible. All that ran through me so fast I couldn't even grab the words needed to say something. Sobbed harder and harder and it was never going to stop.

First thing felt that wasn't fear was my father holding me. Arm across my chest, other across my back because he couldn't reach all the way around. Holding me. Got me to come back from wherever I'd been.

"It's alright," he was saying, at first from far, far away but getting closer. Said it over and over, slowly and slowly, it got me, and I stopped saying "I can't."

Could see again. The nothing I'd been looking at turned into the dashboard. Then could move my eyes to look around. Felt my body, the breathing, the heart pushing in an out, the sweat covering me all. Felt exposed, skin gone, nerves waiting to flinch. Finally, able to move my hand and put it against the car window to feel the nice, cool glass.

My father put his hands on my face and slowly, gently turned my head, so we were looking each other. Sat like that a bit, until I nodded to let him know I thought I was OK. Wasn't. Couldn't be. No one could. Guess reassuring him let me reassure myself.

"All you have to do is try. Do that and no matter what happens you can't do anything wrong. As long as you come back nothing else matters."

Nodded, sat longer, then reached up and pulled the door handle but didn't move to get out.

"Do what you've got to and devil take the rest."

Looked at him another moment.

"And don't forget to breathe."

I exhaled, started out of the car, paused.

"I don't like Uncle Roscoe."

"That's because you're no fool. You're a good man."

Wearing clothes I did my chores in, a work shirt, jeans, a pair of boots. Afterward stories where I wore a costume and a mask. Never happened. Not then or ever. Kluxers wear masks.

Walked down the street and outside sounds faded away again. Chirps of crickets and birds replaced by heart beating like a fast-picking bass. Didn't even hear me opening the police station door. Two cops knew one of them said something from watching his jaw move. Then stood up looking agitated. No matter to me. Walked past him to the iron-barred door at the back of the room.

Something that felt like a flyswatter hit the back of my head. Didn't hurt but same time my hearing clicked back to normal. Turned and saw that cop who'd been talking right behind me, broken nightstick in one hand.

"... God damn nigger! ..."

Big. Almost big as me. Few years older. Probably played football at high school not too long past. Slapped him across the face hard. Too hard. Scared and didn't know any better. He spun, hit off a desk, on to the floor, then didn't move at all. All I thought was he was on the floor right where I'd have to step over to get out.

Saw the other cop now, his pistol out. Would getting shot hurt much? Curious, not worried. Bullets hit me in the stomach were a gentle tap.

Walked towards him and he kept shooting. Yelling something but I didn't pay much attention. Grabbed the pistol's barrel and squeezed until it looked like a beer can got run over. Cop shouted more of the usual shit at me, but I didn't care. Not angry. Didn't want to hurt him, just him to leave me alone. Got to say to a white person what I'd wanted all my life: "Shut up."

He dropped the gun and ran.

Went back to the barred door and pulled it from the wall. Roscoe wasn't hard to find. Six cells and no one in the other five. Passed out on a cot, cuddling an empty jug stinking of moonshine. Got me thinking better of those cops. Letting him get drunk before being lynched almost a decent thing to do. Better than expected by a long way.

Put Roscoe over my shoulder. His small skinny didn't weigh at all to me. Walked out, stepping over that cop's body just like I thought.

Outside quiet. Feeling alright, walking to the car with excitement adrenalin getting me to think how good I'd done. Stuck on myself, so not paying attention to anything otherwise I'd heard the cars.

First I notice was headlights behind me making my shadow fall halfway down the block. Then sounds: brakes hit hard, doors opening, people getting out.

Someone yelled what they always yell at us and I turned around. A shot, another and another and more until they were all one long sound. Terror came again and I went to the ground on top of Roscoe. Crowd screaming everything and worse. Began feeling like in the car but did a big breath and paid attention to bullets hitting me. Started laughing. Hurt now more than rain. Got up, took and Roscoe to the car. Opened the door to put him in the back seat and saw glass all over it. Bullets must have hit the rear window.

"You OK?" Shouted to my father. Said something I couldn't really make out because a pick-up truck pulled right up behind us. Looked into the headlights and wondered why they hadn't run in to me.

Still not even angry. Curious, mostly. Wondered for a while what it'd be like to let it go and slam something as much as I could. Hit the truck about half-way between the headlights. Lousy punch, all wrong. One thrown by a 15-year-old only ever seen fights in movies. Didn't matter.

Truck started moving backward fast and didn't stop until it hit something couple of blocks down away. Shut all of them folks up.

I took a step toward the crowd and yelled, "Go away!"

Another thing always wanted to say.

They ran and I felt joy like never in my life before.

2

Jumped into the back next to Roscoe, then daddy drove away. Stared back through the shot-out window, people running and screaming. Of course they were. Nightmare they'd had for generations was on the streets and laughing hard.

My adrenalin turned to talk. Chatter coming like water and a hose. Kept up until got out into country, and daddy pulled the car off the road half way to nowhere.

"Why are we stopping? I'm OK. Keep going!" Didn't listen for an answer, instead looking out the windows into the night. Scrub pine and fields no one was doing anything with. Far away, far even with my vision, a small light in a small house.

Remember asking why we stopped a bunch of times but don't trust that memory. Maybe it was once, maybe a dozen times. Remember better what didn't happen than what did. Know I didn't ask, "Are you all right?" Maybe already knew.

Eventually slowed down, stopped talking and looked into the front seat at daddy, finally pay attention to someone beside me.

Blood his white shirt from a hole in his chest. Couldn't understand what I was seeing. It was long way away and close all at once. Can't be dead. Impossible. The whole scene intolerable, so focused on little parts. Blood highlighting texture of the starched shirt like canvas ready for painting. His tie a little off center bothered me. Wanted to straighten it but didn't. Couldn't understand why there was no blood on it. Stared at it, trying to figure out how this could be. Then even the whole tie was too much for me and focused on his Mason's pin. He wore it high on his tie and seeing it in the correct place gave some sense to my crumbling world. After a bit, my eyes followed the tie up and I noticed his head was flopped over on his shoulder.

"That can't be comfortable," I thought.

He's small and broken all of a sudden. He'd needed protecting and I should have given it to him but too late. Now wanted him hugging me again, saying again everything would be OK. Wanted to take him in my arms, so easy to carry. Carry us away to some time when none of this was. Couldn't. Trapped in a life where my father is dead.

How long was I crouched in the backseat? No way to know. Long enough to know I'd stopped crying even though I couldn't remember starting. That night I learned about time, how it slows down or speeds up or even almost stops whenever it wants. Capricious time doing as it wants and all you can hope for is noticing.

Out of the car now, sitting against a front tire, trying not to think when a voice comes out of the back seat, Roscoe's voice, and time decides to be back to normal.

"What you crying about?"

"Daddy's dead."

"Where the fuck are we?" Roscoe, out of the car, looking around.

"I said, 'Daddy's dead.'"

"Heard you. Not shit I can do about that now, is there?"

"He died because we got you out of jail," I said, thinking he didn't understand.

"Heard that," he said then did something rare, paused to think. "How the hell you get me out anyway?"

"Your fault he's dead. You got my father killed."

"How the hell you blame me? Minding my own affairs. Having a sip and waiting for the crackers to come kill me." Laughed a little like he couldn't believe he was alive.

"We wouldn't have had to be there if you hadn't got into trouble with some white woman." So angry I even repeated the lie, one we all grew up with. One used to kill us any time.

"White woman? No white woman. Only cracker in all this is one owns the road house. Didn't want to pay all he owed me. Said I was no good with the joint full every night for two weeks. Every night. Not pay ME. Showed him."

"Showed him what?"

"Damn, that shit's shot all to gone."

Looked over and saw Roscoe was around looking at the back of the car. "All those bullets an' only one got your daddy? Some bad luck is what it was."

"SHOWED HIM WHAT?

"Yeah, right. Didn't want his friends knowing where he got his money and how much time he was with us. I go over his grocery store. First, I go back door like I know to. He laughs, shuts the door on me. Piss me right off. I go around out front the store and start telling anyone about his string of girls and which white folks was seeing them all the time."

Took a long pause, shook his head.

"Stupid. Stupid. Stupid! Get riled up and don't think right. Taken what I got and left like everyone was telling me. No surprise police come, put a beating on and take me to jail. Knew it was gonna happen. Whole time I was yelling my stuff knew it was going to happen. But couldn't stop myself. Just had enough."

Wanted to crush his stupid little skull right then but started crying and he let it go on.

"Sorry 'bout him," he said, nodding toward the front seat. "Don't know why Sis liked him but she did. Man never had a day of fun in his life. Work, all he was about, work. Did love Sis though, give him that. Mean as she is, never thought anyone would marry her."

"Mean?" So wrong a word it derailed my grief. Seen her tough but never mean.

"Mean. Always riding me, kicking my ass to get up, do chores when I was barely old enough for walking. Never do anything right by her. No one else could either, until she met your daddy. Maybe they liked being with someone else who'd never laugh."

Never thought of my mother as someone's big sister before, what she might be like.

"She laughs all the time. I can make her laugh," I said, with more than a little superiority.

"Well, ain't you special." Paused and sighed.

"Maybe she doesn't like you," I said, knowing it wasn't true. Loved him didn't mean she approved.

At that the conversation stopped. Its ability to distract run out.

"How am I going to tell momma?" started whispering to myself over and over until Roscoe yelled at me.

"Shit, we got trouble now and you're going and getting more from tomorrow?"

Nodded to his point.

"How'd you get me out of there anyway?"

Question too big to answer, so I didn't. Daddy and I hadn't talked about what to do after getting Roscoe, except putting him on a train going north. Hadn't given a thought to how to explain me, because it couldn't be done.

Car went around looking at the car, seeing how torn up it was. "Nah, really, what *the fuck* happened?"

"Got shot up when we were leaving Hicksville," I said, not really answering.

"Looks lit up by tommy guns."

Change the subject.

"You have to drive us home. I don't know how."

Roscoe laughed so loud it startled.

"Car ain't going nowhere. Even it could move imagine how far we'd get. Couple of darkies driving a shot up car with a dead man in it? Kill me right now and save time. Nah, nah. This? Dump it in the river. If it gets found figure it was Klan. Not that anyone's going to care about another dead nigger."

Went over, grabbed his shirt, lifted him until his face is up to mine and feet standing on only air.

"We are taking him home."

"Fuck that, he's dead. We're not." Give Roscoe this, he doesn't scare a damn.

"You want to join him?" Flicked my wrist gently as I could, and he sailed to the car and slid to the road.

Got up, slowly. Stared at me hard and for a time.

What he saw? Bigger and taller than a couple of years ago when last around but growing up couldn't explain it. More muscles than the circus strongman, a lot more. Bones underneath kept growing too. Take two hands to reach around my wrists and my fist bigger than a brick. Don't know what he made of my color. Until about 10 it was a light brown. Then started getting darker and never, ever stopped. When this all happened it was already into mahogany.

"What happened you?"

I shrugged.

"Nah, really, what *the fuck* are you?"

"I'm me."

"Uh-uh. You were you when you're a boy. Now ... I ... how strong?"

"A lot." Didn't know how to answer, really.

"You pick up front of that car?"

Nodded and Roscoe's eyes narrowed and he's getting an idea.

"Pick up the whole thing, can't you."

"Haven't tried but likely, yeah. Probably more."

"How hell it happen?"

"Don't know. I really don't."

"Nah, you tell me how you got this way.

"I don't know!" Shouted loud enough birds flew out from trees. "Nobody knows!"

Deep breath.

"Remember, when I was little, I had to wear big, thick glasses like daddy's? Then, when I'm around nine, I didn't need them anymore. Daddy's friends with all the doctors at the VA hospital and he took me to see some of them and they said it was impossible. Then, few years later, when I started to get my growth, well, I got all this."

Roscoe shook his head, like its stupidest thing he'd ever heard. It didn't make it make sense to me either.

"So, you like, what, one of those guys in the funny books? Ones who go around wearing tights and fighting villains?"

"Funny books?"

"Y'know, the ones with cartoons."

"Oh, I'm not allowed to read those."

"You're not ... allowed?" Roscoe couldn't believe what he saw before and now couldn't believe what he's hearing. "Who's gonna stop you?"

"Momma and daddy won't let me. Say it's junk."

He looked up, down, side to side, shook his head a long time.

"You fly? Some of them in the funny books do."

"I wish."

"Too bad."

I nodded. Flying away. Give anything for that.

"We've got to bring daddy home," I said. "I couldn't face Mamma otherwise."

"We got to get ourselves home," Roscoe said, but he wasn't arguing.

I nodded.

"You know where we are?"

I shook my head.

"How long you drive before you got here?"

"Maybe 10 minutes?"

"Going fast?"

"Think so. Wasn't paying attention."

"He make any turns when he was driving?"

"Seemed like everyone he could."

"Well, at least he knew to do that. Know anything else?"

"There's a house way on the other side of that field, but that's all I can see."

Roscoe looked around but couldn't see a thing. People nowadays don't know what a real dark night is. Got lights everywhere stealing the sky away. Little light we had right then was a from sliver of yellow moon. The couple million stars hanging out behind it were pretty but didn't do shit. Roscoe – and anyone else who wasn't me – could maybe see the start of the field I was pointing at.

Roscoe started to say something, then looked at me again and paused. "You sure?"

"Yeah, there's a little light in a window."

"How far?"

"Half-mile, maybe little more."

"Wish I knew if they were black or white."

"Voices sound black. Having an argument."

"You kidding?"

"Nope."

"You hear like that all the time?"

"Only I want to. Something I can turn on and off."

Right then actually glad Roscoe was there, a first for me. Spent his whole life skating away from something. Getting out of trouble only thing did better than getting in.

"What they arguing about?"

"Money."

"What else," he said. "You push the car behind those trees. Toss some branches and stuff over it." I started to say something, but he wouldn't let me get more than a sound out. "I *heard* what you said about your daddy. This is so no one driving sees anything. Then we go over that house."

We walked and Roscoe kept pulling up his pants and complaining his shoes wouldn't stay on because they'd taken his laces and belt at the jail. "Didn't want me killing myself before they hung me," he let a sharp, angry laugh.

"Gave you 'shine, though."

"Yeah, those dicks weren't too bad. Didn't beat me up all that much, gave me something to drink. Better than most that way. What you do to them anyway?"

Didn't say anything and Roscoe didn't push.

"We get close, stay out of sight."

"Why?"

"Come on someone's porch looking like you are, they'll shoot if they can and run if they can't. Or run after they shoot, right? Cuz you'd still be standing, right?"

"How'd you know? Thought you were passed out."

Reached up, plucked something off my back, a circle of flattened metal, about the size of a dime.

"What happens a bullet hits something won't let it through," tried to sound all cool but didn't manage. "A couple more of these I can see."

Looked me over again, then few times more. Kicked the dirt. Only time ever saw him up and up not know what's going on, even talked to himself: "But he's right there and too damn big to say he isn't."

Then got back talking loud like it's to me, but really still to himself. Putting the attitude back on, one showed he'd seen more, done more and that he wore like a best suit. "Besides, travel like me you see strange, strange shit in the world. Voodoo? That's almost every day shit. Getting so getting the future from tea leaves and goat livers is as every day as breathing. There's *real* weird stuff goes on and you ain't near weirdest I've seen."

"Like?"

Roscoe's head turned a little to the right, but the eyes slid all to the left to look at me. Like considering if I could handle what he was about to say. Made me think it might be something really happened.

"Once was lost way, way out. Don't know *precisely* but day before I'd passed Nowhere, Mississippi. I was off road in some woods a bit trying to get a squirrel for eating is why I got to see this. Came on some white folks and even for white folks they were ... well, I don't know, but even for white folks, you understand?"

Gave me the significant nod and I gave it back.

"They got a boar. Big, big, with tusks at least a foot long. A mama boar. Musta had a litter recent and not able to let her babies feed cuz her titties is swolled up. She's hanging by back legs from a frame like you'd have to bleed a pig. Didn't know how long it'd hold together because no pig ever as big as this. Animal's hanging up there screaming and kicking like anything with sense. Around it is maybe 10 white folks, men *and* women. Circle around it and take off all clothes and not a nice sight. One of 'em, looks more beard than anything else, has a knife and runs in at the boar. Tries to kill it but the boar got a hoof hard into old man's stuff and he's down bleeding and yelling so loud almost couldn't hear the boar. Another guy goes but all does is grab the knife where it dropped, and crawls fast out. Then an old, old lady with huge, long gray hair never seen a washing. Y'know, all ropey and yellow? She yells at him, no language I'd ever heard. Keeps on yelling like she wants her mind to come out and runs in. Stuck that lady boar right between the tied up legs and pulls down until she can't. Sticks her arm in up to her elbow. Then she found a louder yell inside herself and let it go. Never want to hear again. When she's done she pulled her arm out and starts licking at it. Someone else cuts the neck and puts a bucket under for the blood because ... well, you'll see. After time enough for the boar to stop kicking, a big muscle boy with an axe cut it ass to head with one swing. Then, because I ain't seen enough shit was fucked up, they all get in there – even guy bleeding from his balls – and go rolling around in the guts and pouring blood on each other and start ...”

“No.”

He was right. Even for white folks.

“Yeah. Everyone doing all sorts to everyone right in the front yard. Even with parts of that poor boar.” He took a moment there. Whatever Roscoe was seeing in his mind it wasn't anything he wanted. “Not pretty.”

“The pig?”

Roscoe heard me but didn't seem to quite believe a nice boy me would say that. Side-eyed me again and saw a little smile I had.

“Maybe something to you after all.”

Close enough to the house now for anyone to hear the arguing. A man and a woman and they weren't calming down. Wasn't a house like I'd said, just a shack with corrugated metal walls held together by rust, tar paper roof, windows with wax paper, not glass, and part of a porch someone had given up on.

Roscoe waved me to hide and started whistling as loud as he could so people inside know he was coming.

“Hey there,” he finally had to say a couple of times loud to be heard over the yelling. Sudden quiet inside then a man, probably in his 20s, stomped out wearing dungarees, attitude, and the bottle in his hand.

“What you want?”

Roscoe, head a little bent over and shoulders a little curved in, and a sad, sweet look meant saying “sorry” without saying a word.

“Say, I hate to bother you, but my car broke on that road and I was wondering ...”

“You walked here from the road? How'd you even know there anything here?”

“Well, I just started to walkin' and headed out this way...”

“Through a field? Not down the road? Who you running from? Steal the car?”

“No, no,” Roscoe started to say but right then the other half of the argument came out. In her 20s too and wearing a shift dress. Both had the lean look of too much working and too little eating.

“Who's 'at?” she asked.

"How I know? Just walked up," he said, anger at Roscoe adding on to anger he had before. "Whoever, he's a liar. Says he came over cuz his car broke down."

"No, you got it wrong, I just ..."

"Looks familiar," she said. "Where I know you from?"

"Well, not from around here. I'm on a way to ..."

"You!" she interrupted again. "I know! Guitar player. One played the juke by Uncle Red's. Saw you last week." She slapped the man on his shoulder and went on like he hadn't heard every word she just said. "He's the man we heard. OK? Not real good but OK for a dance. Whyn't you know it's him?"

Roscoe maybe wanted to say something about being better than OK but never got the chance.

"I'm supposed to remember every fool in a bar? 'Sides, wasn't that bad. Got us up and moving." Roscoe smiled, but having a fan didn't help him a get word in. Then the man slapped a wall so hard the whole place shook. "Wait minute. Heard something happened to him."

"What?"

"Talking to Billy Withers today. Told me Mr. Sams was saying that guitar guy'd gone after his wife. Police pick him up yesterday. How you out of jail?"

"Misunderstanding is what it was. Cleared it up down the police station." Only sentence Roscoe managed to complete did him no good. Suspicious stares suddenly turned mean.

"Never happen," she said, not bothering to shake her head. "Not Mr. Sams. You broke out of jail?"

The man started yelling at Roscoe: "Get out of here. Get away!"

"Look, they're going to lynch me! I need help!" Roscoe yelled back.

"So, you want us strung up, too?" She asked.

"No, all I need ..."

"You need? You need to get going, now!" The man shouted.

What Roscoe had said about how I looked must have been right. I walked out of the dark and those two shut right up.

"Can't get going anywhere without help," I said, grateful my voice didn't crack.

"What the hell is that?" the man asked in almost a whisper.

Roscoe snickered, "That's what you don't mess with."

3

The Clarion of Winthrop, Georgia

NEGROES RAMPAGE, POLICE OFFICER KILLED
Residents told to arm themselves as criminal is freed during attack on jail

A police officer was killed by a mob of rampaging Negroes in Hicksville last night. The mob attacked a police station in order to free one of their kind charged with assaulting a white woman. Police Officer George Thomas was killed, and Officer John Fleming was beaten when the gang of at least 20 Negroes stormed the station and freed Roscoe James, an itinerant. Following the attack on the police station the mob set upon a group of men on their way home from a social club outing. They said the gang was armed with bats and chains. Several men were severely injured in that attack as well. Police Chief Hayes Monroe called the attack "cowardly and premeditated" and advised residents to take all measures necessary to protect themselves from this mob. Monroe said State Police were assisting the Hicksville Police Department and that he had not ruled out requesting aid from the state militia.

The Washington Post
NEGRO KILLS POLICEMAN IN JAIL ESCAPE

ATLANTA (UPI) — Negro James Roscoe killed a police officer in Hicksville, Ga., in a successful attempt to escape last night from the jail. Police Chief Hayes Monroe said James killed one officer and beat another in the escape. Monroe said James is armed and dangerous as were the accomplices who assisted James. He declined to said how the Negro had escaped.

The New Amsterdam News of Harlem, New York
LYNCH MOB STOPPED IN GEORGIA

A lynching was stopped in a town near Winthrop, Georgia. There are conflicting reports of how it happened. One witness said a mob was closing on the Hicksville police station where a man was being held on rape charges when a large, masked man appeared and stopped the mob. Other witnesses said there was more than one man. All agree that several members of the mob attacked and shot at the person or persons but were driven off somehow with no injury to the rescuers. A police officer died during the incident but details of how this happened are unavailable at this time.

4

They were Willy and Ruth and everything they had in the world would add up to little more than nothing. Shack's front room had a wood stove, table, two chairs held together with bailing wire, tin wash basin and small battered hutch. Never been in one of these shotgun shacks before. Other than Uncle Stan, my father's brother, I didn't really know anyone who was poor, not like this. Stan was a sharecropper and only times we saw him were when he and his family came to visit. They lived about seven miles outside of town, but my parents never even thought about going to see him. People we knew were doctors and teachers and such. You had to be rich to be poor in Tuskegee, compared to this anyway.

Willy worked as a mechanic, if he could, so he knew people with cars. He was about to go ask around and see if he could borrow one or if someone would drive us when I told him we were bringing a body, too.

Didn't say a thing, just sat right down on the floor and grabbed his head.

"Know what you're asking?"

"Sooner done, sooner we're gone," Roscoe said. "Best for everyone."

Willy thought on that, nodded, asked what we were planning on doing with our car.

"You can have it if you want," I said. "I was going to push it in the river."

"Don't ever even want my eyes on it. Be sure and get license plates off and any paper could identify you. They get you this'll comes back on us."

"They can't get us," Roscoe said.

Willy looked ready to argue but looked at me and changed his mind.

"Even without plates they can still track you if it's found. New cars have ID numbers on them. It a new car?"

I nodded.

"Hope is stays sunk, then," said Willy.

"Where are the numbers?" I asked.

"Usually, one on the driver's door post. Another on engine side of the fire-wall. Those are only tags, so you can pull 'em off. Real problem is one on the engine block. No way to get rid of it."

"Don't matter," said Roscoe, who was getting testy. "Who hell's gonna check out some damn old car been in the river?"

"Long as you know we never met, do what the hell you want," said Willy, then up and out the door.

I was exhausted almost past moving, so just sat, and stared at a wall.

"What were you two arguing about?" said Roscoe.

"None of your business," Ruth said, then sighed. "Money. What else? He wants to go up North to Chicago."

"You don't?"

Ruth shot him a look of "What kind of fool?"

"Course I do. But we barely got enough for one train ticket. I tell him go, make some money, send for me. He wants us both to go. Says we could ride the rails and save money for when we get there."

"Don't see you as the hobo type."

"Me either."

Must have nodded off because the next thing I remember is the sound of a plate hitting in front of me as Ruth gave me a cup of coffee and a bologna sandwich.

"Look like you had a really wrong day," she said.

Then we sat there for a while after that, not talking. I didn't want to do anything except enjoy sitting still but my thoughts weren't cooperating. Finally, I looked up at Roscoe.

"I can't do it."

His eyes opened fast. "Do what?"

"Bring his body back. I've been thinking about sitting next to him on a ride home and I can't."

"Makes more sense not to anyway."

"Who died?" Ruth asked.

"Thought you didn't want to know," said Roscoe.

"Don't but do. Y'know?"

"My father."

She said sorry in a real quiet voice. Nice and hurt to hear at a same time. Nice was the sympathy, which I hadn't had at all until now and didn't realize how much I needed. Hurt was it made it all real again. Cried for a bit, without making a sound. Ruth gave me a cloth to wipe my face.

I sat for a moment after, not quite able to do anything. Finally, asked Ruth if they had a shovel. She showed me where their few tools were kept. Roscoe and I walked back to the car and right near it I found a little opening in the woods. I decided it was a good enough place and handed Roscoe the shovel.

"Me? You could get this dug in like no time, right?"

"Yeah," I said, "but you can't, so get digging." Looked at me once, then again, muttered, started digging. Really, I couldn't have done it. Too wrecked. Dig my daddy's grave? Push me over any edge I wasn't already over.

Pulled the engine out, crushed it easy as tin. Went at the rest of the car until you could barely tell what it used to be, then dumped it all into the river. Took me no time so I waited on Roscoe to get done. When he was sky was starting to light and we put daddy in the ground at dawn. I couldn't speak. Roscoe was smart enough not to.

Willy was waiting for us when we got back, more scared and angry than when he left.

"Damn it! How you get us mixed in to this? A cop's dead, town's filled with state police and talk the militia is coming. You know what they'll do to us?"

"You get us a ride?" Roscoe, as far past caring as me.

"Wasn't easy. He'll take you to Montgomery. On your own after."

"Maybe this can make up for the trouble." Opened up my father's wallet, put almost all the money inside on the table. At least a hundred dollars and back then that was more than most could earn in months. My parents had hoped it would get Roscoe to head North for good.

"That'll do," Ruth said quietly.

✯ ✯ ✯

The truck was going to Montgomery, but we jumped off outside Selma to be extra careful. Roscoe went into town to get me some clothes weren't all torn up and came back wearing a new outfit as well.

"What'd you expect? All my stuff still at the jail. Even my guitar." He looked genuinely sad about the guitar. First time I'd seen him sad that wasn't self-pity or trying to get something out of someone. Another surprise: Said we had to call my mother to let her know.

Hadn't thought about telling her because it was too horrible to think. Entire ride away from Hicksville I went over everything that happened, all I should've done differently. Should've had daddy to park farther away, shouldn't have gone up to that mob. Shoulds and shouldn'ts piled up inside me, each worse than one before. Wanted to blame Roscoe but it was my fault. Should have protected him. Shouldn't have hit that policeman so hard. Time to time a little almost voice in my head tried saying the cop deserved it, but it never got loud enough to hold its ground.

How am I telling mama I let daddy die?

"I can't go back."

"What, you think I'm taking care you? No, you're going home. We gotta get someone else to tell Sis. I'm not doing that either. Call your dad's brother. That'll do."

"Doesn't have a phone. Have to call the Clarks live a couple miles away, then they send one of their boys to get him. Then you call back."

"All right. Whatever."

Found a place with a phone booth. Roscoe said we had to eat first which for him meant drinking. He had one and got up to make the call. I had three orders of meat-and-three, then the waitress came and put a whole apple pie and quart bottle of milk on the table.

"Figure to save us both some time," she said, smiling.

Roscoe gone a long time. Came back he had a drink and then another quick after it.

"What did he say?"

"Say? No saying. Only yelling."

"What was he yelling about?"

"Same things as you. All my fault. Shit, you'd think I'd shot the man from what he was going on. Wants you home now. Didn't seem to care where I went. No surprise."

"He know anything about what happened?"

"Not a damn thing but work on a farm you don't get much news."

"Tell him about the policeman?"

"I told him everything I could to stop him yelling."

"Is he going to talk to momma?"

"What do you think? Now stop asking stuff. Had enough. First, he yells then I have to listen to his crying. No time for this shit."

"Not your fault Roscoe," I said, quiet. "Really not."

Turned his head, looked at me, confused. Maybe trying to think of something to say but never did. Started to go back to his drink but before he got to pick it up, he looked back toward me again. Then slow turn back to the drink, emptied it at one go. Ordered a refill and didn't touch it. Smoked a cigarette half way then forgot and lit a new one. Did it again and then stopped bothering with them. Just sat there, looking at a space halfway between him and the table top, now and then saying something even I couldn't hear.

5

All my strength didn't protect momma from daddy's death.

Or me.

For a long time couldn't think right. Grief rode on top of everything, always reminding me. Evenings I waited for the sound of the car and him coming through the door. Thought it was him walking down a street but just a hat or coat or something else made it seem like him. Grief makes you stupid. People saying things two or three times before I heard it. Always distracted no matter how much I tried. A long shadow between me and everything else, putting my body and two different places.

Rev. Williams came over as soon as I got back. Tall man and high yellow, straight nose, pencil-thin mustache, like a movie hero. Wife was light skinned and daughter Blanche was too. Heard church elders hired him because he could pass and that'd bring the church more "right kind" of people. Lighter skin, straighter hair, more college, more money, more concerned he was about you and yours.

Since he arrived a bunch of families moved to other churches when before that no one could remember people leaving. All with darker skin and dirtier jobs, janitors, maids, yard help, garbage collectors, mechanics.

My cousin Erlissa Doyle isn't my cousin, but we call each other that because we're kin through a marriage of one of my grandparents' uncles and one of her aunt's grandparents. Called her father Uncle Teddy. He was the right kind when he was making money – but his business went to hell and other elders decided Teddy shouldn't be one any more.

Owned a plumbing business so he was definitely dirty. "Only three things you need to know about plumbing," he always said. "Water runs downhill, don't put your fingers in your mouth and pay day is Friday." He's one of those people who made anything funny, even it's the 20th time you heard it.

Most successful plumber in Tuskegee for a while. Truck with his name in big letters on the side and four men working for him. So many white people hired him he was working more than any other plumber – black or white. Reason was he did best work and charged less. Supposed to be how you do well in business. But for us there's doing well and doing too well. Do too well, taking too much from what whites said is rightfully their business, bad things happen. House or shop burn down, maybe beat up, maybe lynched. Why Uncle Teddy sent about half his white business on to white plumbers, saying he was too busy, but he knew someone else could do it. Then their work would always need fixing and he'd come make it right for free. The whole time covering for them. Saying whatever it was was unusual and no one could have seen it coming.

Thought it was enough doing that. One night his truck was set fire to and house shot up. Bullet in the wall where Erlissa and her baby brother were sleeping, not a foot above the bed. He stopped taking any jobs for white people. Let go all his workers, sold the truck, and got a 20-year-old Model T one, always needing fixing. Didn't put his name on it. Right about then is when Rev. Williams and the elders started forgetting to invite him to meetings and barely talked to him on Sundays. Before he left Uncle Teddy stood up in church on a Sunday, cussed out the reverend and everyone else, calling hypocrites and worse. Me and Erlissa were too young to understand what was going on.

Couple years later Uncle Teddy shot himself sitting in his truck. Her mom works as a maid now. Erlissa's trying to get the business up again, damn good at plumbing, but not many will hire a woman.

Parents kept going to the church, though. They've got the accomplishments Williams thinks are important, ones that make us "respectable."

When he came over, I was sitting on the front steps staring at whatever you look at when stare at nothing. Still at it when he left. Don't know how long it'd been or what was said but momma was crying louder now than before.

Stopped the last stair and turned to face me which put us eye to eye.

"Moses, you have suffered quite a blow," he said loud and direct, like I didn't know. "Your father was a fine, fine man. A great example of what our people are capable of when they decide to work. He came from nothing! His family were common and nothing more, but he worked his way out of that. Made himself a respectable man. He had high standing in the medical community. I don't know if you're aware of this he was so well regarded that sometimes white doctors would call and ask his opinion on a medicine. He was blessed indeed."

Paused, looked at me, expecting a response. So, I said the thing you can nearly always say.

"Yes, sir."

Nodded approvingly.

"Your mother is a woman and therefore a fragile vessel." Only time ever heard momma called fragile. I nodded because looked like he wanted me to.

"So, the great responsibility now falls on you. You must guide her through this terrible time with the wisdom men possess. You are young and there's nothing to be done for that. I pray you are ready. The Lord gives us our duty and it is never more than we can handle. If we fail it is because our faith was not great enough and thus, we have failed those who rely on us and God as well. If the burden feels too great, then you must remember to turn to Jesus and ask for His grace. If we are fit receptacles then He will give it to us and our burdens will be lifted, our obstacles removed. It is not for us to understand why your father was taken from us. The Lord moves in mysterious ways and it is enough for us to know that His plan is perfect and take comfort from that."

Three days later, at daddy's funeral, he said the exact same. When I figured he hadn't been talking to me, just rehearsing.

Took a breath then and focused in on me.

"How did your father die, boy?"

"White folks shot him in a town in Georgia."

"I know that, boy. I want to know why they shot him. What he was doing at the time?"

My turn for staring. Hard. He gave it right back and the longer we were like that the angrier he got.

"What he did all the time, be a Negro. That's usually what we're killed for."

"DON'T YOU SASS ME BOY! I ask you a question and you will answer it with the manners I thought your mother taught you!"

I stood. That put top of my head up near the porch roof and I'm three steps above him too. Looking down from some height. Williams didn't flinch or break his stare.

"Your mother said you rescued your uncle." Of course, she did. What you say so you don't have to say I got daddy killed.

"I don't believe it. Bet your father got shot having to save you and that piece of trash uncle. That's the only way this could have happened to a respectable man like that."

Of course, I was getting angrier. Wanted to say something, something hard that'd cut and set him in his place. Also wanted to go and hide because I almost agreed with him. Did speak though because anger had chased words away and because I was still scared of grownups.

Went down off the porch to the walkway lined with rocks daddy had painted white. Picked one up, maybe 15 or 20 pounds, held it out toward him with my arm perfectly straight and crushed it.

He flinched.

"What are you? You're an ape! A gorilla! You're a ..." His words trailed off and he marched fast down to our fence gate, grabbed the handle and stopped, stood still, took a long breath. Turned around. Looked different. Slouched a little instead of the usual shoulders back and chin way forward. Stuck a hand in his pants pocket and walked toward me really casual.

"You know I was in the war?" Back then there was only one war, called The Great One.

Shook my head. Honestly thought pastors were all born with those dog collars on their necks.

"Yup. The 369th Infantry. Harlem Hellfighters." His voice was different, had street sneer in it.

Nodded, impressed. Every one of us knew about the Hellfighters then. They were the best.

"We got to France and the white American soldiers didn't want us anywhere near them, so we were made part of the French army." Talking quietly so no one else could hear. "French were fine with that. They needed soldiers. We were treated like everyone else. Actually, we were treated better than their owns blacks because we were Americans. Civilians loved us. They'd buy us a drink, give us food. And ladies ... well, they liked getting some from us and they liked that all the time. I wasn't a nigger or colored, I was American. Only time I ever been treated like that."

All his high-toned religious act gone now.

"Honest, I loved killing white men. Other guys they wanted to prove they were as good as anyone else. Like it was going to change the shit we got at home. All that made us ferocious. Once the French saw us take care of business, they threw us into some real hell. Know what I learned?"

I didn't speak and he didn't care.

"A man dies then it's on you. You should've protected him. Kept him alive. Bring him back home. You let your daddy down, boy. You're why your momma's crying."

He turned right around when he said that and walked away looking perfect pastor again, like Bing Crosby turned almost black.

6

Next day, Uncle Stan and I went over to Larchmont and Sons, only Negro funeral home in Tuskegee. It changed owners several times but not the name.

Waiting in the office of Mr. Mortimer, the current owner. A somber décor with severely subdued sunlight struggling in to the room through half-drawn shades and gauzy curtains. Too formal for Uncle Stan to feel comfortable sitting on these plush chairs without being told he could, so we stood. He had on dirty overalls, a clean white shirt and turning his old beaten fedora over and over in his hands. Three years younger than my father and same height, Stan managed to have a skinny man's body and a fat man's belly.

Momma should have been there, not us. We were equally ignorant about the world and how it operated. Stan, a dirt farmer, and all he knew of the world he'd learned on the Saturday nights he could come to town, get drunk, and listen to the wisdom of anyone sitting next to him at the bar. Momma ran the house, classrooms, sly-talked principals into a few more dollars pay, knew where money came from, how it moved around, how much we had. But she was at home, confused, untethered in a world didn't have my father in it.

Stan and I hadn't been talking and still the room felt quieter when Mr. Mortimer came in. Went to the closet without a word for welcome. Took off a rubber apron, hung it up, put on a jacket that completed the dark three-piece suit he was wearing. Thin as a banjo neck, he had the sad, solicitous smile of someone wanting to be expensively helpful.

"So sorry to hear of Mr. Crawford's passing," he said, indicating we, too, should have a seat. "A truly fine man and vital part of our community. An immense loss to everyone but you most of all."

Mumbled our thanks and he continued straight on.

"We will handle all the arrangements, if you'd like. Such a difficult time for you. We will do everything possible to ease your burden."

Felt like he had taken us into his confidence when he talked, sharing something very personal. A magic trick done with a tone of voice and a look of eyes that pulled up trust in me and Stan slicker than a rabbit and a hat.

Nodded again and mumbled yes and more thanks.

"I'm sorry to have to ask but could you tell me how did he pass?"

Looked at my uncle and he looked at me, both hoping not to be the one to explain, but finally Stan tried

"There was, um some, um, trouble ... an argument with uh uh some whites."

"Oh dear, dear. Why must we suffer so at their hands?"

He paused for a precisely appropriate length of time.

"Was he ...?"

"Lynched" went unspoken yet still clearly heard. Could happen to any of us, but some proper folks liked to think it there was something improper if it happened to them. They were people with gifts – breeding, education, success – let them navigate a white world. Why Mr. Mortimer delicately danced around the word. Didn't want to say it but needed to know because if so there may be other things needed to be addressed. Would the funeral arrangements need to be adjusted for how badly the body was mutilated? Open caskets were the rule but if the deceased's appearance was beyond rescuing by the undertaker's art then ...

Stan shook his head, so Mr. Mortimer knew the body was in as good condition as could be expected for someone dead.

"He was shot. Once. In a chest."

Mr. Mortimer nodded, again pausing to show a correct amount of sorrow.

"And where did this happen?"

"Hicksville, over in Georgia."

A look of worry flickered across Mr. Mortimer's face.

"Oh. Will you be wanting us to bring him home or do you already have arrangements?"

"We put him under a big oak outside of a Hicksville," I said. "Uncle Roscoe can show you." First time called him uncle.

Mr. Mortimer's eyes went wide, and he coughed to cover his surprise.

"I see. Well, we can certainly assist you there."

"There may still be some problems," Stan said. "Like it to not be known how or where ..." He stopped, crying.

"... he passed," Mr. Mortimer finished the sentence. "I entirely understand." He offered Stan a handkerchief, but Stan looked at it like almost an insult. Crying was not something men did.

"Will you be needing a death certificate? Do not worry about it. There is a very ... discrete ... doctor who I work with. He will say it was heart failure which, in truth, it always is."

Another perfectly timed pause and followed by question he'd likely been waiting on the whole time.

"What kind of casket will you be wanting?" Then carefully, sympathetically told us all the types of woods we could choose. As we looked confused, he followed that on, burying us under a gentle, insistent torrent of further options. Accents and finials for the casket? Wood or metal? Silk or satin for the lining? And that was just the casket.

Sized us up right the moment he saw us. Got talking in a way we'd never think to ask costs because how could we, at a time like this?

Finally, Stan said what Mortimer wanted him to, "You just do right by him, alright?"

Mortimer gave us a sad and comforting smile as he slid over a paper to sign. "I most certainly will."

7

The Clarion of Winthrop, Georgia

GOVERNOR CALLS OUT MILITIA
TO PROTECT CITIZENS IN HICKSVILLE
Acts After Negro Mob Murders Police Officer

Three units of the Georgia National Guard were sent to this town a week after a mob of Negroes attacked and murdered Police Officer George Thomas and freed one of their own charged with an unspeakable crime. The units were joined by a large group of local men deputized by General Whitcombe Forrest, commander of the Guard.

In the early evening the combined force advanced on the Negro neighborhood where the mob originated. Their efforts at restoring order were met with gunfire and savage, screaming attacks by groups armed with clubs. General Forrest ordered the deployment of riflemen and a machine gun squad who returned fire in self-defense. The battle continued for some time and could easily have gone against us had the General not had the foresight to position another squad, so it blocked the only other road out of the neighborhood. During the fighting a Negro set fire to his home in an attempt to distract the militia and endanger any firefighters sent to put it out. Fortunately, General Forrest ordered firefighters not to intervene, thus saving many lives. In the resulting conflagration some dozen or so buildings have burned to the ground. Order was not restored to the neighborhood until dawn, by which time many of the Negroes were dead including those said to be responsible for the death of Officer Thomas.

The Baltimore Sun
NATIONAL GUARD ENDS GEORGIA RACE RIOT
Escape of Insolent Black Felon Said to Be Cause of Tragedy

The governor of Georgia called out the National Guard to suppress a race riot which began a week after a black mob attacked the town jail and killed a police officer. The Guard was attacked by a gang of Negroes. When the soldiers brandished their arms, the group ran away into the neighborhood known as Darkie Town. The soldiers chased the hoodlums and were forced to defend themselves when they were fired on. Fortunately, except for Officer Thomas no more deaths or injuries of note have been reported.

The Chicago Defender
SCORES MASSACRED IN GEORGIA RACE WAR
More Than 50 Dead as Militia Invades, Traps People Inside Burning Homes

8

Day we after buried daddy was day we got the news about Hicksville.

Erlissa drove me in her truck. God looking out for those white police the entire way because I was praying for one to pull us over. She dropped me a few miles away. Told her to head back, I'd get myself home, but she's one who won't listen whenever she wants to. At least she's parked a way off the road. Said to go she heard anything seemed wrong. Way she patted her scattergun was clear she wasn't hearing that either.

We're only let to live in certain places and what they're called was to keep us in our place in every sense. In Hicksville it was Smoketown.

A right name now.

Burned out and dead. Only light was what dropped off the moon, only human life was me. Near every building was a skeleton, charred walls, maybe a chimney was all for most of them. Strange what fire will take or leave. One place was nothing but a front porch and that wasn't burnt at all. Couple of chairs and an old stoneware jug on it, waiting for someone to visit. Few houses not all burned were mostly trashed. One still had table set for supper, serving dishes clean from rats and crows.

Nature always gets its own back and could see in Smoketown how it was going to. Kudzu already working toward buildings. Weeds growing in the roads because there was no one to tramp them down. How long before you wouldn't know this was ever a place?

Overcome by all this my legs were shaking bad enough I sat down in the middle of the road with arms around my knees.

A real hero, like in the movies, he'd have gotten angry, vowed revenge, and that shit. Wish I could have. Would have been nice to have anger or anything else get between me and a crushing feeling of loss. All I could think of was all the people feeling what I was feeling about Daddy. Lost all they had and all that mattered. Felt a dull, stabbing pain in my heart and long, long shudders rolled through my body. Got dizzy after they passed until I figured out I wasn't breathing.

Got up and moved on.

Walls with bullet pockmarks, part of a sign hung down from half the front of a store done for by fire. All four walls of a church still stood, filled with charred pieces of roof. Maybe a quarter mile away and off the main road was a building by itself, never bothered by fire or vandals. Didn't even have to go inside to know it was the juke Roscoe played at. White man owner must have said leave it alone. No matter if they hadn't. With none of us coming back it'd never know another customer.

Willy and Ruth all I could think of. Make it out or get them killed, too? Everything I looked at I saw Willie and Ruth's bodies there, the fear and hope gone forever from their eyes. They were living far, far from any other buildings and that saved them, told myself over and over. Didn't believe it. Were they left for vultures or did someone come get them? My mind giving bad answers to worse questions.

Follow a dirt road toward center of Hicksville. About a mile walk through a small creak and over tracks not seen a train since Sherman was touring. My memory was Hicksville as a big, chaotic place. Really? Small and quiet as dying breath. At center was a rectangle with town hall, police station, and a little park with couple of trees, bandstand, statue of a Confederate soldier, always. Facing that were mostly empty store fronts, dead hotel, living bar. Not a quarter of Tuskegee, never would be. Late enough even the neon at bar had gone home for the night. Two streetlights on but no one using them.

Looked and didn't know what I'd do. Couldn't have told why I was there more than couldn't not be.

Responsibility?

Revenge?

Justice?

Rage?

Not rage, not anymore. Was for all the way from Tuskegee but shattered looking on Smoketown. Once it was gone there was nothing but real behind it. What was real was the horror of knowing. That horror wasn't when shooting started, it was right the instant right in front of it. Knowing what's about to happen to all the people who were just going about their living. Fixing to eat or yelling for kids or doing the nothing at all everybody winds up doing. Some of them probably thinking about what they were going to do later, no reason to suspect that life wouldn't go on as usual. Instead, later was the end of all their worlds.

Not expecting that, not now. Days and days of no trouble since the trouble at the police station, maybe it'd all blown past. 'Sides, it wasn't any of them that did it. The lie we all want to be true while all know it isn't. A lie saying guilt or innocence have anything to do with the punishments we get. Hold on to a hope of justice without a reason to. Living a good, clean life and not being the one who did it do no good at all. They always find us guilty of being us, what they think is the worst crime of all.

All that in front of me, I should be raging. All should be all the time and most are, but it's stuffed, locked down, because it can be our death to show. Rage, reasonable and justified, especially after a look into Smoketown. Gone from me for sorrow, though. Lost, lost, lost, lost. Replaced with knowing, like I said, knowing all the tomorrows never going to be. Felt like a slow wind going into me then couldn't get out.

With that I didn't think, just did. Went in to that old hotel, where deep dust said it'd been a time since anyone else had paid time in it. The basement was a kitchen, laundry machine, and the like. Also, the gas line. Locked. Kicked it open. The same at every store, empty or still in business, facing the town hall. Final place was the bar. Sign shaped like a shamrock read Dew Drop Inn.

Alright then.

Few bottles, some rags, matches. Lit 'em up and got to throwing. Gas running a while in the hotel by then went up big and then kept going on down the street.

Can't be a Southern town without statue of a rebel soldier. Always on a lawn near town hall. Reminder of a noble sacrifice done to make sure they'd always be someone to whip or rape. Always face north, lets whites think they're all set and ready to do it all again. Proud to lose and can do it again if they want is what it really shows. Hicksville had had a general or something because here was a man on a horse waving a sword. Went over, sat down next to it. Waited a short wait until the siren started singing closer, closer, closer. Firetruck, only one town had, speeds in and pulls up. Firemen, nowhere near enough for the flames in front of them, piling out, grab at hoses, and such.

Stood up, jerked statue off its plinth.

No reason for anyone to notice me yet, all trying to make sense of the fires, and they didn't.

Brought that statue down on the firetruck like God's own hammer.

Noticed. Noticed and they're screaming, crying because what was it could do that? Nothing, but there I was anyway and no way to doubt it. A giant, black demon they'd seen running through their nightmares now walking on their street. Hope the fires' lights' and their imaginations made me look like hell itself. Was about to if I didn't already.

Tore up hoses, broke open hydrants, then walked into the roaring hotel. Grabbed up something big and burning, carried it out and a bit toward the church before threw it at and through a big window. Back to the hotel and did it a couple times more to make sure. When the fire was into the heart of that church took burning pews to town hall, knocked through a door and into some offices. Lot of paper in there.

Weren't just firefighters seeing me by then. Fire always bring a crowd and a big one in a small town? People likely come miles for it. Police and guns come also. Didn't notice if I was shot but saw some few raise a rifle or pistol and someone else put a hand to the barrel and push it back down. Didn't seem to take much of a push. Lot of people and all kept quiet.

Don't know if they could tell how this fire wasn't like what they used on our homes and to char skin off us while we're tied and screaming.

Burn all they want and wouldn't burn enough because couldn't burn the terror they created, fed, kept going through a line of centuries. No fire ever big enough to destroy where in their minds it lived, always getting bigger. Couldn't because there's no life in them without it. That fear gone and what all is left of them? Remains of something no one could tell was ever human.

Terror their protection from understanding what they pay to believe we're things and not people. Payment that's torn off their bodies – eyes so not to see, ears so not to hear, skin so not to feel, face so not to recognize what they are. Cannibals, eating what they tear to fuel their hate. Skin, entrails, hair, and nails gone, they crack their bones, suck out marrow, never to notice what they no longer are.

None of it for this fire. It's burning what it's meant to. Turn buildings to ash so they know it can happen and what it's like. What it's like to face something you can't stop, can take whatever it wants from you, and doesn't care to tell good from bad. No knowing where it goes, it just does. Makes it a gentler thing than what destroys us. It has no reason. Fire is air, fuel, heat – not hate. Never cares if there's suffering. It burns all alike, free of the cant of morality. No mind so no reason to think mercy is possible. Where's the fool appeals to the humanity of a flame? Begs it not to steal life God gave you? Doing that means something looks human is doing it to you. Fire is always honest to itself.

Didn't kill anyone that night but no reason why not. Clear I wasn't trying to kill because if I had there'd be a lot of dead. But wasn't trying to not kill either. Someone died, wouldn't have upset me. Not that night. Don't make me out to be better than I am.

I spread the fire and the fire spread itself. All that's left of the town go up? Never bothered to see. Left with the roaring in my ears of the fire and finally that crowd, too. Left when it was so bad none of them was still paying attention to whatever I was that they knew couldn't possibly exist. Before going I put a sign I'd pulled from the town hall on what remained of where the statue stood.

"Whites Only."

9

Gas Explosion Levels Race-Riot Town

Terror Over A Second Negro Uprising

Militia Returns to Aid, Protect Hicksville

Five Counties Declare Negro Curfew and Travel Ban

Hysteria in Hicksville

Residents Say "Demon" Attack Started Fire

10

Years and years before thinking of Hicksville again. Smoketown, though, that stuck tough on me for a long time. Saw bad things and imagined them into being even worse.

What's a thought? A micro of a micro of a micro of a second's worth of energy jumping in your head. Can't weigh a lot more than nothing but doesn't matter. Some can kill you as dead as crushed with a mountain. Takes longer, which makes it worse. A person goes down by that and it's a slow, sad ride.

Got back to Tuskegee and with Smoketown on top of daddy's death spent months and months being as close to that as ever did. Never went all the way to 'I gotta die' but plenty of time imagined a gun going off to my head as a way of getting away. A good thing if you don't understand a difference. Means likely you never felt either.

Life doesn't wait on feelings. Seem as everything's gone wrong? Don't believe it. Always more may be waiting to come visit.

Mr. Ellis, principal of the high school, liked momma, knew she had to grieve. Gave her two weeks off after the funeral, one of them paid. Most jobs didn't even give sick pay then.

Monday after those two weeks momma went to school and came back home like usual. Next day, walked to the school but stopped outside. Sat on a bench watching kids arrive, through bell ringing for everyone to go inside, and long after they had. Finally, Mrs. Dockett, who'd be called the school secretary if secretary meant being a nurse, fund-raising, and coaching the softball team, came out, took mother's hand, walked her back home.

They were sitting in the parlor, tea pot and cups on the table between them, when I got home for supper. Mrs. Dockett stood up, said it appeared momma was going to need some more time, smiled at her, shook my hand, and left. Momma the whole time sitting there, staring out a window.

"It will be OK," she said. "I'll get back."

Next day, fixed herself up like going to work but went to the parlor and into the same seat. Picked up a picture of daddy and held it all day, not even thinking to feed herself. Friday Mr. Ellis came by, left an envelope with two weeks' pay. Said he was very, very sorry about this. Momma nodded. Said glad to give her a recommendation any time and let him know when she was feeling better because he'd take her back immediately if there was an opening. All nodded and smiled when he said it like it might happen. A true, good man, so no doubt he'd hire her back if he could but times as they were people didn't give up a job unless it was for death and who could blame them?

Kept her routine even with not keeping the work. Every morning dress proper for teaching in time to be on time but always went to her same chair in the parlor.

Didn't know what to do but the old ladies from church did.

First came over that Sunday after daddy's funeral and herded Mamma off to church. Going to church didn't only mean the service. Be there hours early to see everything just so: Flowers fresh and in their right places, choir robes ironed, choirmaster and reverend told what was wrong about the day's readings and hymns. Always polite.

"Well, that's a very *interesting* choice you've made there reverend. I'm sure it will be alright."

Also in charge of seeing to that folks were doing what they should setting up for the coffee after the service.

Enough cakes?

"Hopefully, we'll get by."

This cake for front and center?

"Well, I don't know, who did you say baked it, dear?"

Here for the tables and chairs?

"If you can be happy with it like that." Meaning no, no, no.

Then they "saw to" the cleaning and putting away getting done right, while also seeing to saying a little about a few people.

"Such a bright hat Rachel Mason had today. Didn't know feathers came in such an *unusual* color."

Always polite.

Then they'd walk momma home and send her in to get me because of a sudden people were wanting to have us for Sunday supper. Visits got every day when momma stopped working. Not all of the ladies then, one or two. Some with a chore or errand needing momma's help. Others sitting quiet with her for hours, sipping tea, knowing that was needed sometimes because of when others did it for them.

Old, old, some couldn't see, some couldn't hear, some couldn't even much walk but so tough nothing in life would kill them unless they agreed to it. Children of slaves who'd cheered when Union soldiers burned the land. Grew up with the nightriders who came after the soldiers. Buried family and friends who'd made the mistake of believing government promises. Didn't trust outsiders and lived by you had to take care of your own. Raised to love Jesus and Lincoln, not always in that order.

The parlor chair momma was in was from daddy's family for a wedding present. Close to an heirloom as we had, taken from the plantation's master house during the war. Before Union soldiers fired the mansion, they handed the chair to "some damn darkies" who had nothing. They were laughing as they gave it away so maybe a joke to them. Story told in the family is they stopped laughing from seeing a look on the people they'd given it to, people for the first time got to be the owners and not the owned.

Family took the chair back to their dirt-floor shack but not for long. Lots thought everything fixed now the Union had set them free. Grandfather didn't. Didn't trust anything a white man did. Knew it didn't matter if he's owned or not. Nothing good would come out of him having that chair when the master got back. Didn't mean he'd give it up, though. Built a crate, put the chair in, buried it deep in the woods. Didn't go near it for years, not until the Union soldiers started going away. Seemed to be expecting it would happen. That's when he got together the family, dug out the chair, put it and what else we had on a wagon, and in the middle of a night started it all moving east and out of Mississippi. Why stop at Tuskegee? All he ever said was wanted to be someplace he'd never been a slave when there were no more soldiers around. No fool. Soon new laws making travel hard for us, then more laws making it harder, and finally white people patrolling to make it impossible.

Lost the war but fought to be sure not to lose the peace. Doing whatever to keep things as close to how they were before as could be. We couldn't move from where we lived and had to work on the same plantations, only this time they called it sharecropping.

Don't trust a white person, grandpa said, don't trust a white.

11

DADDY DID OTHER THINGS for earning money besides the pharmacy. One was selling life insurance for the Greater Connecticut Mutual Insurance Co. Tuskegee had more of our people making more money than probably anywhere else in the South – doctors, nurses and administrators at the VA hospital, professors at the Institute. A good, good place to be selling insurance, especially if you were the town's only pharmacist. Every couple of years daddy paid his way up to Hartford and met with the insurance people. Became something like a person to the people there which is why his policies got paid. Couldn't count on that all the time, which is why people got insurance from him. Companies selling policies to Negroes would "lose" the claims or send checks that never arrived or all of a sudden "discover" some missed monthly payments, so the policy was no good now.

It's what happened with us. Without daddy birddogging the claim it vanished. Wrote to all the people who'd known daddy but now we were just another sucker. Had to resubmit at least twice. One time said they wouldn't pay because the death certificate "looked suspicious." Then came letters about it being looked into and how it shouldn't be long. Then no letters came at all.

Also figured on getting some money out of the pharmacy. It had done good for years. He had a partner, Mr. Desmond, and they'd known each other since being kids. Daddy went to college and became a pharmacist and Mr. Desmond, well, he did a little of this and some of that as we used to say. Must have been good at it, because he always had cash. Loaned daddy money to pay for school and setting up the pharmacy after that. The VA hospital was just being built then, so a pharmacy seemed like a sure thing and it was. Daddy ran the medicine side of things and Desmond had an office in back where he did what he did. I didn't know all what that was, but he ran numbers, which was another sort of insurance business. For the first few years it was like daddy worked for Desmond but then he paid what he'd owed.

I loved it in there. A pharmacy then was special. Floor was black-and-white diamond-shaped tiles, washed and polished every day. Glass-front cases on the walls reaching all the way up to the ceiling. A high ceiling so there was a brass rail put in for a special ladder with wheels for getting at the top shelves. Counters all dark wood, except in front of the soda fountain where they were marble. Four tall chairs of fancy twisted metal in front of the soda fountain so you could sit and have ice cream floats and Cokes. All nice enough for guys to bring dates to the pharmacy. I worked the fountain and saw some guys propose right there. Only one got shot down. I didn't charge him. The middle of the shop had wood cases of shelves and on top were giant glass jars, called show globes, filled with green and red and blue liquids. No real reason for them except that's what people expected to see when they went into a pharmacy. When daddy had down time, he'd try at different solutions to get different colors. Said some pharmacists guarded their formulas, never sharing them with anyone. Asked if that's what he did. He said that would be foolish and gave me a wink saying he was one of those pharmacists. Then he laughed, enjoying the silly of it. First time I ever understood that grownups weren't all grownup, had some kid left and sometimes even had fun.

You could get pretty much everything at a pharmacy: medicine, of course, stuff from the soda fountain, newspapers, books, magazines a cup of coffee, candies, chocolate bars, make-up, hair coloring, hair straighteners, skin lighteners, herbal extracts, toys, and games. He even sold condoms, which were illegal back then, but you couldn't ask for them right out. A guy had to sort of indicate with a nod and say something like, "I also need a few of *those*." Daddy wouldn't sell to anyone under 21, which is foolish. You could even get alcohol during Prohibition. If a doctor gave you a prescription saying you needed it for "medicinal purposes" you could get any booze you wanted. Didn't know it then but that's why Mr. Desmond kept the office at the pharmacy. Had to have a real, certified pharmacist for that to be legal. Back then all a lot of pharmacies had was someone wearing a white doctor's coat saying he was a druggist. Sell anything and maybe didn't care if it killed you or cured you. Daddy with a degree and certified by the state brought in the of business.

At the funeral I heard people say Mr. Desmond needed to give us money we were owed and maybe buying us out so he could have daddy's half of the store. I really didn't understand what all they were talking about so I hoped Mr. Desmond would come by and give us whatever money we were supposed to get but he didn't. Weeks and weeks went by with me wanting Mr. Desmond to show up mostly because I was really scared of talking to him. Didn't make him special. Any time I had to ask something of a grownup who wasn't kin I usually almost threw up and couple of times did. Had to wait for my fear of us not having money to get bigger than my fear of him.

Saw him at the pharmacy and he was really nice about it. Thought he might be – never seen him without a smile and cigar sticking out of it – but thinking on things like that never made me any less afraid. A mostly round man about medium height, always wore a fine clothing – black homburg pushed back on his head, two-tone shoes, silk vest over fine shirt with a button-on collar and all of it going along with pants that cost.

Said we should go in back to talk about it so he could explain some things. Put up the closed sign on the front door so we wouldn't be disturbed, even asked me if I wanted a Coke.

"I'm sorry, Moses," he said. "You shouldn't have had to come see me, I should have come to see you, but you know ..." His voice seemed to trail off into grief.

"That's OK, Mr. Desmond. This is a very hard time for all of us." Barely got the end of the sentence out before I started crying. So embarrassed. Said "I'm sorry" a couple of time but couldn't help myself. He got me tissue and let me alone until the crying stopped.

"I understand, Moses. Nothing to be sorry about. We all loved your father. He meant so much to all of us and to this business. He had – has – a fine reputation and he earned it. That's one of the reasons I didn't want to talk to you about all this," he said, motioning at couple of big green ledger books.

"What? What do you mean?"

"Moses, I don't know how to tell you this but," he paused here like he was about to say something horrible. "Your daddy was a ... gambler."

"No, he wasn't!"

I couldn't imagine that. Daddy was someone who thought through everything he did, usually a couple of times. Hated spending money. Seemed like if he had a nickel in his pocket at start of the day it'd still be there end of day.

"Afraid he was," he said. "And he wasn't a good one. Now you must know that I run some numbers now and then. Let people put down a little money for a chance to win a lot of it. You ask anyone and they'll tell you I always pay on the spot to the winner. And if someone wins and doesn't come to get their money quickly, I go and find them! I know running numbers isn't the most honorable thing to do but I do my best to do it honorably. That's why this is so difficult for me to say to you."

Opened one of his ledger books and got an envelope with daddy's name on it, held it over the desk and let contents spill out, little white slips of paper fluttering slowly down to the green on the desk blotter. Lot of them. I picked one up. An IOU with daddy's signature for a few dollars. Picked up some more and several were for quite a lot of money.

"I begged him to stop," Mr. Desmond said. "Begged him. I even said I wouldn't take his money anymore, but he said he'd find someone else to gamble with. There are some very, very bad people who are bookies and I was afraid what they would do to your daddy if he couldn't pay them. I knew it would be better he owed someone who would be kind with him."

What Mr. Desmond told me, and I'd seen made me dizzy. Thought I was about to pass out. It must have showed because Mr. Desmond got that Coke, and I drank it and we sat there silent.

"So, you can see why I didn't want to talk to you about this," he said. "Truth is he owed me more than his half of the pharmacy. He was back on salary, in fact. Now I know how tough a time this is for y'all and I don't want to put you in a worse way. I'm glad to settle all this for only his half of the store. It'll cost me but you and your mother are like family to me. I'll even do what I can and give you a little something each week for a bit."

"What do I tell momma?"

"I know!" he said. "I worried about that too. I would do anything not to hurt your daddy's reputation or your mother's memory of him. Because of that I've thought about this quite a bit, in fact, but I don't know what to do."

We sat again until Mr. Desmond clapped his hands.

"I've got it!" he said. "Why don't we go ahead and say that times being as hard as they are – and Lord knows that's true – I don't have enough cash right now. In fact, I will have to wait to find someone to sell your father's interest in the store to. How does that sound?"

I'd have agreed to anything right then.

"That way we can keep all this between us. Nobody else needs to know," he said.

All made sense to me and felt like a relief too. Weren't getting any money but at least we weren't owing.

"Thank you, sir," I said. "Thank you so much."

Started to leave but he stopped me, got his wallet, and handed a $20, which was a lot of money.

"You take care now."

12

At least with daddy being dead people stopped asking me all the time why I didn't play sports. Too busy working or looking for work. Any and every job I could. One of daddy's friends at the Institute got me a job as a janitor. Only a night or two a week but something. Mr. Desmond gave me a shift running the soda fountain and others came by with odd jobs needed doing. Wasn't enough but it was some. Momma made me promise I wouldn't do anything that would show my strength. Terrified she'd lose me, too.

Before I turned 10, I never even thought about playing sports. Eyesight was terrible is one thing. Wore big, thick glasses, always falling off and breaking if I tripped or walked into something and that was most of the time. Even if they stayed on it wouldn't have helped. Hopscotch and jacks too hard for me. But then...

Eyesight started getting better around when about 8 years old. No doctor could figure that. At 10 I'm not even wearing glasses. Then of a sudden I was good at sports. Better than good really.

Went from a joke to being the slick shortstop, the flying outfielder, the pitcher everyone wanted on a team. And hitting? Throw it nearby and it was gone. Started too small to hit a real, out-of-the-park home run, but I put the ball anywhere I want. Easy to see, easy to hit. Pitch coming looked big to me. Could almost count the stitches on the ball. I was speed, too. Anyone else's single my double. A double? Bet on me making all the way home.

Weird going from a no one to the best so fast. Before I'd get picked on because of my glasses and clumsy. Favorite things were reading and math. And telling others how much better I was at them. Probably picked on for that, too. Or maybe they picked on me and that's my way of getting back. Maybe both. Got good at sports and I acted the same. Difference was now other kids would put up with me. Didn't make sense. My cousin Erlissa was only friend I really had. She'd yell at me and all a few times. Can't blame her. But they were one-day fights and next day it wouldn't matter a damn to her.

Mamma didn't like me at sports. Worried about injuries. Whenever I left the house, she told me to be careful. Dad's friends wanted to know what he was feeding me. He'd smile at the joke, but always seemed worried. Puberty was unreal. Started sixth grade about five feet tall. A year later, six feet and going. Went from skinny and wiry to carved out of a big piece of a mountain. My skin got darker, too. Like someone kept putting another coat of stain on wood. Eventually *real* black, no brown to it at all. It didn't stop till it got a color Uncle Stan said was blacker than lights out at the bottom of a mine. Called it the color everything was before God made light.

I was 12 a scout from the Black Barons, the Negro League team in Birmingham, came to see me play. Talked after the game and his first question, "Any other scouts seen you?" I said no and a look on his face like Christmas morning. Said Barons *might* be interested, and I started smiling exactly like him.

Got home it was all I could talk about, so I didn't notice my parents being sad but then dinner and my father interrupted me.

"You've got to stop playing ball."

"Baseball?"

"Any kind of ball. Any sports."

"Why?"

"You got too good too fast. First thing that man asks is if any other teams have scouted you. Said they *might* be interested. He's already called his bosses. You could play for them right now. I know it and he knows it and you aren't even shaving. This is trouble."

"Are you kidding?" As close to raising my voice to my parents as I ever. "Momma, I'm not going to get hurt. This man said I could be really good. I could get paid to play baseball!"

Went like that a while longer then momma said, really quiet, "It's not about you getting hurt. I'm scared you could hurt someone else."

Made sense even though I couldn't have explained, and I went from angry to confused fast as falling down stairs.

"Remember last week, we were working on fixing that door frame?" my father asked.

"Uh huh."

"You were sawing and cut your hand," he said.

"I know!" Didn't mean to snap but couldn't stop. That age where I got frustrated faster than knowing why. A constant flicker between knowing everything and everyone knowing I didn't know anything.

"I'll be more careful." Like he'd hurt me for bringing up my mistake and I'd hurt me by making it.

Put his hand on top of mine, very gently.

"That's not the problem," he said. "Let me show you something." Walked out then came back holding something behind his back.

"First thing to know is you were sawing faster than if it had a motor on it," he said. "When the saw hit your hand, how much of a cut did you get?"

Looked at the back of my hand. "None, I guess."

Brought the saw from behind his back, laid it out on the table. Middle had a big patch with all the teeth gone.

"What happened to it?"

"Remember? I took it as soon as you cut yourself. Saw should have cut you deep. At that speed it should have gone right through your hand."

"No! You are trying to pull something on me because you don't want me playing ball."

"I wish we were," he said.

"No, no," I said, getting scared. "That's impossible. Why are you saying this?"

"Moses, I need you to do something for me. OK?"

"W-what?"

"Look at your mother for a moment."

"OK," I said, turned my head and looked at her. Suddenly, something like a slight, dull bump against my hand and mother breathed in fast and loud. I looked at my hand and couldn't make sense of what I was seeing. Daddy had a big knife that was against of my hand, like trying to stab me. The blade bent to one side. That little thing I felt had to be because my father tried to stab me, but I literally couldn't imagine that. The knife didn't make any sense either. It was a big sharp kitchen knife, but it was bent and right against my hand. There was no blood. No mark at all.

"I'm so sorry to do that to you, Moses," my father said, his eyes shiny wet and almost crying. "I didn't know how else to make you see what's happening to you."

"What do you mean, happening to me?"

"Do you remember anything about that time you got lost? Anything at all?"

I shook my head. When I was 8, I got lost in some woods, found my way home. Parents said I'd been gone for three days. Didn't believe them. *Knew* it had only been a few hours. A few times since my parents asked if I remembered anything else. I didn't. Never gave thought to why they asked.

"Since then, we've noticed things about you that were different than before," my mother said. "They were all good things, but they didn't really make sense. Eyes don't fix themselves. And it's not only that you don't need glasses anymore, you also see things so far away it shouldn't be possible."

"So?"

"I saw you juggling some bricks the other day," she said. "How long have you been doing that?"

"Only that time," I said. "I saw a man do it when the carnival came through and when I saw the bricks, I thought I'd give it a try."

"You'd never done that before?" She asked and I shook my head no.

"Did you drop any of them?"

Shook my head again.

"Honey, it takes a long time to learn to juggle."

"No," I said, knowing she had to be wrong. "Juggling is easy. At least if it's only three or four things. Now when I was juggling the five bricks I could see where that might be hard."

"Five? I missed that."

"I just did the same thing that carny man did."

"Moses, most people can't juggle anything," daddy said.

"And those bricks," momma said, "you were tossing them like they didn't weigh any more than a pebble."

Caught me there. Threw the bricks around for an hour or more and arms didn't feel any different than at the start.

"What's wrong with me?" I said, getting scared again.

"Nothing's *wrong* with *you*," said my father. "*You* are a good person. *You* don't lie. *You* don't sass. *You* work hard. *You* care about other people. *You* do everything mother and I ask of you and more. You go to church and what's more you try to put the Lord's teachings to work."

"You're different is all," momma said. "Very different. Already faster and stronger than anyone I've ever known. You're already big even though you're an age most people are only starting to get their growth."

"I don't understand," I said. "If I'm so much better than anyone else, why can't I play ball? I could be the best ever."

"You're thinking like a person," my mother said.

Being a person. The best, most dangerous thing to be. A person is as good as anyone else and not Colored or Negro or whatever else white people said. The truth and the truth can set you free and can also get you killed. Dangerous. Being a person is intoxicating. Places it's safe to be black and a person and places it isn't: Barbershop, home, church, a bar, maybe not on the streets outside them though. Our neighborhood not as risky as their neighborhoods but anywhere outside could turn, even as you're watching. Police car always might drive by. Maybe good ol' boys show in a place they never are. Natural for a person think they're person everywhere, at any time. Right to think it. Nothing more important than being a person. Why it was worst crime we could commit. Why they made a whole world to stomp it out.

"We're scared of what could happen to you," momma said.

"What could happen to me?"

He paused and shook his head.

"Think the government is just going to let you be? They find out about you they'll snatch you up and do whatever to try and make another. If they can't, they'll just lock you up. You're getting bigger and stronger almost every day and we don't know how long that will go on. If you grow like ..." He paused here and I knew he was trying to think of any word he could use that wasn't "normal" or "human."

"Everyone else?" I said.

"Yes, like everyone else," he said. "If you grow like everyone else then you still have some more years of growing to do. But even if you don't, even if you were to stop growing today, you're already stronger than anyone I've ever heard of. You might even be bullet proof. If you are or if you're not, won't matter to the government. They won't let you be. They'll want you under their control or dead."

He let out a little, unhappy laugh.

"Who would have thought being invincible would be dangerous?"

"What do I do?"

First response was a long, sad quiet.

"Be careful and quiet," daddy said. "Don't do things that draw attention."

"Like sports."

"Yes."

All sat silent again. I wanted to argue but nothing to argue about. These were facts. Wanted to say what so many of us have said so many times, "Why? I didn't do anything wrong." True. Makes no difference. That's the inescapable weight. Dreams would always be crushed, sometimes before you know you have them.

Glanced at my parents, looking heartbroken and afraid, wondered what they'd had destroyed.

"What was it for you?" I asked my mother.

"Harvard. Or Johns Hopkins. Or the Massachusetts Institute of Technology. One of them. I was the best in all my classes. Especially chemistry."

My father nodded.

"Didn't even answer my letters. They weren't going to teach a Negro to be a chemist. They probably don't think it's possible. So, I applied to Musgrove College and that's where I found out *they* weren't going to teach a *woman* to be a chemist. My own people. I roared. Roared at them all. I lectured the professors about Marie Curie, about knowledge, about them treating me just like whites. They just laughed. Laughed. Told me it was a silly idea."

More silence, this one like after the first shovel of dirt hits the coffin.

"What about you, daddy?"

He shook his head no and I wish I hadn't asked. Knew all I needed; he'd had it happen too. Everything else only details.

"What do I say about why I can't play anymore?"

"That your parents are afraid and won't let you."

There was a moment and we all looked at each other and started to laugh. No one have any trouble believing that.

I ONLY PLAYED BECAUSE kids asked. Always happier with a book than a ball.

School's library didn't have many books and no public library let us in the door, front or back. Reread some books so many times I'd memorize it all. Nothing to do for it until when I was 10 and momma gave me keys to the universe: A Tuskegee Institute library card.

"But that's, that's for college students," I said.

"Means you will have to work harder to read them."

Institute library was big, not as big as it is now, but bigger than a 10-year-old's imagination. Three large rooms up to the ceilings of books. I'd sit way in back and read. Didn't want a student asking what a kid was doing in *their* library. Happened once and guy who did it ... well, I started crying and he went straight at feeling terrible. Apologizing to me over and over, then to the librarian who was very not pleased. Next time saw me brought his friends over, said look at this kid so smart he's reading our books and one of them gave me a candy bar. But I stayed scared it might happen again.

One day I heard someone say they were looking for the book I was reading. Sound was like next to me but was no one there. Went around, up and down aisles of shelves, no one in the room or next room. Finally went out to the checkout desk up front, so short I could be seen over the counter. Put the book on it and asked someone was looking for it.

"Yes, a couple of minutes ago. How did you know?"

Shrugged and went to look for another book.

13

Money.

Except for daddy's death all I could think about. Didn't know how much we had only that it was running out. Daddy's funeral cost was a lot of the reason and another thing I hammered myself about being my fault.

Got so bad for a few days had voices in my head, little gray whispers from somewhere and something I couldn't ever see. "You shoulda known, shoulda known shoulda known." Even when they stopped they were still there. Remember them and think they were back and once I figured out they weren't, I'd worry about what it would be like if they did. Thought on killing myself they came back. Didn't know I couldn't.

Big arguments with momma about quitting school for a full-time job. Wouldn't hear that, thought we could take in a border or two. Sounded good but it was the Depression and other people had the same idea, right when there was no one to rent to.

Tried telling momma sorry for getting daddy killed but words turned clay in my throat, and I couldn't breathe. She had to hate me. Had to. What I thought even without her showing anything like it. Didn't matter. Even she didn't hate me, I did. These damn powers most of all. All their fault. Hating them could make me feel better by letting daddy's death be the fault of whatever had done this to me.

Hated them not just for that. No good to me at all. Maybe could've made money with 'em. Join a freak show or something. But I had to hide so no money from them. Money. All everything came down to.

Mr. Desmond gave a $10 or a $20 for a few weeks then said business was bad and no more for me.

In the end no reason for all those arguments with momma. No full-time work to get. For a while had little job loading milk trucks early in the morning couple days a week. Came home from it as momma was going out the front door, in a Sunday church coat on a weekday. Told me there were muffins in the oven. Smiling I said thank you and about to ask her where she was going but saw she was using the coat to hide wearing a maid uniform. She tried smiling too but it didn't work. Did my best to act like I didn't see it.

Momma was fierce when angry, intimidating to anyone anytime she wanted. She'd told her father she was going to go to college, he said it was a waste of time. They were at the dinner table and she went stood down to the end of the table directly across from him. That's all. No fuss or saying anything. Stood there, staring, not letting the conversation be over. He was a hard man raised by a hard man and lived a hard life. Didn't know he'd raised a daughter even harder. No way through to getting up from table without an argument that'd be as useful as arguing with an avalanche. Last he coughed, mumbled about it "only being a thought and he'd go talk it over with her mother and see what she thought."

But there momma was, handbag in hand and going to clean and fetch, do as she was told. Stood a moment, both trying not to cry until she kissed my cheek, said she might be late home and went.

So many different ways to die. So many.

14

Day everything we owned was sold sky looked like it wanted to rain but didn't have the energy. A day too hot and too humid, day a storm would clear up, taking away damp air like sweat. Maybe it'd even bring a relieving breeze but no storm to stop everything continuing awful.

By then we'd discovered a thing worse than momma being a maid: Not able to do that. Went to the job a couple of weeks but then grief or nerves or whatever were back again. Went back to her chair in the parlor, holding daddy's picture, watching nothing on the street.

Said I couldn't find work but maybe I could've. Started telling momma I was looking for work but go off and sit somewhere, looking at air like she was. Jobs I had I didn't do very well. Washing a floor or bailing hay then think of that night and stop. Stand still with my head seeing, hearing, feeling it all like a movie playing so slow a second took a minute to pass. Time let me think on could've and should've. Sometimes I'd see the same little thing happen over and over until someone shook me or said something. Other times nothing would happen. I'd just see the policeman's body and his neck bending in that way it shouldn't. So, the jobs I got I lost pretty quick. Felt I didn't deserve them, anyway, didn't deserve anything.

Tried selling our house before money ran out but no one buying. Bank foreclosed and a court order gave them what was in the house too. So, they auctioned what we had to get some money back.

Momma and I stood across the street watching, arms around each other. Auctioneer, fat little white man wearing seersucker and a boater hat, stood on our porch. A deputy sheriff there, too. Wasn't uncommon. Auctions happening all over, sometimes people get up family and friends and try taking it back. Deputy a little ways away from us, leaning against the police car, chewing tobacco. Now and then spitting a gob of black stuff on the street. Not just spitting anywhere either. Aiming at a little area about half way across the street and mostly hitting it. Never seen an adult serious spitter before. Boys, we're always bragging on how far and how accurate. Someone called you on your bragging you had to back it up. So, we practiced a lot, all time not wanting parents to find out. Said it was disgusting and common, both true and both were reasons we were doing it. Deputy had a real rhythm to the way he went at it – suck on chaw, suck on chaw, push it to one side of his mouth, push it to the other, suck on chaw, suck on chaw, then ready to spit. Same every time. Fascinated me. Also watching it was an improvement on anything else there was for watching right then.

That all was horrible. Everyone turned on us. People buying what was ours were all from the church! About 10 of them, dressed in black clothes they probably wore for daddy's funeral. Working together to see they only paid a bit more than nothing for what they got. Even though we weren't going to get any of the money that made it even worse.

"Fine sofa. Beautiful condition," the auctioneer called, shirt blotchy with sweat. You could tell he was a bank man, not a real auctioneer as everything was said normal instead of the fast-singing way it should be done.

"Start bidding at $5. Five dollars! Who'll go $5?"

"Four seventy-five! Who'll go $4.75?"

"Four fifty."

"Four and a quarter."

"Four dollars."

"Three seventy-five."

"Three fifty."

"Three and a quarter."

"Three dollars."

His face getting redder with each price drop. At a dollar all he was an angry apple with mouth and eyes. He paused there, took a sip of something from a flask and looked straight at the deputy like he had something to be doing.

Deputy looked right back at him, loosed a brown ball of tobacco spit up and up and almost to the other side of the road.

Everybody hated the bankers.

That was the longest spit I'd ever seen. I sorta looked over to the deputy and gave a little nod and smile, acknowledging the shot. Must have caught me on the corner of his eye. Did his own little nod and even smaller smile. But then remembered who he was, who I was, what the world was. Sent a chunk of spit right in front of momma's shoes.

The auctioneer was calling out twenty-five cents when he got his first offer.

"Dime," someone said.

Auctioneer looked over to the deputy, but he was busy not giving a damn.

"Once, going twice, going three times, gone ten cents," he said, took another nip, let out a long sigh and right then his face started back to a normal color.

Auction went faster then on, as the auctioneer started everything at fifty cents. Watched for some longer, don't know why. Because it had been ours probably. Left as they brought out Grandpa Jordan's chair. Reverend's wife had first bid on it.

Uncle Stan would've taken us in but had a new wife and three kids from his earlier marriages. Maybe other people offered help but my mind doing better than mamma's so if they did, I ignored them. Honest, right then I didn't want help, didn't even want to exist. Not killing myself, disappearing. Gone from my world and anything that reminded me about it. If there wasn't mamma to care for I'd have gone on the bum, riding the rails anywhere. A car I'd have driven, wings and I'd have flown.

Couldn't do any of that but one thing I could do, one place to go as good as falling off the earth.

15

There's town poor and there's country poor. Country poor is invisible.

"You're a big one all right. What you say your name was?"

"Moses, suh."

"How old you, Moses?"

"Don' rightly know, suh."

"Don't matter, really. Ever done farmin' before, boy?"

"No, suh."

"Oh you'll pick it up fast. Nothing to it really. Now, can you read or do numbers?"

"No, suh." Tomming is easy. Bow your head, look at the floor when you talk. Never in their eyes. Talk slow and mush mouth, like your tongue's half asleep. Pretend you don't understand so they have to repeat what they said. Might irritate them but it's what they want. Really. Shuffle some when you walk. Make it seem you don't know if you should be doing what you're doing. That was easy for me. Leave words out of sentences now and then. Call them suh, not sir. Call them boss. Every time you speak. Give them what they want to see, and they only see what they want. Let's you hide right in front of them. They're not looking at you, they're looking in the mirror. Don't tell them anything true. Watch everything, hear everything. They'll tell you who they really are and who they think they are, even though they don't know it themselves.

I'm tomming in a barn that's a hard wind from falling down, in front of a man who thinks he's important because he's sitting at a desk. Doesn't matter it's warped from rain and bleached by sun and only still standing because no one bothered to kick it into kindling. Still a desk and he knows a man at a desk is important. That's all he has. Boss or maybe his boss's boss is Beaumont the owner. This guy looks close to the nothing he is. Small and lean, skin the color of the ash at the end of a cigarette about to burn your fingers, straw hat half-way back his head, clothes like any other shit kicker. Trying to act like someone. Someone slick as goose shit putting one over a half-wit darkie.

"No ciphering? OK, you gotta sign this contract but you can just make a mark. That'll be fine. I'll tell you what it said though."

"Thank ya, boss."

Sharecropping. Sign a piece of paper, get a share of land on a plantation – yeah, that's the word – to farm and live on. Even comes with a shack. Except you don't get the land, it gets you. Pay rent at harvest with crops you grow and working the owner's crops. Anything you need? Have to buy from the owner. Anything. Not only seeds or a plow or a team to pull the plow or what it took to farm. Clothes, furniture, tools, wood, food, pots, pans, buckets. Owner knows you've no money so get what you get on credit. Has be paid back at harvest too.

Owner sets prices on what you buy. Sets interest rate on credit he gives. Sets prices he pays for the crops you try to pay him back with. Changes those numbers when he wants so it's never paid off. Who's going to argue or even know? Not poor crackers and Negroes never been to inside a school. Back then there was public schooling for everyone but there wasn't. School was free, books weren't. Have to pay for those. No school for the poor. Over in Louisiana, Governor Huey Long had the state pay for all the books and rich people wanted him killed for a Communist. Poor people voted for him though, which is what he planned.

Anything you sign your name to, all the numbers are changeable. Why the owner says your signing a contract for a year but find out later it's five or 10 years. Not that what the words really said matters. What they really mean is you are here for life. Owners are backed by laws don't let you move off the land without a say so. Try and go to prison and you're rented out to doing the exact same work and putting the money in a warden's pocket.

That's just one way to prison, plenty others. Missed payment, don't have enough for a whole payment, or do everything right and a plantation owner said you didn't pay. He can take everything you have – even clothes on you – and throw you out. Police are already there, and you got as much money as a catfish so you're guilty for vagrancy. Joke goes that it isn't illegal to be poor in the U.S., but it might as well be. The hell it isn't.

Thing is, if you want to disappear this is the place for it. Plantations separate from anywhere else, sealed behind poverty and despair. Not much reason to go off the plantation except maybe a Saturday night drunk at a juke joint, if you can afford it. If not, you stay at home, drink there. Takes a lot of extra hands to work a piece of land big enough to pay but those hands all have a mouth that need to eat and bodies that want clothes. Means all you're about is getting enough to feed the family. Who has attention for other, bigger issues? Not you'd likely know of them. No radio and even people who can read can't afford a newspaper, so might as well be no outside world. Disappear from the world and the world disappears from you.

"That's everything what's in the contract," man said. "Don't have to remember all that. Come look at any time. Just ask. Glad to show it you and read it again. You put your mark there. I'll get someone to take you to where you'll be at."

I used my wrong hand to draw an X. Don't know why I bothered. I signed my whole name in Sunday-school cursive best he still would have seen it as an ignorant man's scrawl.

In return for my mark and my life we get a shotgun shack sitting on a land of weeds and dust. Three rooms in a row, windows with no glass. Trench out back for a lavatory. Front room has an ancient twist of flypaper black with dead flies and a wood stove with a busted seam. The walls half-covered with newspapers to plug cracks where winds and dirt blow in, so someone gave up, moved on or died in the attempt. At least the tin roof looked alright and we were near a creek to get water.

Moved what little we had in and fixed the stove by pinching the metal. Momma insisted on going and getting wood and making us something to eat even though I don't think either of us wanted to.

"We will return to become ourselves," she said as we sat on the porch pretending to eat while really watching a sun set. No pretty in the sky either. Just a pale-yellow fighting to be seen through a sky gone brown from all the dust.

"I'll make us something here," I said.

"I know you will, son. I know you will."

We were nobody and nowhere and that was all I wanted right then.

16

In addition to giving a portion of what we grew to Mr. Beaumont we also had to bring in his cotton. Put about as a way for us to earn some extra money if we wanted, but nothing optional to it. As we had moved in at harvest time only way to make money was in his fields.

Got up some time deep in a night and went where I'd been told to. I don't know how many of us there were, but it was a lot – men, women, and children. We got to the fields and you could almost see the sun tipping over the horizon. A white man, the overseer, told 10 people they were captains in charge of about 15 people each. Followed ours to the field we were working, and he put us each to a furrow. When he started hoeing down the side of it, chopping weeds without hurting the cotton plants, everyone else started too.

After that came picking. Don't know how people who aren't me can do that. Horrible hard work, bent over the whole time to get at the cotton. Only choice besides crouching is all day on hands and knees. Do it dragging an enormous sack, at least six feet long, gets heavier as the day goes on and you fill it with cotton. If you're real good it can get to 200 or 300 pounds. With an average picker it'll go a hundred easy.

Cotton doesn't want picking. Grows inside a boll, little thing size of a golf ball. Can't be picked until it starts to open, and you can see cotton out the top. Boll has four or five sharp stickers to protect itself. Be as careful you want, still going to get cut over and over. Also have saw briars cutting your legs and cockle burrs sticking to clothes, the sack, and the cotton. Thing to really look for is a little worm called a packsaddle that eats cotton leaves and has a real mean sting.

Best pickers have small bodies, so women, older kids, and small, skinny men. Normal person even close to my size? No way they're any good. Hands to big, knees and back too sore. Me? I didn't even notice all that bending over.

First day I slowed myself and was picking just bit slower than the fastest person, woman named Irene. Life had been hard and harder to her. If you told me she was 25 I'd have believed it and the same and if you told she was 45. She'd have been faster than she was but for carrying a sling with a baby. Never mind about me, that's real strength. She had a sister about my age called Juneybug. Always a look on her face like picking was a personal insult. Slowest picker out there by a good margin.

Took our first water break and I wound up near to them. Irene looked me up and down a couple time and finally said, "Big man mostly worthless out here. Groaning and complaining whole time. Seen some walk off half-way through a day. Never one as good as you."

"Thanks," I said. "Don't think I could do what you do. Not with the baby and all."

She nodded.

"This my sister, Juneybug,"

"Jet," the girl said really loud.

"What?"

"Jet," she said. "Call me Jet."

"Don't mind her," said Irene, irritated. "Thinks she's too good for her real name."

"Do not," said Jet. "It'll just sound stupid. Who ever heard of a professor called Juneybug?"

Irene let out a long, long sigh. "You never even been in a classroom."

"I'll be at the front of a classroom," Jet said. "I will." Not said as boast or argument. Said it as a certainty.

Like everyone else here she was skinny from too much work and not enough food, dirty and sweaty because impossible not to be. Wore a washed-out blue thing more patch than dress. Tall, real tall, and all angles and sharp edges, which wasn't just about not getting enough to eat. More than any-thing her eyes got my attention, different than all the rest were out here.

Sharecroppers – white, black, brown, whatever – got a look like old mules, plodding along to survive. Can't blame them, it isn't a life about big plans for the future. Not Jet. Eyes were moving, smart, intense, alive, fiery, all the time.

"Don't pay no mind," said Irene.

Too late.

Looking at her quick then looking anywhere else so she didn't catch me staring. Me being me I'd rather have died before talking to someone I didn't know but had to say something and had to be right then. Had to get her to know I existed and maybe even make her smile.

"You're about the worst picker out here, aren't you?" I said real flat and even, not a tease or joke.

Her head snapped around and she stared up into my eyes. "So?"

Really quietly, hoping my voice didn't crack, I said. "Meant that as a compliment."

Continued looking at me and had almost started to make what I thought could have been the start of a smile but then she walked away.

"Figured her out quick," Irene said, raising an eyebrow and not letting me know if that was a good thing or a bad thing. Then we got back to work.

That one time talking to Jet used all my braveness. Avoided her the rest of the day, spent my time thinking I'd said the stupidest thing ever. Once or twice I actually felt something like awe when I thought maybe she understood, and I wasn't a *total* idiot. That didn't last long.

Finally figured something to say which I hoped didn't have too much of a chance of making me look like a fool. Jet's dress had one red pocket in the front where she kept a small, old book with covers that were barely staying on. Whenever there was a break, she'd pull it out and read it.

Next morning, she was sitting on the ground reading, so I went over and asked what the book was. I was hours coming up with this idea. "Twelve Caesars," she said, not looking up.

"Suetonius?"

Head didn't shift from the book, but an eyebrow raised, and eyes looked at me for a full second before going back to reading.

"Know it?"

"Read it."

"English or Latin?"

"Latin. Momma was always after me to read more Latin, but it never grabbed me much. Twelve Caesars is probably the only thing I liked. It's fun. Has all sorts of gossip like stuff in it. Makes all those guys seem like real people, y'know?"

"*Praesidibus onerandas tributo provincias suadentibus rescripsit boni pastoris esse tondere pecus, non deglubere,*" she said, still not looking up.

"OK, give me a second," I said, and she rolled her eyes.

"A good shepherd cuts ... nah, shears ... something, probably sheep but I don't remember; he does not ... beat ... them?"

Got me a full head turn away from the book.

"Shears *the flock*. He does not *flay* them." She said, more irritation but less contempt.

"Oh. Yeah. It's been a while."

"You got the tenses right, though." Like she was deciding if I'd made up for the vocabulary.

"How'd *you* learn Latin?" Really suspicious, like maybe I had cheated.

"Momma and daddy made me. Momma wanted me to learn Greek too, but I didn't really have the time..."

Jumped up and started yelling.

"YOU COULD HAVE LEARNED GREEK AND YOU DIDN'T? WHAT IS WRONG WITH YOU?" Tried to hit me with the book. "The mother tongue! If you know Greek you can read Plato and Homer..."

"Bible, too." Trying to sound like I knew something.

She nodded and took a deep breath.

"Tell me, what is more important than learning Greek?" Contempt wasn't dripping from her words, it was spitting.

Fear was right back with me. I was a fake and she was about to know it, which is why I mumbled my answer really quietly.

"WHAT? Your giant head is up there somewhere so you need to speak up if you want normal people to hear you."

Ouch.

"I wanted to study trigonometry..."

"Greek word," she said.

"What?"

"Trigonometry. From the Greek *trigonon,*" she said. "Never mind. Go on."

Ever been in class, up at the blackboard, everyone looking at you, know the answer but feel like you don't? Where I was.

"I wanted to study trigonometry because I like math but I'm not really great at it, so momma spent her time helping me with geometry..."

"Another Greek word."

"... instead of teaching me Greek."

"Your mother could have taught you Greek?" Now she sounded confused.

"Well, she taught me Latin. She's a real good teacher."

She stood there a moment, considering everything I said. Finally, she gave me a little nod, like what I said was almost reasonable and walked away. Toughest exam of my life.

"That's a first," Irene, who was nearby, said.

"What?"

"Usually, it's the boys leaving ... at speed."

17

BACK TO PICKING AND thinking about Jet, not what I'm doing. Singing going on and me along with them to make time go by. Not going pleasantly even so. Regular people do this months and years, but how?

"Stop it! Stop it!"

In my ear loud, startle scared and go from hunched to standing. Heart and breathing shot right to too, too fast and hold there. Brain beating faster than either, straining for a threat, any threat, there must be a threat. Ignore the shouter, too small. Turn around once, then again. Looking, only sort of focused, at half-way to the horizon. Looking for motion to tell where and what. Arms set to fight. Later, later, in bed that night, realize there was no thought for flight and understand: Running is over. Finally, breath slows. Brain crawls back to the present from where it had been, a place of waiting for bullets from guns fired months ago to arrive now.

Then notice the person next to me. Irene, who was too small to be considered, standing there, shaking, more terrified than I am.

"Stop what?" Really quiet and calm, trying to let her know everything is OK now.

"That. You can't do that." Waved her arm at the row I'd been picking.

Didn't understand until I looked over the field at the other pickers. Best were about done their first row and most everyone else about half that. I was on my fourth row and we hadn't been there long enough for sunlight to be more than wishful thinking.

"You're making trouble for all of us. Beaumont sees what you done he'll yell at us as lazy and why aren't we working fast as you?" A desperate voice now, loud but still sounding like a whisper. "Fine us for not doing as much or say we gotta pick as much as you each day or something else. It won't be good."

Beaumont was supposed to be one of the better owners but better wouldn't stick around if it came to getting more money.

"Problem," I said, nodding. "Real problem."

Waited after that, giving Irene more time to calm down.

"Thing is I want my money too. Can we figure some way out of this for everyone?"

She nodded, started crying out her fear.

First time understood people were scared of me. I was afraid so much my only thought of others was, are they laughing at me? Knew I was big. Hard thinking otherwise when all I see is top of heads. But it's a kid's knowing. Being small and uncertain was what was big in me. Sometimes wanting to be noticed, sometimes to be invisible, sometimes both. Never occurred to me it wasn't obvious to all the world, that people being scared was nothing about how I felt.

Didn't make *everyone* afraid. Not Jet, then or ever. Suddenly there next to Irene like being conjured.

"Whatcha doin' my sister?" Shaking a finger up at my face and no quiet in her voice. "Don' be giving her no grief." So mad talking where she was from, not where she wanted to go.

Caught herself doing it, eyes went huge and honest to God put her hand over her mouth. Irene shook her head and let out a little laugh. Made me come out with a big one. Jet started to say something but then was laughing too. All did for a bit.

"What if I picked it all and we divide it when I'm done?"

"You can't do that," Jet said, a little contempt back in her voice.

"Yeah, I can," I said. "Honestly, I haven't even been trying. I can go twice as fast easy."

Irene looked at me, chewer on her lip a bit. like Jet nodded like she didn't know to believe it.

"Today was me picking without paying attention. Yesterday I was going slow because I was scared."

"Scared?" Irene said. "What can *you* be scared about?"

Way too much question for me.

"How old are you?"

"Sixteen, last month."

"Younger than Jet," she said, shaking her head. "You really do all what you said?"

"Yeah."

"What are you?"

"Wish I knew. Think about that a lot. All I've figured so far is whatever I am is me."

"You'd do that? Pick it all and give most away?"

I nodded.

"Why?"

Shrugged. Hadn't really given that much thought.

"Because. Because I can. Because it's just me and my mother and some of y'all got whole families. Because Jesus would. Because that's how my mother and father..." My voice cracked. Couldn't even mention my father without all the hurt coming up again.

Irene reached out and put her hand on top of mine. Started to cry and put my hands up over my face. She put her arms around my waist and held me. Little woman t comforting someone my size probably looked silly, but it didn't feel that way.

Jet was gone when I stopped. Crying and hugging never would be much of her thing.

"Problem is someone coming around with water during the day. Some-times Beaumont will do it himself or send his boy out."

Getting water for the croppers working his ground was only one thing made Beaumont different from other plantation owners. Thanksgiving, Christ-mas, New Year's he put on a big feed for people working his land who didn't have enough. Sometimes at the store him or his wife wouldn't charge for some-thing and kids always got a penny candy. He came out and gave me advice when I was starting. Told me what crops to plant, how to lay out a field and a lot else. Not talking to me like an equal but not condescending or insulting.

Didn't make him a good man, just better than others. He'd still screw you on your contract, changing terms whenever he wanted, and set the price low at harvest when you were selling to him. Those people Beaumont fed, if they couldn't pay what he said was due he'd turn them out the day after, keeping everything, they thought they owned except the clothes on them. Didn't really matter if someone was charged for something since the rest of their debt was on them forever. Sick how many of us talked about him being nice. That's making a slave of yourself.

Irene and others figured out a plan, put some in the fields keeping an eye for anyone. That brought up a real problem: Had to be hollers and singing as usual. That wasn't the problem. Early morning Irene and couple of others walked up looking uncomfortable. Waited for them to talk but it was a lot of looking at each other and at the ground until Irene said: "You can't sing."

"What do you mean?"

"I mean you *can't* sing. Don't join in on it. Your voice is really loud and … and there's no melody in you. So bad it messes up everyone."

I started laughing.

"No rhythm either," Irene said, and I laughed louder. Felt good to not be able to do something.

Only close call we had was when Mr. Beaumont's son came around on his little pony cart with a big bucket of water. Everyone not picking wasn't sweating much and we all got scared he'd notice, which he didn't.

Scared of a little boy, maybe seven, eight years old. Why? White.

Baptized in the fear at birth. Press it harder and harder against the heart every day until it's running up and down your veins. Jesus was crucified to show us His sacrifice, thousands and thousands of us sacrificed so we will never forget we could be crucified, too. Instead of rosary beads we have our footsteps down any road at any time: "Mother of God what will they do to me? What will they do to me, now and at the hour of my death?"

An eight-year-old kid.

✮ ✮ ✮

Got home to momma agitated like I'd never seen. Going back and forth, back and forth on the porch and all the time muttering.

As soon as she saw me: "Have you met this girl Jet?"

Cringed. "Yes. She's a little rough on the outside."

"Rough on the outside? Rough on the outside! What does that matter? That girl is a genius!"

Mouth opened to say something but there were no words to come out.

What?

"Taught herself Latin with nothing more than a grammar book!" Talking to me or herself? Didn't really matter. Her eyes lively like before daddy's death. "Fluent like it's her native language! Never even been to a school. Had to steal books from libraries but she's read so much!"

She stopped, sat down, looked about. Looking at possibilities, not a shack sitting on dust.

"I must wash my Sunday dress. I am going to town tomorrow, to the Institute. I don't know if there's anyone who can teach her Latin there, but she wants to learn Greek and really, she has no knowledge of history other than what all those Romans wrote. We must do right by her! How will her tuition get paid? Well, that's nothing, once they meet her, they will see and she will be taken care of."

Idea of Jet making a good first impression or second or third made me laugh but momma was listening to a future, not to me. She kept talking for a while then started a fire in the stove and goes off to the creek to wash, smiling. Momma is making plans. Momma is back. Momma is back.

Next day goes to town, first time since we'd left it. Comes back in the evening, carrying a new dress. "It's for Jet. I do hope it's the right size." Day after goes to town again, Jet in tow and stunned at the speed of happiness coming down at her. Right reaction because she was gone. Never again set foot on the plantation.

18

Sharecropping just a different type slavery. Not owned directly but might as well be. Paid scrip only good at a plantation owner's store, at his prices. Working on a contract where terms can change on his whim.

Strange thing? Parts I really liked. Farming was it for me. Soon as I'm messing around in that dirt, plowing, planting, weeding, seeing it all grow, I felt right. Not many people, get born knowing that. Not me either. Even more once I learned about my powers. For a bit I thought it marked me as someone with a purpose. Chosen for something. Maybe. Shit that died in Hicksville with daddy.

Here's a weird thing: At the time I'm talking about I'm seven-foot tall with shoulders you can land an airplane on and basically nobody knew about me. Because I also had the power of Negro: Invisible until and unless I'm to be fucked over some way. The power of shuck-and-jive. Power to stay small by acting as if you don't matter. Never let them know you might have a want and whites only notice you enough to cross the street, lock the door, spit at you. All look alike and all nothing to them.

Invisible and found something I loved doing, made me feel right. Like putting on a shirt that fit when you'd only ever worn ones that didn't.

Stupid to say there were things to like about sharecropping. Stupid and true. Liked the people. Too easy for memory to make the past nicer than it was. Always be looking out for that. "Better back then." 99.9 of the time that's stupid thinking. Same here: Everyone wasn't good. Assholes and liars and folks with all sorts of problems from alcohol to being plain wrong in the head. People got nasty drunk and started beating on their wife or kids. Neighbors would come to me late at night about that, family too scared. 16, so I didn't know what to do. Broke up the fight mostly or dragged the asshole out of the house but couldn't stop them from getting back together next day. Plenty stole from each other. Having nothing you steal from the nearby to get more. The nearby don't have anything either. It's a rake or a bottle of 'shine gets stolen. There was stuff going on I never knew about: People were getting it with someone married one way or another to someone else. Even all that stuff and it still felt a lot like we were in it together. Didn't all like each other but knew we were the us in us vs. them. Seemed if people had a little extra they'd give it with no one thinking worse if you didn't. Could just be memory.

Spent more time with whites then than ever else. Later, looking at lynchings and more I couldn't believe one person would do to another, I remembered them. Ones who wound up as brown as we were because all covered in dirt from working the same fields. Whites who'd let you have the first drink of water on the hottest days and drink from the same cup, never thinking they'd catch Negro from it. Some days had to work real hard to remember that.

People of all types all they want is someone below to know they're above. Not just whites. Difference is they built the whole society around that. Have money, guns and law all working for them, even if they're poor. Negro wants to make another Negro less is an asshole. White does it and they destroy, even if they think they're not. White going after a black is backed up by a whole world of every insult, beating, and all that ever done to a black. Not just done to one they're going after either, done to all of us. Living in a community where everyone's living with that and even if no one's ever laid a hand or said a word to you, it's still happening to you. Hear the stories, see the bruises – you know it's just a matter of when.

END OF DAY, FEW months after Jet went to The Institute. Come to the shack and find Roscoe is out on the porch with Mama. Sizeable old jug at their feet and only one thing it could be was moonshine. Never had any but smelled it and it made turpentine smell good.

"Moses," said momma, "Roscoe's here and he brought us a fine, big ham. Isn't that nice of him?"

It was and I told him so. The first time I could think of that Roscoe brought something other than wanting money.

"There's this 'shine, too," he said. "I was thinking you could..."

Momma kicked the bottle off the porch. Fell right onto a rock and broke. Always had good aim.

"Why don't you and Moses go wash up and I'll finish making dinner," she said like nothing just happened.

Roscoe didn't know whether to shit or go blind. Wanted to yell and trying not to. Momma dared him, giving a look to have settled a rabid dog.

Roscoe took a few deep breaths instead.

"Kit, I didn't bring it here for drinking. A gift. I thought, Mo being gone, you might be wanting cash. Could've sold it." Mean as he could be, Roscoe never raised his voice to my mother.

"I know you meant well, Rosie." Hated being called Rosie. Anyone else and he would have had his knife out. "I don't like having it around. Can't imagine selling it. Why that would almost make me a moonshiner, wouldn't it?" She gave a laugh saying, "Now, isn't that silly," through a smile saying, "Don't you ever even."

He nodded surrender. The jug wasn't going to get any less broken and he wouldn't have won the argument anyway.

"Guess we'll go wash up then."

A moment I was actually glad to see Roscoe, that changed when we were a ways away from the shack. He took off his hat started hitting me with it and screaming.

"WHAT WRONG WITH YOU, BOY? My sister NOT live like this. NOT live in some damn cropper's shack. MY SISTER is someone! She's A COLLEGE SMART LADY, not a NIGGER! WHAT YOU DONE, BOY? Why SHE here with CRACKERS AND MORONS? She's NOT ABOUT THIS. WHAT ARE YOU DOING ABOUT IT, BOY? My sister IS A TEACHER! PROPER AND LIVES IN TOWN! IN A REAL HOUSE!"

"Where were you? Where were YOU?" I said it until it interrupted his ranting.

"NOT my job! NOT her child, not the one looking after her!"

No argument from me. I'd been thinking it for months. All my fault.

"What did you expect? I'm a kid. I don't know what to do."

Roscoe got a hard, hard look on him.

"YOU'RE NOT A BOY, boy. No kid. Seen a man die. KILLED A MAN. No sweet baby child for you after that. STOP PRETENDING. You just want someone feeling bad for you and going to keep doing this until they come along. Hiding out here. Shit, when I'm your age I've been out on the road three years and fucked a hundred women."

He paused then, slumped a little, rage and its energy gone. Rolled a cigarette, smoked about half before he talked some more.

"What happened to the money, the house?"

Told him everything. Only thing wasn't said was momma being a maid. Some things aren't said for very shame.

"What about money from the pharmacy?" He asked. "Place brings in the cash."

So embarrassed to talk of daddy's gambling I stuttered. "I-I-I w-w-ent to see Mr. Desmond and he said daddy had been gambling a lot for a long time. He showed me all these IOUs ..."

A loud, loud laugh, a donkey's bray from a mean donkey, interrupted me. It went on a couple minutes or so before Roscoe could stop long to speak.

"Maurice Crawford? Your daddy? Maurice Crawford gamble..."

Laughing again until he was even more worn out from than from the yelling. A deep breath, splashed water on his face from the creak, moved hand to mouth to smoke only to find he'd lost his cig laughing so rolled another.

"Your father hated borrowing and owing. Hated getting a mortgage for the house. Hated it. Wouldn't have done it at all but your momma said she wasn't raising a family in an apartment. You know how hard it is to find a bank lend money to a nigger? Put 50 percent down. He paid *cash* for his cars. Go down the dealer, trade the old one in and buy a new one. Didn't get shit for the trade and had to pay more for the new because he was Colored. Knew it. Didn't care. Go in, look that white man in the eye and count out the money straight down on his desk. Man didn't like a nigger looking at him like that, but he liked that cash money more. Mo always brought more than he needed so everyone could see him drop a big old roll into his pocket when he was done. Chopped his own wood, fixed his own clothes. If the law had let him, I bet he'd kept a cow so he didn't have to pay for milk.

"Wanted everyone to know he earned his money, proper. Stupid pain in the ass about it, too. John D. Rockefeller himself was giving out his shiny dimes and your father hadn't eaten in a week he still wouldn't take one. Getting money from Desmond to open up the pharmacy ate at him. Saved every cent he could. Paid it off long before Desmond wanted. Meant Desmond didn't get all the money he was counting on from the interest.

"Desmond's a snake – didn't anyone tell you that? Can't you see it for yourself? Think you're running numbers in three counties any other way? But he owned half that pharmacy and wasn't going to give that up. Mo hated being his partner. Hated it. Tried buying him out a bunch of times but Desmond knew better than to sell. Gives him legal cover for having so much money."

Stuttering again, said I didn't know any of that all.

"What wrong with you? This is what happens when you raise a child right. Don't know anything he needs to."

He took a deep breath and got mad again, but it didn't seem to be at me.

"You're eight foot tall AND bullet proof. Don't you know? What can stop you? WHAT? No one tells you how to do. You tell. Do what you want, say what you want, take what you want. Like to see 'em try and stop you. Pay good money to see that. Hell, I'd sell tickets.

"Sis and church and all those proper ones said don't be like that. All sin and Jesus didn't do none of it, so you don't either. Case you hadn't heard Jesus is dead and being a fool got him that way. That's all there is to it. You don't think that's right and who cares because your momma is living in a fucking crap piece of a shack and what's gonna fix that ain't to get nailed to a cross. You'd break the nails anyway. Just go down there and shake Desmond until money falls out. Then beat him for a while. No one will mind if you do. Believe me, that'll make you friends, and a lot of them."

Hardest part of what Roscoe said was I already knew it. Known since before momma and I moved from town. Then I didn't want it to be true. Easier to go along with whatever happened, like I had no choice, that let me pretend it wasn't my fault. Now Roscoe had said it and I couldn't pretend like I didn't know. No more certain things would go all right than I was before but certain I couldn't keep doing like I was.

"C'mon, let's go see Desmond," I said.

"Why don't you go by yourself? Been walking all day. I'm tired."

"I need you to do the talking."

"Can we at least have supper first?"

I just looked at him because I knew he already knew the answer.

"Damn. Should've waited till after we ate to give you some sense."

19

WELL INTO EVENING WHEN we got to Tuskegee, but the pharmacy was still open. That and so much else showed daddy wasn't running it anymore. Pink and blue light from a new neon sign spilling onto the street and jazz music on the radio playing loud through the open door.

Roscoe, suit and homburg covered in road dust, went in first, with me behind having to duck to get through the door. Kid I didn't know behind the counter. Roscoe said to get Desmond and the kid gave a yell. He gave the kid a look and jerked his head toward the door. Kid didn't need telling twice.

Been a while since Desmond saw me and I liked the look as he saw how big I was. Shop had tall ceilings and still had to lean forward not to bump into the lights.

"Moses, good to see you my man! And brought Roscoe," he said, sticking out his hand. "It's been too long."

Roscoe stared at the hand until it dropped.

"We come to talk to you about some money." Roscoe threw a fierce, steely eye at Desmond likely would have gotten him a beating without me there.

"Oh, I know, I know. I said I would help out Moses and his mother..."

"My sister."

"... yes, your sister, too. I've fallen woefully behind on that and do apologize. Hope you will let me make it up."

"We ain't for charity," said Roscoe, quiet, the way he only got when talking money. "We're here for cash you stole from *my sister.*"

"Did no such thing! The boy tell you about his father's gambling? I showed him all the notes I got from Maurice."

Roscoe spit, shook his head, and used a look like he'd stepped in pig shit.

"Dog won't hunt. Mo Crawford wouldn't have laid money if you gave four-to-one on the sun going down in the evening. Cut it. Just cut it all and right now. Fast talked a fool child out of what you owe." He paused, stared around a moment. May not have been a great guitar player but he could use a stage. "I know 'cause exactly what I'd a done. Too bad for you the *boy* is gone and the *man* wants his."

Desmond's smile went from his face faster than blow out a match.

"SONNY BOY!" He yelled.

A man you would've called big if I wasn't there came out the back with a snarl and a sawed-off pointing straight to my chest.

I smiled.

Desmond threw a bill on the counter.

"Here's $20 because I feel sorry. Take it and git."

Put my hand behind one of those giant jars of colored water my father kept on the top of the shelves and gave it a little push. It was probably 30 pounds or so and moving at speed. Hit Sonny Boy in the chest right before he pulled the trigger. He went backward until being stopped by the wall. Hadn't even landed when there was a small sting in my side. Desmond had a revolver talking fast as it could. There were spring rains I've paid more attention to. Walked over, waited for him to shoot all his shots so he'd know he didn't miss. Took the gun, crushed it easier than a beer can.

Desmond didn't know what or where, staring at me because nothing else to do. Returned him a smile to make an alligator nervous.

"Got you faded, fucked and laughed at," Roscoe said, pulling out an emery board to work on the nails on his picking hand. "Forgot the first rule of poker. Sit to the table and don't see a sucker, means you're it."

He went over, looked at Sonny Boy, and let out a laugh. "Good thing this place has bandages. He's gonna need 'em. Be a bit before he wakes up, too." Still laughing he came and handed me the sawed off. Put my hands on either end and brought them together. Nothing but toothpicks and a flat bit of metal left.

Give it to Desmond. All that and still slid a smile back on like nothing at all. Cool as Coke he looks at me, takes a cigar out his pocket, bites off the end and rolls it around his mouth. "Do what you want. Won't get you any cash. Told you I don't have any. Look at the books if you want."

My turn for laughing soon as he said that. Didn't know but he fixed a problem I'd been thinking about all way to town: What to do if he flat out refused to give it up. Sure, I could hurt him, and I wanted to. Question was, could I without killing him? That policeman lying on the jailhouse floor bent in ways no one should be. It's first thing through my mind when I want to hit someone. Didn't want Desmond keeping the cop company the rest of my life.

Still with a smile, go over to Roscoe, whisper in his ear. He nods and walks out. Not being able to hit Desmond I had to figure out to enjoy myself in another way. This right now was part of it: Take away being in charge, leave him confused and nervous. He could understand all types of threat, not this. An hour waiting on Roscoe and Desmond spent most of it talking, trying to figure.

"Why aren't you dead? I hit you with all six."

Shrugged, picked up the marble counter top from the soda fountain, broke it into pieces then crushed those to dust. Something to do.

"Gonna have to pay for that, y'know?" Like he said it because he thought he had to. No heart behind it and both knew it wasn't true. Rest of the time he just kept at me with questions and I kept not answering which bothered him more and more.

Roscoe came back alongside a well-dressed little woman carrying a briefcase. Not short, little. Acorn colored skin and gray hair, wearing a gray pinstriped dress and jacket, not flashy but look at it and you knew it cost.

"Who the hell is this?" he said at no one.

"I am Mrs. Terry," she said in a clear teacher's voice that would have carried into corners of the largest classroom. "I teach accounting at the Institute. Dr. Robbins called me and asked if I could do him a favor. Now I do not like going about late in the evening and normally I would have asked if this all could be handled in the morning, but Dr. Robbins said it involved the family of my friend Mr. Maurice Crawford. I cannot claim Mr. Crawford and I were close, but we had spoken several times when he visited the Institute and of course I saw him when I needed anything from the pharmacy. I quite enjoyed our conversations and still have great respect for Mr. Crawford."

At that she turned and looked to me. "You must be Moses. You look so much like your father." She held her hand out to me and said, "I am so sorry for your loss. I deeply, deeply regret missing his funeral. I was out of town and did not learn about it until I got back."

I remembered daddy saying it was polite to kneel down when talking to a small person so you can look each other in the eyes. I didn't know any so I always wondered why he said it. Now I knew. Knelt, which meant my head was still two feet or so above hers, and we shook hands.

"You do not remember me because I have not seen you since you were this big." She held her hand about a foot above her head and gave out a laugh. "You have grown a bit more than I expected. Now where are these books I am supposed to examine?"

Desmond led back to his office and Mrs. Terry stepped around Sonny Boy without surprise or concern. At Desmond's desk she asked for a stool, which she got on gracefully, opened her briefcase, pulled out pencils and a sharpener, checked their tips and sharpened the ones daring to not meet her standards. Only then did she ask for the business ledgers.

Desmond handed her two large black ledgers from a cabinet. Mrs. Terry looked them over for a couple of minutes then said, "Very nice. Now the real ones, please."

Not a request.

"That's them," he said.

"Mr. Desmond," she said with a slightly disappointed sigh, "I began my career in accounting many years ago at the firm of Josiah Finch and partners in Birmingham. That name means nothing to you, nor should it. However, the name of one of our clients should. It was Mr. Haley Earle, Sr."

No idea who that was but a big grin slid onto Roscoe's face and Desmond began to look worried.

"Mr. Haley Earle, Sr.," she said to me, like a teacher catching up a student, "was a very well-known businessman. He ran a funeral home and owned a restaurant as well. He also had several other businesses which were in the nature of breaking the law, such as gambling, illegal shipments of alcohol and whore houses. He was successful at these. I do believe that any such operation in the Colored communities of Alabama needed his approval if it wanted to remain in business. That approval came at a price, of course. Although his operations were illegal, Mr. Earle required they all keep the strictest records and follow all the requirement of modern accounting.

"Mr. Earle and I got along wonderfully, I must say, and Mrs. Earle never did find out about it. She was a sweet woman but by then she had had a stroke some years before, so she was paralyzed all on one side of her body," she said and paused, a slight smile on her face. "Needless to say, this was before I married Mr. Terry.

"I was hired to oversee the accounting for his operations and those that he worked with. It was quite the time." Her eyes lit up and I would have dearly loved to know the stories she was thinking of.

"Mr. Haley provided me with a big black limousine and a driver. His name was Little Willie Milligan. He was about the size of that gentleman on the floor there. We drove all over the state, Willie and I, to see some very bad people. I think they either were already killers or likely preparing to become so.

"Do you know something? I scared them. All of them. Willie and I would pull up at their establishment and the people would dash out to the street, straightening up their clothes while they ran, so they could give me a proper welcome. All of them asking after my health and offering a drink or the like.

"I scared them because if they tried to hide anything, I always found it. Always. Many of them were scared that they had made a mistake and I would see it as stealing. I did my best to put them at ease over that. I didn't mind mistakes. Those do happen, as much as they shouldn't. Some of these people simply didn't know anything about accounting. Can you imagine being in business and not knowing accounting? So, I taught them. That's where I realized I enjoyed teaching. But that's nothing to do with this.

"Of course, some tried to bribe me and Little Willie. That only made Willie mad and put them into more trouble with Mr. Earle. Once one of them pulled a gun but it's one thing to pull a gun and another to use it. Not everyone is up to the task. He wasn't. Little Willie was. So, don't think I haven't seen it all. I tell you this so you know I understand your *real* business very well. Now, get the true ledgers, the ones I suspect you must show to whomever Mr. Haley Earle, Jr., sends."

Desmond knew he was beat. Moved a couch, uncovered a safe in the floor and pulled out two other ledgers. Mrs. Terry was about an hour going over them. When she finished, she gave Desmond her best teacher's smile of approval. "These are very well done, Mr. Desmond," she said and then pulled out a large certificate from a pocket at the end of one of the ledgers.

"This is the deed to the Crawford's house, isn't it?"

He nodded yes.

"Very wise of you to purchase it Mr. Desmond. Real estate is always a good investment, especially at this price. Keeping your overhead low. Very smart. Now I will need you to sign it here and here to transfer it to Mrs. Crawford."

Desmond looked up, angry again. "I'm not doing that and you can't ..."

She interrupted him without even raising her voice. "Let me tell you something about Mr. Earle, Jr., who took over the business when his father passed. I took care of him on many occasions when he was growing up. To this day he calls me Auntie Terry. You wouldn't know it from the scars on his face, but he really can be so sweet. He invites Mr. Terry and I out to his summer place every year so we can spend time with his children. We're godparents to Emily, his oldest. And he always sends me a gift on my birthday and at Christmas."

Desmond started signing before Mrs. Terry finished speaking.

Then she handed him a second piece of paper. "That's what I calculate you owe Moses and his mother. If it seems a bit high that's because it is. I added charges for interest because although the money was in your possession it was not yours. Therefore, it must be considered a loan and people in your line of work always charge a high rate on unsecured loans. You will also notice another charge. It is for the suffering and inconvenience you caused them, which I believe was considerable. That's why *that* charge is so high."

Desmond wasn't happy but there was no fight left in him. "I'm sure Moses won't mind accompanying you as you make the rounds to collect all the cash you owe him. Moses, please let me know when you're done with that, won't you?"

Then the pleasant tone dropped from her voice. "Mr. Desmond you should know as soon as Moses tells me he has his money I am going to place a call to Mr. Earle, Jr. I am going to explain what happened tonight and, even though your books are as clean as could be wished for, I will tell him you have been stealing from him for some time. He will take my word for it."

With that she put the ledgers, her pencils and sharpener into her briefcase, snapped it shut and hopped down from the stool. She wished us all a good night, waited a moment to make it clear Roscoe was to escort her home. He offered his arm, she took it and they left, and I felt like I was watching a battleship recede into the night.

20

NEXT MORNING I WAS woken up by people yelling from out front of our shack. There was a wagon carrying one of the old church ladies and a couple of big old boys who were likely her grandsons – maybe great grandsons – and it was being driven by my cousin Erlissa.

"Mrs. Crawford! Mrs. Crawford," the old lady crowed. "Your house is your own again! We've come to bring you back to it!"

Didn't take me a second to figure that Roscoe had gone around telling about Desmond's demise to everyone he could. Didn't take me another second before I went blood angry and started yelling.

"WHAT ARE YOU DOING HERE? ALL Y'ALL STOLE FROM US AT THAT AUCTION! GOT EVERYTHING WE OWN FOR PENNIES!"

First time I'd ever let it all out, got as loud as I could and turns out I'm thunder when I do that. The two grandsons or whatever they were just about jumped off the wagon, the church lady looked over and set her jaw hard and straight at me. Erlissa, standing on the wagon bench which put her right about my height, was shouting as hard as I was even though she couldn't make as much noise.

"How could *you* bring them here!" I hissed. "They took all we had!"

Crazy as I was Erlissa wasn't having it, got right in my face and screamed to scare the devil. Even so she had to grab me by the ears and shove her face up against mine eyeball-to-eyeball before she could get my attention.

"What wrong with you!" She said over and over until I shut up. "Nobody taking nothing from your family! You idiot! They been keeping it all so you'd have it back. Why you think they scared anyone else off at the auction?"

"No, no, that's not it," I said, sputtering out the words. "Can't be. Soon as we lost all our everything, we weren't good enough to be in their church. Just like happened with your daddy."

"Even for a fool you're an idiot," Erlissa said. "You think the old women turn on someone over money?"

Soon as she said that I knew it was true and I'd been wrong by a lot.

"Long time I thought the same about my daddy," she said. "Then last year my mom told me daddy started drinking hard, right after everything got burned down. That's what cost him down at the church, though I'm sure reverend asshole wasn't sorry to see him gone."

I looked at the old woman.

"I didn't know... I thought..."

"You were lost child, we all knew. Lost and going fast. Nothing for it, so we just watched it and let you go. You're good stock though. Knew you'd find a way back."

"I'm sorry," I said, and she gave me the same look of "what's this foolishness about" that she'd given when I was shouting. Then mamma came out of the shack and the two couldn't stop grinning and talking except for when the old lady yelled for one of her boys to come give mamma a hand getting seated in the wagon. The old woman kept apologizing for not being there sooner, but they had had to clean our house before everything was put back in it. Made it sound like it was all the old ladies done all the work but bet you it was daughters-in-law and grandchildren up through the night getting it done. A half minute to move the things worth keeping out of the shack and into the wagon.

"Coming with us?" Erlissa asked.

"I got some settling to do first," I said.

"Well, I'd say watch yourself but ... y'know," she said with a grin, and they all went off on the road.

Watching them head back I gave half a thought and more to living in the shack by myself. Horrible place but comfortable to me. Here I didn't have to bother too much about other people making me out to be something. I was only a Negro when I had to deal with Beaumont and his people, and he wasn't an always throwing it in your face type.

Part of what I liked about farming was I could just do it by myself. That and being able to say I'm a farmer if anyone asked what I was. Mostly if I asked myself what I was. Being here had helped me with my grief, too. But all those thoughts passed, and I saw where I was for what it was: a horrible place where only a fool would stay if he could leave.

So, I brushed the dirt off my jeans and went to have a word with Beaumont.

The sun wasn't high up yet and it was already hot enough days where animals, plants, even the air seemed to be looking for shade.

Beaumont was in his barn talking with some other men and they all started laughing when they saw me walking up. He was sitting with his feet up on a ratty old desk that may have seen better days or maybe not.

"Well, hey there Moses," he said. "Boys just telling me they saw your momma and a wagon full of stuff headed back to town. You know you got a contract to honor, right? Not the brightest way to break it. Most folks try to run off in the middle of the night when we're sleeping."

More laughter then but not mean or vicious like it might have been. Lot of plantation owners would have come right out to the shack and been yelling and threatening if they'd even thought someone was considering leaving. Beaumont never was that sort. A good reputation for a plantation owner. Despite how he lied and cheated them, many of his sharecroppers genuinely liked the man. Chains you don't see kill you first.

"Not leaving, are you Moses?" he said, slightly amused. If I was leaving why would I come to see him?

"Yes, I am, Bill," I said, shuck and jive all gone and looking in direct in the eyes like we were never supposed to.

His smile gone then. His boys were about to jump me but he held up his hand to them, telling them to hold off.

"Now Moses, what's wrong?" Honestly concerned, not upset or angry. His attitude was no reason for a white man to be upset by us poor, ignorant people. Knew he was in charge, was the boss. Had the upper hand and never needed to show off. That's someone all confident in themselves going about things. As an owner, which he was, it made him a rare thing. So, he just kept speaking gently, like there was a simple misunderstanding needed working out.

"Signed the contract. Remember doing that, right?" Said in a slow way like I was wrong in the head. "It said in return for getting to live here and farm my land you have to do things in return. Only fair, isn't it? Can't take something without paying for it, right?"

Maybe I should've been insulted but I was kind of enjoying listening to him think like he had power. Gently explaining to me how the world works was his way of doing good. Easy enough for him to do as he was sure I could do nothing about it.

"... and signed that contract, didn't you?" More he talked though, faster my enjoyment ran out. Shutting up is never taken advantage of as much as it should be. "You agreed to 10 years of work for me ..."

"Now Bill, it was one year when I signed and we both know that." Matching his reasonable tone because it'd bother him. That smile wasn't sitting so easy on his face now.

"Difference between you and a slaver? None. Have yourself a contract say we can't work for anyone but you. You're only one we can sell our crop to. The only one we can buy anything we need from. All you aren't selling is us. Nice getting to set prices the way you want. Even better, you change the contract whenever you want because *darkies* can't read, can't even count much. So, tell them they owe more every year or a one-year contract is now 10 year. Slavery with enough trimmings to not call it what it is."

While I talked listened to the heartbeats in the room speeding up from anger. I knew they were going to move on me before they did. Didn't care, though. Didn't stop talking or move much at all.

A sledge hammer hit my shoulder blade and Newton's physics hit whoever swung it: An equal and opposite reaction bounced it off me right back to his face. Someone digging in to me with a pitchfork got a bunch of bent tines. An axe handle shattered on one of my legs. Whoever it was sucker punched at my kidneys started screaming. Let them go at me until they figured out it wasn't doing anything. Didn't take long.

I looked at them and all I felt was fatigue.

"Tired of this," I said, mostly to myself. "Every day. All I want is go on with my life. That's all. Every time there y'all are, telling me I can't. Sometimes it's said, sometimes it's spit, sometimes it's just a look. So tired of it. I ... we ... all we want is living. Do for ourselves, go home, go out again, all without having to think who we are. That's all. So little is being asked for. Just not thinking all the time about how we're *Negro*. That's freedom. You don't have it any more than we do. Don't even know it, do you? You don't think white unless you see black. Even then you've got a choice. You can go on with what you're doing if you want. I'd love a day where I could do that. God, I am so tired of this."

Doubt they understood of word of that.

Their mind couldn't deal with their eyes seeing something happening that couldn't. A black man they couldn't beat to prove he's wrong? That's the morning the sun doesn't rise, the Mississippi runs north and Jesus himself said their sins aren't forgiven. Maybe would've enjoyed this too but was just irritated.

Might as well get to it then.

"Who's got a gun?"

Silence.

"C'mon, six crackers and no gun?"

More silence.

"Beaumont?"

Hearing his name snapped him back to being able to do. Nodded, started to move, real slow, making it clear he wasn't doing anything that might be trouble, moving just like how we all have to with the police. Carefully reached back and pulled out a pistol which he'd had tucked into his pants. Tried to hand it to me.

"No, you keep it. Shoot me."

Froze up again at that. Can impossible be more impossible? "Your gravity fails, and negativity don't pull you through." Heard some guy sing that about 30 years later and flashed right back to the look on Beaumont's face.

Put the pistol on the desk and backed away. Tried handing it to each one of the other rednecks but they weren't having it. Almost laughed. Six honkies with a gun and a black man can't get shot when he wants to. Tired of waiting so shot myself. Held it about a foot away from the side of my head and fired all six shots.

"Can't stop me. Can't. Doesn't matter if all y'all and all y'all's friends grabbed every gun you could get. It's been tried. Didn't bother me. Didn't even slow me."

Picked up that old desk with one hand and threw hard. Punched a hole in the barn roof on the way out. Don't know where it landed except it wasn't any bit nearby.

"Know how lucky you are now? Could kill you easier than a fly. Remember. Remember, people sharecropping here are my friends. Good friends. Kind to me and mine and there was nothing in it for them. I'll be back out, check on how you're treating them."

Walked away like a movie hero. Slapped one of Beaumont's wagons on my way through the yard. Turned it to kindling wood.

Heard later Beaumont gave the whole plantation to his walleyed sister Hannah and headed outward to Texas or Arizona. Hannah changed all the rules. Let people buy things wherever they want to. Even set it up for people to buy land they worked, paying off a little every year. She didn't do that because of me. That's who she was, who she'd always been.

Upset a lot of her neighbors, though. Other plantation owners came over one day tell her she couldn't do what she was doing, their darkies wanted the same. She didn't mind them, started reading at them from The Gospels, the Sermon on the Mount. Soon rumors started among the whites about how she'd gone crazy. An uncle tried getting her declared incompetent to take the plantation away. Sheriff came out to serve papers, but when he pulled up in his car there's a whole bunch of sharecroppers in front of the house looking angry. Hannah Beaumont was there, too, sitting on her porch and drinking iced tea. Invited the sheriff to join her. He said no thank you. Said he suddenly remembered some business back in town. Not long after the uncle moved away.

21

After we moved back to our house, I went to the Institute to look for Jet. Hadn't seen her since she left and not because I didn't want to. With her gone every day was dull and dusty. Other people to talk to but no one else I wanted to.

Only went to town a couple of times when we were sharecropping. Wanted to see her but was afraid. Telling myself I'd embarrass her to all her new friends because of how country I looked. Least that's what I was ready to tell anyone if they asked, which no one did. Truth? Longer I didn't see her more I wanted to and more I thought she wouldn't want to see me.

Afraid this day too and might have talked myself into not going but momma used her best teacher's voice and said, "Go find her. She how she is."

Saw Jet before she saw me, of course. Sitting out on a bench reading. Easy to see there's been changes. Some of it outside stuff – she'd been eating regularly maybe for the first time in her life and had on nice clothes and her hair, which she wore natural, wasn't coated infield dirt. Big thing, though, she was smiling. Never seen that before, her happy and almost relaxed.

Got closer and hollered to her. She looked up with a surprise and then got up and ran toward me. Stopped a foot away, then reared back and hit me with her book so hard it broke.

"Where have you been?" She yelled, then threw the book down, went a bit away and started walking in small circles. All the while muttering to herself, not knowing I could hear her perfectly well. "No, no, no, no. Not how it's supposed to go. Not at all. Not what I wanted."

Came back over, took a deep breath, looked up at me with smile so false it broke my heart.

"What's wrong?"

"I don't know these people," she whispered like afraid someone else would hear. "Don't know how to dress or what to say or what to do. I'm an ignorant nigger girl from the fields. Never been in a school before, not a real one."

Thought I'd thought a lot about her since she was gone. Right then taught me I'd really been thinking about me, about me missing her. Never once concerned myself with what she had been feeling, doing, going through.

"I'm sorry," I tried to say.

"No, no, no," she interrupted. She looked me right in the eyes, waved her arm at the buildings and said, "Thank you." Then she put her arms around me and hugged tight. Right then I knew what perfect was.

After that we started spending time together, never talking about why. Then one Saturday we're sitting out in the Institute's yard, leaning against a big elm tree, and reading because that's mostly what we did. I brought a big pail of sandwiches and Cokes which I eat most of and then have to remind her to eat hers. She's got her usual pile of books and a notebook. Read something in one that'll remind her of something in another, then there's something else in a third one and when she's read all that she spends a long time writing in her notebook in Greek. Says it helps her think the right way about what she's working on. Jumps between books like a cat playing with mice almost, pouncing on one like she thinks it might run away.

"Moses," she said, not looking up from her book.

Right away nervous. Only two of us and we never use each other's names. Grunt something that sounds like "uh huh" and don't look up from my book because I'm trying to act cool.

"Why don't you ever try and get me to go down to the river like other boys do with their girls?"

"Down to the river" meant a place people our age a lot more confident than I was went to make out and screw. Right to be nervous. Whole sentence is a trap. She asking me to ask her? Did she just say she's my girl?

"Whaddya mean?" I mumble. Stalling. Hoping for a tree to fall on me or anything else might change the topic. Except I keep thinking on what she said about "with their girls." That definitely meant something – maybe something good.

She looks at me. Raises an eyebrow. She knows I know what she means.

Take a deep breath and look up into the tree which still isn't falling on me. People I don't mind talking about sex with is a small group consisting a few other boys don't have any experience with it either. Talking about it with the girl who I want to be my girlfriend when I haven't even figured out how to go about that? No, no, no.

"After you breathe in, you're supposed to breathe out."

I nod. Exhale.

"The thing is ... I don't think you're someone who is going to put up with someone else who tries to talk you into something. Pretty sure that a fella who tried that, well, all he'd get is you walking away."

Long pause. Try to figure out how stupid that was. Then, I jump in. From height.

"And I don't want to do anything that means I might lose you."

She stood up, brushed off her skirt, walked over to me, held my head between her hands and kissed me long and hard – with meaning and passion and everything else I didn't know that I wanted to be part of my first real kiss.

"Moses Crawford, you cannot lose me."

22

Thought moving back to town would be good. Wasn't. Tuskegee was foreign now. Nothing and everything had changed. Everything looked familiar and strange all at once. Stories about Desmond and Beaumont got around fast and got bigger by the telling. Folks known me before talked nervously, like we'd never met. Some avoided me altogether. Folks I didn't know wanting to be friends, telling me how great I was, offer liquor or a meal. Made me uncomfortable. I get to know people slow. Here being shy got useful. Back as a kid I was afraid to talk to people and got known as being I was stuck up.

But top seven-feet-tall and not talk to people? Call that intimidating.

Not the all of it, though. Tuskegee not my place anymore. I didn't fit. Or it didn't fit me, literally. Walking around everything felt too close. Worried about bumping into cars or buildings, maybe break something. Hated a crowded sidewalk. People got out of my way, but I was too aware they'd get hurt if I so much as turned around too fast.

Finally, didn't know what I was supposed to do. Didn't have to provide for my mother now and that was all I'd been doing. No going back to school. Little chairs and little rooms, that was behind me. Didn't take long to figure on farming as what I wanted to do. Wouldn't need to hire help. Could be my own plow and harvester, do my own haying. There's a lot of room on a farm, too. Nobody to trip over.

Momma wasn't happy about me not going to school but when I told her about how I was feeling she understood. Momma said I should take some of the money we got from Desmond and find myself some land to buy.

23

One day Erlissa and her friend, Tammy Jo drove out to the farm I was building on the few miles outside town and drop off a big canvas sack.

Tammy Jo, Erlissa's girlfriend at the time who I didn't know was her *girlfriend*. Should have known Erlissa, best and many times only friend since ever, was a girlfriend-getting girl. Should have been plain. Probably was to others. Her and Tammy Jo together all the time and slept over at each other's a lot and I'm just stupid is what it is. Broke up and back together twice, then a third time and that break up stuck. Wasn't until after that, when I noticed 1 + 1 = 2. Not like she could've told people because it was when it was. Then we really, really weren't cool with lady or a guy of ours doing what's their own business with another lady or guy. Better today, though. Better enough I'd only use one really in that sentence saying how it is.

"Here ya go," Erlissa said, handing me a big, bulging canvas sack like I was expecting it.

"What is it?"

"Your mail."

"*My* mail? Who's writing to me?"

"Dunno but it's lots. Been piling up at the post office for a few weeks and they didn't know what to do with 'em. First tried giving it to Rev. Williams on account of *he's your pastor*." A big smile saying that. "Pissed him off good, I hear. He told 'em I knew where you're at and to bring it all to me. So here you go. Hope you're paying me to deliver because post office wouldn't give me a dime even though it's their job."

Bet she asked him for it, too.

"Still don't understand ..."

"The addresses," she said, pointing at the sack. "Look at the addresses."

Pulled a handful of envelopes out. All had same thing on them: "John Henry, Tuskegee."

"John Henry?"

Right then Tammy Jo showed she had a good voice

> *Lissen to my story, it's a story true*
> *'Bout a mighty man, John Henry was his name,*
> *An' John Henry was a steel-driver too*
> *Lawd, Lawd,*
> *An' John Henry was a steel-driver too*

> *John Henry said to his captain,*
> *"A man, he ain't nothing but a man,*
> *Before I'd let that steam drill beat me down,*
> *Oh, I'd die with the hammer in my hand."*

> *An' John Henry was a steel-driver too*
> *Lawd, Lawd,*
> *An' John Henry was a steel-driver too*

"That guy? He died when the mountain fell on him."

Erlissa rolled her eyes.

"Gotta get out more, Moses," she said. Loved busting on me. "Should buy one of those *new-fangled* radio things. Or maybe you don't need one. You tried pickin' up stations with your ugly ass ears? You did and you'd hear the new John Henry songs."

Tammy Jo cuts in with a whole different song.

> *John Henry get up on the mountain*
> *John Henry look out on the land*
> *John Henry sees work to be done*

John Henry got a hammer in his hand

"All say instead of being dead he just lay down and went to sleep. Waiting until we needed him to wake up."

Shook my head.

"Need him for what?"

"What we always waitin' on? Being led to the promised land ... Moses."

"Fuck."

Erlissa and Tammy Jo nodded to that.

Surprised but shouldn't have been. Daddy and I had talked on it. Parents didn't only worry about whites finding me out. Thought our people would be trouble, too. Different trouble but still trouble. Said people would want me as a prince, king, hero, savior. They figured right and warned me. Minute they started explaining knew I wanted nothing of it. Just another way of having to be what someone else says you are. Already too much of that.

Reached in the sack, took out a letter. So did Erlissa and Tammy Jo and then we went to reading.

"Shit."

"Oh, Christ."

"You poor fuckers."

Then reading more and more until we couldn't anymore.

All the letters different and all alike. Different situations but what's the same: Wanting. Stop a lynching, stop a beating, stop the police, stop the trouble, stop the trouble. Wanting revenge, justice, retribution. Punish the wicked. Punish them all. Give us a voice that's heard. All sad, decent, reasonable, normal wantings. Wanting me to be their words made flesh.

Supposedly why there are laws, to take care of this. Ask a professor, she'll tell you laws are society saying what it believes. She'd be wrong. Laws are society saying things to cover up what it does. Politician loves the Constitution, on and on about it making us free to say whatever we care, to protest even. It says police can't beat us up. Everyone can vote. Government can't kill you just because it wants. Slavery is ended. Law says all that and not a true word to it. You're white and money likely it can be. Sure, a better chance than you're poor. Poor and wrong color on your skin? Don't bother.

Even so, even I knew laws were needed more than me. All I can do I can only do if I'm there. Law *should* be anywhere, any time. Could, should, might. What we needed even more than laws was everyone believing we should be treated by it like they are. What comes first, though? Will the people believing change the law or will changing the law get people to believing? Either way, it depends on people.

People.

Law alone isn't enough. Already had laws saying we could vote and that didn't do any good. I knew that's where I came in. Not a savior, but something to scare those white people, give them a reason to be sure they enforce it.

Walking down a road, looking for what I didn't want to find.

Pretty road in May near Greensboro. Box elders and red gum trees, jonquils, ticklegrass, creeping spotflower and peppervine, all alive and growing as only happens in the South in spring.

There because Erlissa got a call. Whites out looking for a couple of us for the crime of doing something.

Somehow Erlissa's work was told as the number for people to call. Didn't get lot of them, not so many they interfered with her business, but regular – one or two a week. Calls from all over: Arkansas, Oklahoma, Indiana, the Carolinas, Florida, Minnesota, California, New York. Nothing I can do. People wanted me flying or running fast like a train to get to them and who can blame them? Wanted me able to do anything. I knew better and it wasn't a good knowing. Could only do anything I was nearby and no guarantee even then.

Lynch mobs form up and go to it in no time over nothing. Eliza Bryant killed because her business was more successful than was right for a colored person. Mary Turner, speaking about *her husband's* lynching got her lynched. Roscoe's rescue was a fluke.

Wish I'd done all said of me. Probable the stories helped more than I did. Gave some hope. Found out my being there seemed to help people, didn't matter if there was anything I could do. So, when I could, I went, even knowing it was too late.

Best chance for me to help was someone in a jail and cops didn't want to see them lynched. Didn't happen a lot, likely barely at all, but surprised me how often it did. Surprised it happened at all.

This wasn't one of those.

Henrietta Dorsey, maybe 30. Maybe. Her son, Hayes Turner, around 14. Maybe. Never asked what it was said they did. Why bother? Always the same, really. Guilty of alive and black.

Last seen driven out this way. Why I'm walking the highway – hoping for something to show me where. Something was a burnt, greasy, wrong smell. Never smelled before but knew right away what it was.

Clearing in the woods, not easy to see from a road. Middle has a phone pole, not for wires, not there a couple of days before either. Tied to it: Something didn't look like people at first but stared a moment and could make out what once was arms, hands, a leg, two heads. All that's left of a mother and her boy. Henrietta and Hayes tied together around the pole, facing each other, set afire, looking into each other's eyes, if they still had eyes. Fire burnt away anything showing if they'd been mutilated and tortured, but my bet would be they were. What usually happened. We all knew that.

Don't know how long it takes fire to make bodies into what can't be seen as human but it's how long they were burned. Faces gone. Shape of bodies gone, shrunk down to bone and whatever somehow fire didn't take. Here and there, pale spots where something was cut away after the fire.

Pieces taken for souvenirs like that's a thing you do. Didn't happen all the time and make whatever the fuck you want from that. Sometimes it was killed and done. Shot, throat cut. Sometimes. Hanging was never fast. Watch us kick and squirm and struggle as we choke to death, more thrashing the better show they thought it was.

We're all raised knowing "lynching" the word is too clean, too simple for all it covers. Real definition can't be written in a dictionary, can't barely be said. It is horror like this and more, then making sure news of it carried to us all, better to keep us in our place.

One thing to hear about and another to see. Different by a factor of infinity. A camera! Wanted all of a sudden. Not for pictures to show the world, bastards took plenty of pictures. Didn't hide either. Make sure to be seen front and center, the entire family right there – grandmother holding a fresh new baby in her arms -- and smiling before the corpse hanging on a tree. Mailed and swapped like trading cards to make even Satan puke. Nothing so horrible to not want everybody knowing how happy they were at getting to take part. Wanted a camera right then. Wanted for putting between me and what I saw. Give me distance from it. God, give me distance. Fool myself with thinking it's a photograph and somehow not real. If not a camera, take anything else could do the same. My birthday that day. Turned 18. Too young for this. Could be turning a thousand and still be too young.

Even though nothing much looked human of what was left of Henrietta and Hayes, it was enough to get me imagining horror of their thoughts, their feelings. Stood looking for I don't know long, then took my knife and cut them down, gently and respectfully as could be done and lay their bodies on the ground.

Heard some cars stop on the road. Six black men come out, some had rifles, others pistols. Absolute surprise on them when they saw me.

"Any of you kin?" I said.

One old man nodded yes.

"I'm sorry. I'm so sorry for you. I wish I could have found them sooner," I said, started to cry.

He shook his head no and started crying too. One man walked to the woods and threw up, others sank to their knees. All lived our lives knowing of the murders, the rapes, the tortures. Never forgetting a whim could destroy our bodies without warning. Hard to think this body is your own because of it. Think about it little as you can is all there is to do. Try. Continue on. Make plans, have dreams in the face of knowing they and you are worthless, worth less than a spittle of tobacco happens to splash on a white person's shoe. That or less and someone ends your life. A mighty action they'll face no consequences for. Other people's lives have value, but yours?

We all warn each other: Think about it too much and go crazy. Really it makes you go sane. Can get an understanding of the world so clear you know it's not your fault and then how do you go on living with that?

Blankets and tarps to wrap and hold Henrietta and Hayes with a deep care, dignity now mattering more than anything. They were taken to the cars with a gentleness and attention that was more than their due.

Then I hear, "What are you gonna do now, John Henry?"

First time called by it and for a moment didn't know who they meant.

Before I answer someone else said, "Let's get everyone and their guns and go to town!" Looking at me, sure I was here for leading them.

"Then what?" I asked. "Say you kill every last one in that town, then what? There's still more. I'm supposed to stay here forever? That's what I'd have to do. Otherwise, they'll wait 'til I'm gone."

"Hicksville," said another man.

I nod.

"Maybe they'd wait a long time. Word is getting around on me now, so might make them think on it a while. But they'd never forget. It would be Hicksville. It would be Tulsa. It would be East St. Louis, Omaha, and Rosewood. They'd use the militia, the Army. Tanks, airplanes, machine guns, all of it. They'd know they had to make a big example because this time they'd be making the example for me. Want me to know even if they can't kill me, they can kill everyone else. I'd come back then. Promise. Avenge all of you and it wouldn't do you any good because you'd all be dead."

Had to say and hated saying it. Their bodies slumped as I spoke, another hope extinguished. Wanted to give them their hero, one who could make it right. They deserved it. I'd have given it to them but for understanding I could do anything but not everything. Gave them what I had, the knowing enough to be afraid for them.

"So, what do we do?" asked the old man who was kin to Henrietta and Hayes.

"Why do you think I know?"

Snapped at him, frustrated because I wanted to have an answer. Wondering what good I was.

They left but I didn't. Stayed there doing I don't know what that night and all the next day. The following night I knew.

A forest fire at night is a beautiful, horrible thing. It burned acres and acres and acres, leaping, and pawing at sky. A fire to greet the end of days. A fire to light the sun. Whoever came to find where it started found something else. Where Henrietta and Hayes were tortured and murdered now there was a great tree. Only living thing for acres and acres around. Swinging from the tree from a noose around its neck was a Confederate soldier statue. Used to stand in Greensboro's town square.

Stayed in the area for a while but no reaction. Or maybe there was. Never another lynching in that county.

24

WHAT ARE YOU SCARED of when nothing can hurt you?

This. Absolutely this. More this than I can say.

Wearing my best clothes. Starched white shirt, dress pants ironed to shave with the crease, jacket, a blue tie so big and long it could probably be used as a lasso. Even shoes! Wingtips. All have to be custom. Tailor gives me a discount on labor but all that material, it costs.

Even a flower in my boutonniere.

Cool night and sweating anyway.

Taking Jet out to dinner and then some dancing. Not our first date. Not by a lot. Even so I feel like I'm pretending to be a grown up. Nervous all night. Stuttering when I talk and starting sentences but forgetting the end.

She just smiles when I do, instead of laughing. Usually laughs and I laugh with her but not tonight. Not even a smirk tonight. Looks great. More than great. A pink-red dress type thing, nice and tight on her and a matching short jacket. And her pearls. Always them. A gift from Mrs. Terry. Won't open the door for the paper without pearls.

Sitting at a table in the club – got a special chair that can take my weight. Start looking at the pearls and then lost in thinking until finally she snaps her fingers a couple of times in my face.

"Sorry."

"That's fine. I need some air. Can we go for a walk?"

Was about to say the same thing.

Moon seems bigger than any before. Walk down the street, into a little park with a gazebo. Go on in and she sits down, and I start to get down on one knee, pulling out the box in my jacket pocket.

"Yes," she said.

"Not even going to let me ask?" Really irritated, which is dumb.

"Did I answer the right question?"

I nod.

"I trust that was the answer you wanted?"

Nod again.

"But I had a whole thing I was going to say. Been thinking about it for a long time." I knew. I knew exactly how stupid this sounded, like a kid on the verge of a tantrum.

"Well go on then. Go ahead and say it. I'll listen. Hope it doesn't make me change my mind." She's sounding reasonable and understanding which isn't helping the situation.

"No." I'm sulking. Can't believe it and can't stop it. "Would have been nice to at least get to ask the question." Mumble that because I know it's stupid but I'm saying it anyway.

"We're having an argument about my accepting your proposal?"

"There something else you have planned for the evening? Somewhere to go?"

Shakes her head no with that little smile she only ever gives to me. Was going to mention it, if she'd let me talk, because every time it tells me it's just us, just her and me in that smile. Know I'd have messed up all the words if I tried to tell her ... but still would've liked to try.

A long silence starts but gets filled with a kiss pretty quick.

"You are an idiot."

"I'm an idiot? You're the one said yes."

Another long silence, which is to say kissing.

"That jacket looks really ..."

"Terrible?"

"I was going to say ... 'interesting.'"

Rag on my clothes all you want, can't make me care. It's a farmer thing.

"Not like I can buy stuff off the rack. Anything my size is going to look ... 'interesting.'"

"Doesn't have to. I'll get you something nice for the wedding."

"So now we're arguing about clothes I wore to propose in?"

"That's us."

"It is."

More silence.

"You said 'wedding,'" I said, and we start to giggle because it hits us now for real.

"Wedding," she said again, and we giggle some more. "Wedding, wedding, WEDDING!" She's jumped up and is stomping her feet as hard as she can and shouting. "WEDDING! WEDDING!"

Some guy walking down the street said, "Am I invited?"

"WOULD I LIKE YOU?"

"Prob'ly not." You can hear the smile.

"THEN YOU CAN SIT ON THE GROOM'S SIDE!"

A big laugh rises up to the big moon and keeps going, fading as the man walks away.

"Y'know, I'd shout too but ..."

"Scare half the county because everyone will think it's the tornado siren."

There's a lot more silences.

"I'm not doing farm work. Ever."

"No, ma'am. You're OK with living on one?"

"Not one pig slopped. Not any hoeing. No mucking. Nothing that sounds like mucking. And none of it, not so much as a blade of hay, is to ever enter the house."

"So that's yes?"

"Idiot."

"No doubt about it."

25

Scottsboro never be anyone's guess for a place where the world would change. Shithole and always had been. Even road dust wanted a good wind so it could go anywhere else. Everything about to happen only happened there because the county courthouse had to be somewhere.

Whole thing was about an empty box car going Chattanooga to Memphis and who got to ride in it when no one should've been. Depression and no money didn't stop people going places. Empty freight car was lucky luxury riding if you got one. Unlucky was underneath by the wheels or hanging on top. Lose a grip on those and best thing would be being dead fast. Still, lots rode there, kids to old folks.

This time it was kids, teens, maybe a couple dozen. Plenty of room in a freight for all them but they were split black and white, making it way too crowded. Someone's got to get out, but who and when was the question. Maybe our teens were noble, stoic, and wanted only being left alone but were set on by white boys. Maybe they were savages crazy on attacking the pale and church going. Both stories and a lot of others got told and none really mattered. Whatever else went on, the thinking money said much of it was teen boys being teen boys. One thing known positive: It was whites got off first and weren't happy for it. When you're white you can go get the law for help even when you've been breaking it. The sheriff knew there's only one side in this argument. Still, could be the sheriff knew the case was sounding too stupid if said aloud. Railroad might say put those other boys in jail to for riding where they shouldn't have been. Somehow once the law comes into the story so do two white girls. Maybe they really were there all that time. No matter because like a man said about God, if He didn't exist, we'd have had to invent Him. Those girls had to be there, and our boys had to be accused of what we're always accused of because that's how it always goes.

Law deputizes half the men in town and for some reason they didn't have a proper on the spot lynch party and all the wild sexual beasts actually get to jail. Worse for a hard wearing but still alive and that's more than nothing. Trial is two days later at a nearest courthouse. Scottsboro. Would end there but someone gets word to NAACP. They scream all they can and there's a surprise because for once people listen. Boom, news for all the nation. Big city reporters squint and squint at a map, finally locate the shithole then overrun it like fat sweaty coyotes. Why interested this time like they never are otherwise? Novelty is a guess. So many and so young – oldest is 15 and youngest 12 – getting shafted together. One of us is never enough, gotta get killed in bunches to get on the front page.

Press has uses though. Gets a governor thinking, 'Do this right, look like I care and possibly my career is national.' Another trial scheduled. Strictly playing the North, of course, because the boys are still getting lynched. This time done fair and proper and by the government.

Press has other uses too, as that's how I heard about it. On the road right after that.

Don't even have to ask Erlissa. Pulls up in the truck without needing me to ask.

Nothing usual when I get there. Troops, regular Army not militia, on the ground in numbers. More than patrolling and standing guard, dug in hard around jail and courthouse, which is square, brick, three stories tall. Serious trenches, bob wire, sand bags, machine guns, like waiting on a war. Even a tank. What's it for? Too much for just lynchers. Way too much.

Almost laugh out loud. Trying to figure what they're so afraid of and go, oh, yeah, me. Been time since Hicksville and I think they forgot. No. No. No. Even if they don't know what I am, they know I am. Call us spooks and they finally got one. A haunt bigger than all their imagining.

Know what white papers said made Hicksville burn? "Freak Lightning Strike."

Made me into an act of God.

Part of the code their papers and they use to avoid having to say what really happens.

"An outrage." "Unspeakable act." Happen to white woman by black man. Supposed to be rape and never was. Really meant they only set to murder one of us, though they're always up for more.

Other words, too, not even subtle as that. "Disrespectful." "Uppity." "Didn't know his place." "Brutes." "Animals." "Savages." All for whites reminding whites we aren't human, so anything needs doing is OK. Weren't human and needed teaching of the right and the wrong. Go ahead and do whatever, just be certain a lesson for us can be used to say why it was done. Couldn't straight out and say what they thought, what they did. Had to cover every horrible thing with thick coats of moral. The doings of decent folks. The God-fearing. More and more and more words to hide one thing.

Terror.

Terror of us and the moment coming when we're rising up and killing and raping. Why their boots kept so hard on our necks. They say us being "savages" is why we'd do to them so bad. Easier to say than what's true: Blood is the only coin to pay for what they've done. All they can think is if they were treated like we were, that would be what they'd do.

Knew what they'd done was wrong, all of it. From when first they chained a person, they knew. Why we weren't allowed as human. Buried the guilt by making black, colored, Negro, nigger as something will never be human. Didn't work. All those words can't bury it far enough to keep them from knowing it's there. Knowing makes the rage, makes the inferno that eats their lives. The inferno fed by the trying to escape it. Each denial makes it worse. Worse for facing, worse running from, worse sitting with. So, they do more killing, raping, beating, all for proof of us not being human. For if human what a reckoning and worse, knowing it is a just one. Hard earned.

Some afraid Hicksville was the start of that reckoning. Witness stories not in the papers but travel on word of mouth. Not making sense but have to be believed. Negro giant can't be stopped, skin darker than a preacher's heart. Came and did whatever he wanted. Tore up that whole brick town hall and the police station too with his giant's hands. Tell themselves can't be true. Say it all they want, again and again and again and again, but doesn't help. They know what they've done. They know what they deserve.

They know I'm real. I'm the price for all they did and didn't do. All the things they turned away from to not have to see, not to have to know. All they pretended in order to allow themselves to go to church and say they're godly people.

All these educated Christian white people believe in the devil, magic, and curses. Believe we got a special gift for it. They'll ask Mammy or Unca Ben to get them a charm for love or to keep away the cancers.

Savages all worship a devil, it's well known, now Old Scratch giving them something back. Maybe it's Toussaint L'Ouverture's ghost come over from Haiti, where he did what Nat Turner and so many others tried for here in mother America.

Because blood was their only understanding, it must be ours, too. No other way for anyone to think. Impossible to imagine even after the slavery, the rapes, the murders, and the destruction, we wanted to live our lives in peace more than an eye for an eye. Impossible to imagine they weren't so important to us.

Maybe they thought not talking, not printing about me, meant the servants wouldn't know. We're not smart enough to understand. We know, of course we do. Know code words, what it means when they say something, what it means when they don't. Know more about their world than they do. Had to. Have to. Surviving requires it. Maids, house cleaners, drivers, "mammies," hear everything. Anything heard and told everyone. Grapevine carried our news. Some gossip and some exaggeration too. Word got around on me fast, a lot wrong. Made me stronger, bigger. Had me flying, 50 feet tall, breathing fire, walking on water. No loaves and fishes. Yet.

Time for me to make myself real, I decide.

Court is in session so that's where I go. Soldier boys pick up on me as soon as I come out the woods where I was. Who'd miss a giant black nightmare walking straight on to them on a clear sunny day? They start screaming and warning me before I'm anywhere near. Wherever they decide is too near is when the business opens up.

Imagine going to see fireworks and there's a real tall building there and you go on the roof. Means there's not enough of not much between you and the sky. Know those big boom fireworks? On the ground when they go off there's a deep shake all inside of your chest. Up there, it's like your insides are a bass drum with someone stomping the pedal. Heart is moving, jumping with each blast hits me. Me right then.

At first.

Felt somehow the body, my body, change something. Blast waves getting to me less with each one. First time ever felt the body do that. First time ever thought like me and body are separate, it doing what it needs.

I keep walking at them, and machine guns and grenades and rifles aren't doing a thing is when the tank comes in. First the smaller cannon in the turret. Then I'm still coming and the big one in the chassis let's go. Good aiming. Dead center chest. Tore the shirt all up and I'm still coming. Got something else, though, something I hadn't seen, though. Airplane fast dives from the sky, all its guns going, then drops a bomb and pulls up fast as it dove. More good aim. Right next to me and almost makes me break stride.

Almost.

Soldiers keep at me, even as I'm through their line and at the tank. Twist the big barrel around until it breaks. Shooting stops right then and they're running. I'm on the tank and standing, grab the turret on both sides and pull. Comes up and man inside falls out screaming. Got that turret over my head to let the world know all I am. Heave it at least 50 yards, hits asphalt and there's a deep, deep hole.

Cameras everywhere film all that. Got motion pictures from a bunch of different angles. Press has its uses.

THOUGHT ABOUT PUNCHING A wall to go in. Took the front door.

Two stories. Court room I want is one with all the police in front. Break and run as I come toward them, so I walk in as easy as white. Two bailiffs, one pissing himself, the other one against a wall wanting not to be noticed. Judge is a crazy old fool, hammering the gavel, screaming at me. Two sets of lawyers. Prosecuting pair doing the no-sudden-moves thing, like with a cougar or wild bear. Defense is standing still out of confusion, not fear.

The boys?

They're boys. A moment to figure then they're cheering and yelling. Chained at feet and wrists! Oldest doesn't even look the 15 years he is. Looks like neighbor's boy you ask to come look after your kids. Pinch the iron off and then it's out and gone. Boys start whooping even louder seeing what's done to that tank. No other noise but them and a lot of cameras clicking. Every person in town is gone elsewhere except those press people. Say it: Got brass. Shouting questions not knowing what I'll do. Don't get any answers but give it to them for the try.

Go a ways through the woods I came out of and there's Erlissa and the truck. All in and drive away not in any rush. Drop the boys with a few different folks who see to their getting far away and that's all. For me, anyways.

26

New York Herald-Tribune

!!!EXTRA!!!

NEGRO RAMPAGES AT ALABAMA COURTHOUSE

Unharmed by Bombs, He Destroys a Tank

Birmingham News

EXTRA EXTRA EXTRA

NIGHTMARE IN SCOTTSBORO!!!

Chicago Defender

JOHN HENRY

IS

REAL

27

I'm home and going about life as regular only to find out later the entire world lost its mind.

Home's not done but getting there. Parlor, kitchen, bedroom, bath all finished. Why Jet's moved out here after living in the old house with momma. Making to fit: Doors 10 feet tall and five wide, ceilings at 12, halls are eight across. Take a usual house, make it all a quarter or so larger. Going up fast because I can push a nail in with just one finger. Working on it is all I'm about until a week later, that's when "then what" pulls up in a big black car.

White chauffeur gets fast to opening the door for two men in back. First is short man, red hair, a three-piece, trilby, and skin paler than pork. Bantam. No other word to do for him. Other man, dressed similar, one of us, and walks like he's used to people listening as he speaks. Everything about them said come from far, far away.

Red in the lead. Strutting energy, chest out and clear-the-way. His foot hits our steps and what a change – still pleased for himself but makes himself over from someone come to tell to come to talk and certainly does

Already started as hat goes from head to hand as is proper. "Good morning, Mr. and Mrs. Crawford, I'm ..."

"Mr. Tommy ... the ... Cork," Jet said, silence between each shows she's not impressed. "Roosevelt's fixer."

Almost doesn't show surprise on his face. Almost.

"Did you not know we can read?" she said, her voice extra, extra heavy on the Southern. "Mail brings us newspapers and magazines. Got radios, too. Just like real people."

Small smile comes and goes as Thomas Corcoran nods, acknowledging Jet counting coup.

"Pardon me, Mrs. Crawford," he said. "Press outside of Washington don't pay me much mind and the press inside pay me only a little more. So, yes, I'm surprised someone who doesn't spend time in the District bothers to know who I am."

Other man steps forward to shake hands, face fixed so Tommy the Cork won't see the smile was there right before.

"I'm James Gunner. An honor to meet you both. Really."

There's a big stink eye look starting in Jet. Gunner sees it.

"My father was a tenant farmer over in Georgia. About 10 miles from Hicksville, as a fact." First he sounded all Northern but there's Georgia backwoods in it by the time he's done. Can't fake that.

"I read in The Defender you are in that Black Cabinet old Roosevelt has," said Jet, gets a nod in return. "What is it you do when you are not being a cabinet?"

She knows. And unless he's a fool he knows she does. Not asking for finding out, she's announcing the pecking order.

"I'm a sociologist. At Harvard." Jet makes a little look like she's been sucking at a lemon.

No, I'm not saying anything. You don't tell Satchel Paige how to pitch. She got a mind to she can filet anyone and outstare the Sphinx.

"Well, all come in," she said, looks at me. "Let us hear what Massa Roosevelt wants us to do."

Show time at The Apollo.

SETTING ROOM DIDN'T HAVE much for setting on. Jet took the Good Chair, Corcoran a kitchen stool, Gunner leaning at a door jamb back behind him. I'm down on the floor at the other end of the wall from Jet.

Cat onto Jet's lap, velvet-gray Siamese with eyes color of jade green and mean. Showed up day Jet moved in. Said she brought it from the Institute but never saw it there, didn't see it when we put Jet's belonging's in Erlissa's truck either. Called Cat because Jet said so, not it pays any attention. Cat and Jet together always look like a secret just got shared. Not a good one. Say Cat doesn't like me but that's too much credit to me. Cat doesn't like the world. Wouldn't say it likes Jet either, closer to tolerates. Can't hurt me any more than anything but, honest, can make me nervous. Like Jet.

"Mr. Crawford, the president asked me to come here to ..."

"Why only talking to me?"

"My apologies," he said and had to turn his head from me to Jet as he's talking.

"President Roosevelt has sent me here to discuss the situation we're confronted with and see if we can find a way to make the best of it." A Northern voice sounding in charge and like anything it said is reasonable and won't even allow you might not think the same.

"What situation, Mr. the Cork?" Jet asks, regal in her voice now where the South was thick before. "No situation to us. No situation to our neighbors. We are all getting the farming done just as we always do."

"What happened in Scottsboro is causing..."

"Oh, you mean when Mr. Crawford helped those poor boys out by stopping a trial that started with a verdict already decided? Is that the situation you are referring to? Are you offering to buy my husband a new set of clothes? Because, if so, it was not necessary to come all the way here for that. It is very polite of you, but a check would have been fine."

"Clothes?" Confused but knows it's a setup.

"Yes, clothes," she said. "They were quite damaged when those boys shot at Mr. Crawford. Shot at him for no reason, I might add. Unless walking toward a courthouse is now a capital crime."

"Too bad about the tank," I said. "Y'all gonna be able to fix it?"

Gunner putting a hand on his mouth so not to laugh out loud. No need, Corcoran wouldn't have heard it over his own. His is loud and true.

"Mrs. Crawford, would you ever consider running our congressional liaison office? It would be like what Mr. Crawford did to that tank."

I smile at it, but not Jet. Fixed a stare saying she wasn't having bullshit friendly talk.

"Mr. and Mrs. Crawford, may I tell you about a problem President Roosevelt has? First, please understand, the President shares your opinion about that trial."

"Really? There was nothing in the press about it," Jet said, suddenly innocent like she doesn't know.

Enough decency in Corcoran for him to blush and look down before saying more.

"To what end? It wouldn't have helped those boys and having a Northerner, even if he is president, interfering would likely have made it worse for them."

"Worse than what? If my husband had not done something, they would have put those children in an adult prison for all the time they still had on earth. Least they might have had the comfort of knowing the president was for them."

"It would have cost him votes." Gunner said and Corcoran got a look like hearing a fiddle out of tune. "He's not going to get any legislation through Congress if the Southern states don't go along."

Corcoran didn't let him go farther. "Yes, that's true too. It would make it impossible for him to pass the legislation that will truly help the Negro people. We got the Southerners in the House and Senate to agree to assigning a percent of funds explicitly for Negroes in the Works Progress Administration and Civilian Conservation Corps. The president doesn't like those people – just ask Mr. Gunner, here – but he's stuck with them. So, he had to choose between making a statement that wouldn't help those fellows or not making a statement in order to help a lot of others."

I gave a grunt sounded close to uh-huh. Cat and Jet ignoring Corcoran to look at Gunner. "How do you feel about that?" she asked.

"Everything looks different when you're in Washington," he said, shaking his head. "It's a place that can warp your priorities. Politics, winning the game, can be how you ... was how I judged everything. Even peoples' lives. I'm ashamed to admit when I heard of the boys' arrest, I wondered how it could be used for political leverage. Knowing the president wouldn't speak out, I was trying to guess what we might shame him into. Trying to figure out what we could get from him for that guilt. That and promising him our newspapers wouldn't be too hard on him. Politics, all politics. What's the angle? How can I work this to our advantage?"

"Were you able to?" she asked.

"No chance to find out. John Henry arrived, and the apple cart wasn't upset, it was gone. No one, white or black, knows how to figure things anymore."

"Mo," I said. "Everyone calls me Mo."

Gunner nodded but not like he heard.

"Tom was in those conversations with us, figuring how to work the president. Mrs. Roosevelt pushed him too. Please don't think it was an easy decision for the president."

"Not easy," Jet said as Cat got bored, curled up to nap. "But not as hard as being 13 knowing best thing you might expect is spending the rest of your life in Kilby Prison."

"You're right," said Gunner. "That's what I mean about the warped thinking. People stop being people. They become things to be used, chips in a game. Seeing John Henry got me out of thinking that way."

Gunner walked up now and stood next to Corcoran.

"I happened to be at the White House when I heard the news about you," he said. "There are newswires in the press office, and they have bells that go off when something big happens. How many bells tells how important the news is. They didn't stop for hours. There were so many of us crowding the machines that someone read the stories aloud as they came in. I didn't believe it. It was literally too good to believe. Right then I thought, 'If I believe this and it isn't true, I don't know if I can stand it.' So even as reports kept coming in about what you did, I wouldn't risk thinking it was real. And what we were hearing was all confused. Some had you killing all the soldiers, tearing down the courthouse, killing the judge. I think that was because the reporters couldn't believe it either... and they were right there, looking at you. But then, finally, there were pictures. I started crying, Mr. Henry. In front of all those white people and I didn't care. Kept the first picture that got sent. You're standing on top of that tank, holding the turret over your head. I knew I'd never be the same."

Not just him, either. Next thing Gunner tells me of movie theatres all around – North, South, everywhere – showing the newsreel stories of me.

Some run it before and after every movie, some it's all they're running. Longest one of the newsreels is maybe 7 minutes. Theatres getting rich because lot of people coming to watch it again and again and more. Wasn't only us either. In Jackson, the mayor tried to stop the showings, said it was giving the wrong people wrong ideas. Police chief said the lines were so long closing the theaters might start a riot. In Jackson, Mississippi.

Shook my head and looked to Jet. "You know?"

"Of course."

"Why didn't you say?"

"Not my job. You said tell you if it sounded like there was something for you to be doing. You want to be ignorant, you are going to be ignorant. All you had to do was turn on the radio."

Nodded, because she's right. Scared of another Hicksville. Ready to go if it happened but knew if I started, I'd just be sitting by the radio all day, listening in fear.

"What else happened?" I asked. "After Scottsboro."

A moment for Gunner and Corcoran to understand, maybe even believe my question or really fact behind it: Had no knowledge of all what I'd caused.

"You just about shut down the country," said Corcoran. "Everyone thinking Scottsboro was the start of a war. That you were going to go attack somewhere else. All Southern and border state governors call up the militia and Mr. Roosevelt puts the military on alert, saying it's ready to go anywhere it's needed."

Don't know exactly what he would've sent. Wasn't much military at the time and best part of it was big Navy ships. Most of the troops were away protecting places most people didn't even know were ours.

Once they were called out, all the militia and police and all did was run around to wherever people said they saw me and there were a lot of people saying they did.

"No one knew where you'd gone, Mr. Henry," said Corcoran. "Impressive that a man of your size can hide so well."

"No hiding," I said. "I was right here. What else happened?"

"Nothing," said Gunner with some surprise. He didn't only mean nothing else in the nation but nothing to any of us and I was surprised too.

Nothing never happens to us.

Back in the not long-ago Jack Johnson beat a white man boxing and across the nation we were murdered everywhere. Pulled off streetcars, hunted on streets, trapped in bars. Beaten 'til no blood left inside, knifed, shot, hung from streetlights, burned in houses. All because a wrong man won.

How could there be nothing now?

I'd beat their army, broke their court, freed their prisoners, and nothing?

Gunner said while they were doing nothing all of us were celebrating. Big, noisy, Juneteenth is now real! type parties. Roxbury, Harlem, South Side, Black Bottom, Watts, East St. Louis, D.C., Bank Head, North Central, Gary, Rosewood, Lower 9th, East Baltimore, Red Bridge, Omaha, Hayti, East Cleveland, Deep Deuce, Homewood, South Memphis, South Six, Tukwila, Rufus King. It was ON.

Before now they'd call that a "provocation." That's when it was our fault they were killing and raping us. If only we hadn't done whatever then they wouldn't have had to do to us. Keep our place. Why didn't we keep our place? Always our fault for forcing them in to it

Not this week.

No mobs, no white riots.

Yet. Always a yet. Lives spent waiting on the white yet.

Tommy the Cork made sure to let us know all the work has been going into making nothing happen. President federalized the militia and called it out in all the other states. Sent into cities with orders to see to it we were protected. Patrolling not just our neighborhoods but places where we work and the roads in between. Lot of shitkickers got their shit kicked so they'd stay in line.

That made most police departments, not all but a lot – a lot of a lot, be real careful around us. Almost treating us like we're almost white.

Corcoran made it clear the president was doing more than that. When the news came out there was a lot of screaming and race baiting on the radio and papers, but of a sudden it stopped. Roosevelt twisted down the volume knob fast, leaning hard on press, politicians, preachers, anyone with a big enough soapbox who, if it was all normal, would be talking the shit on us. Now it's either give the official line or go away. That line: Keep calm, we'll find him. Most all parts of government saying it, but none doing anything much in the way of looking. Because they're all thinking, "Then what?"

"Arms are being twisted hard," said Corcoran. "Radio stations reminded they got licenses we can pull. Publishers asked about what the tax guys would find if they were to look real hard. It's mostly worked. It's mostly all illegal, too. But FDR's not worrying about that. It's not for you. Pretty clear you can handle yourself. We're worried about what happens if they decide to go after other people because they can't do anything to you."

Jet, she sees through everything.

"Corcoran, you're pretty proud of this, aren't you?"

He is, but stutters no.

"Proud the government is protecting *all* its citizens for once," she said. "You want us to think better of you because you did something you should be ashamed had never been done before? You only did it because you are afraid. Afraid of what might happen if someone does not like how you behave. Whatever fear you are feeling is not enough, Mr. Corcoran."

"I was under the impression the Negroes like the president."

"I was under the impression the Irish are always drunk."

"Sometimes we just wish we were."

Jet wasn't letting go. Cork still thought this was negotiating, thought showing they could treat us like people would show we're all friends here. People get nothing for a long time supposed to be glad they get anything, right? Those days done but he hadn't figured it yet.

Jet, though.

"Seeing as there are two of you, what was the play going to be, Mr. Gunner?"

Gunner told as Corcoran tried hiding being unhappy about him telling. Plan was Gunner talking about how much our people thought of Roosevelt, done more for us than any president since Grant. Same time Corcoran was gonna be about how I created opportunity to bring a nation together against the Great Depression. Be a hero giving all people hope, getting them believing in America again.

Jet, not impressed, scratched Cat's neck – even its purr was threatening.

"Now we know your game, tells us your offer," Jet said.

"You can talk to President Roosevelt directly about what you would like, and we guarantee, at a minimum, more money going to Negro communities and business, more Federal jobs for Negroes." Look on our faces wasn't what he wanted which got him talking fast even by Northern standards. "As I said, that's just a start and the president *asked* to talk to about it."

"And in return?" she asked. Damn, were her and Cat blinking at same time? Seemed so.

"John Henry meets with the president, preferably at the White House," said Gunner. "Then he gives a statement to the effect of the United States has some problems but it's still the greatest nation ever, you're proud to be an American, and you're going to work to make it better and will follow the laws from now on."

Jet and I look to each other and it's a race to see who rolls their eyes first.

"If Moses will not say your magic words?" said Jet. "Mr. Gunner, what is the plan then?"

"Mr. Roosevelt and the Secretary of War said to do whatever we can, politely, to get John Henry say he's willing to work with the government."

"Secretary of War?" Only time in all this Jet sounded like there's something she hadn't already figured.

"Yes, Mrs. Henry," Gunner said. "It's not only our politics that's gone upside down. Every government on the planet is waiting to see which way this goes. If John Henry says he's with the America, it gives us a weapon no one else can match."

"I'm not fighting in any wars."

"That's what the White House expected," said Gunner. "They just don't want you saying that publicly. The belief is that as long as you don't say anything either way you are as big a worry to any foreign enemies as you are to the president."

"After Scottsboro, they thought I'd stand with the government? They say why?"

"That wasn't addressed," Gunner said. "After the meeting, Mr. Hull, the secretary of state, asked to talk to me privately. He said, 'There is one sentence every diplomat relies on: We have had a frank and honest exchange of views and are continuing to discuss the situation. If Mr. Henry won't agree to any of our proposals but will agree to this, then I will consider your mission a success.'"

I would've gone with it, but Corcoran didn't give it a chance. He was up and talking fast like tap dancing across a burning roof. Going on about there's no reason to discuss what wouldn't be happening in the future. Let's talk about how we can help each other, make something good happen now. We're fighting for what's best for Negroes which is just as it should be. That's what makes America great, that everyone does that and can do that. How he wanted to be sure the nation could see me as someone going to help America, see that I want to make it a better place. America this and America that and all working together like we should be.

Meanwhile, Gunner's shaking his head and Jet's gone from amused to irritated but Corcoran can't tell. Set of her mouth and hard of her eyes changes only the littlest. Her sitting, gone from regal queen to more, call it empress, empress of whatever she wants. Like Cat.

Way, way past irritated for me. Man acts like he pours enough words on the ground they'll get agreed to, like only the words right now count, not everything that's happened for centuries before.

"No," I said. Should've answered any more questions but Corcoran's desperate got in the way of his smart. Also, hard to hear in one word how low my voice had gone. Jet and Cat heard. Cat moving suddenly and away. My voice is always down there but Jet said I get angry and it's like the ground is talking.

"Please, sir, I don't think you understand. The president will give..."

"Give?" Later, Jet told me floor boards shook at that. "No give, here. No handout. No, 'See we are letting you have something.' There is owed. We are owed. We are owed because we were stolen."

Deep breath out. "Where you from, Corcoran?"

"Rhode Island."

"Where?"

"New England."

I nod.

"Not a lot of slaves in New England, was there?"

He nods.

"Lot of slave money though. It was all y'all's ships carried molasses, up there from Caribbean. Make it into rum, fill those ships, then to Africa to fill with stolen people. Fill isn't right word. Packed. Packed so thick and close there's not an inch to move until people start dying. But dying is coming. It's part of the plan. So many in there because so many are going to die and need some alive to make your money. Rum treated better than we were, because bottles got to be kept whole. Not us. Live for months in our own shit and die in our own shit. Our bodies aren't ours. We become chum when we're dead. Bait.

So, someone else can eat. We are raped. Our children are stolen. Families broken again and again because our bodies needed to be sold for money. Sold. We are stolen. Our work stolen. Our value stolen. Stolen to make your land. Stolen to make fortunes and then sold when the fortune falters. Stolen to build your cities. But then jubilation arrives, and Massa Lincoln said we can no longer be stolen. Now we are not stolen, we are cheated. Cheated of getting to be people. Cheated of being paid the same as people. Cheated of getting to live where people live. Cheated of laws only can be used by people. Cheated out of those additional two fifths that would make us people. Now the thief and the con man comes telling what he will give. Thieves do not give. Thieves owe. That should be clear even to an educated man like yourself.

"What are we told? 'Roosevelt is doing all he can. More, much more anyone else. Be patient. There are political realities to face. You can't expect everything to change at once. Be patient. We promise you crumbs from the table as soon as can be. Be patient. Your children will be people. Or your grandchildren.' Cheating us of time. How do you give back time?

"Course you said it. Why not? All you were faced with was 'moral suasion.' Appeals to a sense of decency. Reminders of how you said it was a nation built on justice and equality. But now you're here and ready to promise anything. Why? Because moral suasion is done. I am a threat. That is why. You are here to negotiate and my answer to your offer, any offer, is no. We are owed. We are people and we are owed the price of not letting us be people. We are owed everything stolen from us. We are people. On the day this nation treats us that way it will have begun to pay what we are owed."

Longest ever spoke all my life.

Nothing said after, as if anything could.

Gunner had a look of someone reminded of something didn't want to be reminded on. Who would? Think white people only ones don't want to have it talked about? We don't, more than they don't. Because we don't want it to have ever happened. Who wants to say this is how we were destroyed? We don't. Have to because we are never allowed to forget.

"What do you want me to tell the president for you?" Corcoran, like he might be getting a clue.

"Get all that minimum offer moving. Now. Show me what he's doing. That anti-lynch law. Get that through. Give it teeth and use those teeth. Does that I'll give him the international. Get on radio and say America made its problems, America fixes its problems, and no one should mess with us and ours."

"How soon would you be willing to make that statement?"

"We will let you know," said Jet.

"Until then?"

I give Gunner a look.

"We've had a frank exchange of views and are continuing to discuss the situation," he said.

ONE MORE THING TO say before Corcoran goes.

"Want you to tell something to all the people government has trying to figure how to kill me."

He sputters a denial, sincere. What he really, truly believes. A quiet when he stops. Three of us being embarrassed for him.

"Tell them to ask themselves one thing: What if it doesn't work?"

Corcoran nods, charges out the door, Gunner doesn't.

"I told them to send Mrs. Roosevelt," Gunner said. "Or Secretary Hull. Didn't because they were afraid she'd be on your side and that he was too high-level, government couldn't be seen negotiating with an individual."

"Your ride just left," I tell him.

"Just as well. I don't think Tommy wants to talk with me right now."

"Mr. Gunner..." Jet starts.

"Jim. Please."

"Jim, can you stay around a while? Be useful to have your advice."

"Mrs. Crawford – and I insist on calling you Mrs. Crawford – I'd be glad to but might do you better being an ear for you in Washington. Besides, you can always call."

I point out there's no phones, no electricity here.

"There will be soon. White House wants to keep you happy and make it easy to communicate. You'll never see a bill, either. They'll pay for it. Want a new well? Get the roads paved? Won't have to ask them twice."

"Tell them we want all that and anything else you think of," I said. "Same for all my neighbors, including the never paying for it. Forever."

28

Always stupid around.

Can't find it?

Ask for the police.

This day it was delivered right up to the house in five police cars. Five – two more than Tuskegee has so one's State and one some other town – all packed tail to snout, at least 20 cops. Chief got out first, looking like a cliché: Stomach slopped out way in front, maybe tip over if he leaned too far. Jowls fall and pool on to shoulders, and everywhere dead pale skin with red blotches. Mush mouth when he talks, sounds like words drowning in grits. No understanding them but knew the meaning. Wasn't for me, anyway. Never is. For self and crowd, so know what they do is right, that they're people, not me.

All others come with him tapping fingers on batons, shotguns, pistols, but for two who're casually moving back and away like setting a speed record for nonchalant. One a state cop, other that boy from the spitting contest. Kept going until were across the road and about a third of the way into a neighbor's yard.

"No," I said, without knowing what he said.

Chief's face got redder than his blotches and eyes almost crossed because no way one of us interrupted.

"No."

Didn't feel like getting shot for no reason except teaching them what they ought already learned. Instead put my hand on a police car roof and leaned until it crunched down into floor. Next ripped the entire wheel from an axel then toss and bounced it off another car's hood hard enough knocked its engine out. Finale was pulling engines out of a couple other cars using only two fingers and thumb on each hand. Carried like bowling balls over to that last car and dropped one on a hood and other on a trunk.

At that, all the police, except the two faded way in the back and the chief, run and scream like didn't know if shitting or going blind. Finally, the headless chickens figure out enough to all leg it the way they'd come. Chief didn't join them on account of being busy being face down on the ground. Seemed for a heart attack.

Walked over to those other two who stood up straighter, arms across their chests to show their hands had no interest in their guns.

"Chief looks to be dead," I said.

"Yeah, ain't moved since you started all that body work on the cars," said the state cop who was half-way to a smile.

"Save mayor trouble of killing him," said the Tuskegee one.

"Mayor didn't know?"

"Was 100 percent all chief's dumb idea," Tuskegee said. "I told him, too. Said he should go down to the Bijou and see the movie where you opened that tank like it was a of beer. He said it was just the Hollywood Jews tricking us again."

Impressed me how cool both these boys were. Might as well been wondering when the next rain would come by the way they sounded.

"How come y'all came out then?"

"Miss this?" Tuskegee said, now showing his smile – a mean one. "Not for mamma's Sunday dinner. Must be 10 times or more I went to the theater to watch you. Had to see what you'd do to the moron brigade."

State cop nodded and we all thought on it, way you do when letting the talking take its own time.

"Got a chaw?" I asked.

Tuskegee got out a bag of Cannon Ball and a pocket knife, started cutting me some from the plug.

"You still spit all way across a road?" I asked.

Stopped what he was doing at that, wrinkled his forehead looking me up and down a couple of times, then broke out in a pair of wide eyes.

"Damn b...but you can grow fast." We all knew he didn't start out meaning to say "but." Caught himself, though. That's sign someone can learn fast.

Offered up the chaw and I took it.

"Hope it don't stunt my growth."

"Might you could use it," Tuskegee said. "I'm Ray Dandril. This is my brother, BG."

Nods all around.

"I recall your last name is Crawford? Don't know I got told your first name."

"You can call me, Mr. Henry."

This time the cop brothers' nods were a slight bit slower in coming. They were used to being on the other side of that exchange but weren't fools either.

"Pretty sure the chief there is dead," I said.

"Yeah, that'll happen," said Ray.

"Didn't like him?"

"Liking people don't take up a lot of Ray's time," said BG and his brother nodded.

"You didn't much like that banker when our belongings were sold off," I said. "Think he wanted you to stop all the people from the church who were keeping away anyone they didn't know. Why'd you do that?"

Another long pause. This one awkward, not just a killing time type of pause. Ray kicked at the dirt.

"Wasn't first time seeing a family have everything sold out from under them," he said. "Wasn't first time seeing neighbors low-ball a bank like that. Came down to it and knew I'd never be the one running the sale, but it could easy be me losing my stuff."

"Even though it was Negroes?"

"Don't make too much of it," Ray said, irritated. "Was a matter of who I didn't like the most."

"So, let me ask you a question, but hear everything I got to say before you answer. You think you'd be able to not like everyone the same, no matter what? I'm asking because I hear the police chief job just opened up in Tuskegee. Not gonna be like it was before, being chief. New chief has only one responsibility: Making sure I never have to have a word with him. One way to do that is not liking everybody all the same. No more Negro law. Has to be one law, one way of treating everyone. Otherwise, I have to come around. That's why you need to think on your answer. Mayor and town council listening very carefully to what I say, and I say someone's gonna be chief, they'll be chief."

Ray's pause now was a thinking pause.

"What happens when I gotta arrest one of y'all?"

"Man breaks the law, that's why we have police. Thing is the police better make damn sure they got the man who broke the law and not someone they said broke the law. Everybody gets arrested the same, don't forget. No confessions beaten out of somebody. No beating somebody for minding their own business walking down a street or because someone thought they were sassing. And don't tell me a lady got raped when it's her daddy or husband found she's pregnant and been hiding a boyfriend who's got dark skin."

Ray sucked in his breath hard. "That won't be easy for some folks to take."

"Sounds like being police chief will be a shit job," said BG.

"Being the chief's deputy won't be a pile of happy either," said Ray. "But you're still gonna have to do it."

"Awwwww, Ray. I have to?" Cry of every little brother.

Told him think a little longer because new chief would be replacing all the officers and some of the new ones would be Negro to work our side of town.

That last was what this visit was about. Old chief didn't come out to the house and be stupid for no reason. Done it to show me what's what because two nights before I'd gone to the city council meeting and said one sentence.

"Got your separate, now it's time for the equal."

City hall, like any normal building, not built for likes of me. Getting in the door, the front door, meant bending over a bit and sort of sideways. Didn't stand up proper again until got in the council room with its high ceilings. When I did my head was up past the light fixtures so none of them could even see my face.

No surprise everything stops when I came in. Finally, one of the boys up front who knew manners is a thing you can use no matter what said, "What can we do for you..." Could tell he wasn't sure if to call me Mr. Crawford or Mr. Henry. "...sir?"

That's when said what I said. Done with it, turned around and gone. Jet's one figured the whole play: "Let them guess."

That was all my part to it.

Next day, a Cadillac, baby blue and brand new, pulls up. Passenger getting out of the front seat is Mayor somebody – never did remember his name. Driver gets out and it's the city councilor with the manners. Didn't really focus on him or anyone night before because of being so nervous. One reason Jet knew to not give me more than a sentence to speak. Now I saw him, knew who he was. Dr. Stuart. A Ph.D. doctor, not a real one. Small and wearing suit, tie, pocket square, fedora all perfect match to the car's baby blue. Hair silver and likely trimmed at least weekly. Confirmed bachelor, as was said then, which no one took a mind to because he was the only remaining of oldest, most pedigreed family maybe in the entire state. Daddy's great-grandfather was Jeff Davis' godfather and momma's was an aunt to Bobby Lee, which made him practically a Washington which, for the gentry, was almost as good as being a Lee. Such a standing if he'd shit on an altar, white people would just laugh and say ain't he colorful. Wouldn't do that because, like he showed, he had manners. Why I knew about him. He had manners to everybody. Treat his yardman and his maid as same as a bishop – except he'd be asking them to do a thing or two. Always asked. Always please and thank you. No report ever of him using any wrong words to us. That'll make word get around on a person. Didn't know if he liked or hated us, same as you'd never know how he was about the bishop.

Dr. Stuart just about bouncing up our steps and gave a happy knock on a door. Mayor walked like going to his own hanging.

Dr. Stuart holding his hat over his heart when Jet opens the door. She's dressed for her best because she knew we'd be getting a visit. Mayor kept his hat on until Stuart hit him an elbow to the gut, and he hurried it off. Me, my part all done, I'm sitting on a sofa where can't be seen.

"Pardon me, ma'am," the doctor said, "I'm Winthrop Stuart of the city council and this is our Mayor Davis."

"Pleased to meet you Dr. Stuart, Mayor Davis," she said. "I'm Jet Crawford."

"Oh, Mrs. Crawford, I am delighted to meet you at last. I have heard so much about you," doctor said.

"You have?"

"Why, of course. You see I get to be on The Institute's board, and you are mentioned regularly at our meetings."

"I am?" Not easy to surprise her and he'd done it.

"The president and the faculty are – and I do not say this lightly – a bit in awe of you. The president said to me, and please don't let him know I told you, he said he's always afraid he may say something stupid in front you."

"He is?" Not even my hearing can hear a blush but tell you I heard her blush.

"And he is not the only one," said Doctor Stuart, the mayor still behind him looking like eating a toadstool. "No reason you should know but I took my degree in ancient philosophy, and I do hope there comes a time as we could have a talk on it. Unfortunately, our business today concerns your husband. Do you mind me asking, does he prefer to be called Mr. Crawford or Mr. Henry?"

"Dr. Stuart," she said with consideration, "you should call him Mr. Crawford. The mayor can call him Mr. Henry."

"Then is *Mr. Crawford* at home? We'd like to speak with him concerning the city council meeting last night."

"He is," said Jet, conversation now more in line of what she'd been expecting. "But he is in a bit of a temper just now. So, it is best if we talk and leave him out of it. Will you have a seat?"

Had some reasonable good chairs on the porch since that where we did most entertaining and talking. Mayor Toadstool sulked his way over to sitting down and Cat followed Jet out the door.

"Well, to be direct about it, Mrs. Crawford," said the doctor, "we'd like to know more detail about what your husband meant when he said, 'Now it's time for equal.'"

Swear I felt her eyebrow go up.

"Why Dr. Stuart, I would think these truths to be self-evident to an educated person such as yourself," she said in a tone to make a smart man nervous. "Look at your schools. Look at our schools. They should be in equal condition, should be equal in what the students are supplied with: the quantity and quality of textbooks, the desks, blackboards, hallways, the entire building. The faculty and administration should be paid equally. Look at your streets, paved with sewer lines beneath and electrical lines above. Ours cannot be different than that anymore. Look at the fire department, you know they only put out our fires if the building is owned by a white person? Fortunately for us, in our neighborhood many of them are white owned. Do you know why? The bank almost never gives us a mortgage and if they do it is at twice the interest rate and requires twice the down payment. And that was before the Crash. But now, and Dr. Stuart since you are on the board you must know this, The Institute's president cannot even get that offer on a mortgage. Nor any of the doctors from the VA hospital."

Mayor Toadstool clearly couldn't take quiet any longer.

"Look here Mrs. Henry Crawford," he said and there was a loud cough from the doctor, sharp as the gut elbow. "We can't tell the bank what to do! It's a private business. And for the rest, well what with The Depression and all we barely have money for what's already done. Can't afford what you're asking for here."

"Is that what you want me to tell my husband?"

Silence with nothing but Cat's evil purr getting louder. Cat always comes around when talk gets "interesting." Just seems to know. Silence went on as likely the mayor was thinking about Hicksville and Scottsboro, too.

"A Siamese!" said Dr. Stuart. "I have one, too. She's horrible to everyone which is as it should be. What's this one's name?"

"Cat. Yours?"

"Beast."

"Things like these have to be called what they are," said Jet, sounding like she'd found someone else who knew the truth of the universe.

"Exactly. Otherwise, you are calling a tornado Mr. Silly Poo. That kind of mistake will come back on you."

"I believe Cat makes my husband nervous."

Not supposed to tell!

"Mr. Crawford is no fool."

A loud sigh from the mayor who just figured this was a capitulation, not a negotiation.

"Mrs. Crawford, how long do you think Mr. Crawford would allow for things to get 'equal'?" said Dr. Stuart.

"Gentlemen, may I show you something?"

They nodded and her pocketbook snapped open, I didn't have to see it to know what happened next. She reaches in, takes out a handkerchief, spreads it across her lap in her finest lady-like way. Next – and wish to see the look on their faces – a 1911 Colt .45, polished and cleaned to beauty. Puts it on her lap delicately. Not in the pocketbook just for this meeting, either. Mrs. Terry got it for her soon after Jet arrived at The Institute. Had to do with something from before and Jet won't tell me. Few months later, on Jet's birthday, Mrs. Terry gave her a necklace of pearls. Doesn't go out, not even to mailbox, without pearls, pocketbook with gun, and an appropriate ensemble.

"My husband can become very fixed on a thing, gentlemen. Now when he does it is usually something like plowing or planting. When this happens there is nothing will turn him aside from it. He will not even hear me when I try talking to him, which is why I have this pistol. In order to get his attention, I must fire at least one and sometimes two full clips into him. Then he will pause what he is doing and listen but not with much grace and when I am done, he will go straight back to what he is doing. I am telling you this so you will understand what I mean when I said he is fixed on this. He is fixed on this maybe even more than he was on those poor boys in Scottsboro."

Those two must be paler than mayonnaise ghosts by now.

Not it matters but most everything Jet said was beautiful bullshit. Except the gun and the shooting. Y'know the two of us have arguments like anyone will. Jet, in a mood, will give an argument to tear bark off a tree. Even so, it's me she's arguing with and size comes as an issue. With my big I can stare louder most people scream. On a day we're setting in to it she pulled out the Colt and shot me up. Only one clip. Never even ever once has she put another clip in. When the first shooting was done it got us both to laughing like better than anything. Since then, she'll use it anytime she needs. Wonder what a kid will make of that?

"You know the president's man was down here," she said. "Made an offer. Pretty good one, seemed to me. Wanted John Henry to say he loves America and was willing to follow the law. That man put a check on our kitchen table from the United States Treasury and signed by old Roosevelt himself. Did not say how much it was for, though. That was blank, could be filled in for however much. That man got thrown out by the ear, so hard almost got him all the way to Washington."

Check? Had to put a hand on across my mouth not to laugh.

"So, what would you like me to tell my husband?"

Never did find out. I'd run out to the backyard and put hands to my mouth to try not to howl. And when Jet came back in, we were laughing hard enough to cry and barely breathe together. Even damn Cat was almost smiling.

29

"You're a fool, Moses," Mrs. Terry said. "What could possibly cause you to say that?"

Never been on this end of a Mrs. Terry firestorm before and please never again. Stood my ground, though.

"You really think they're gonna let us sit next to them? Use a front door? Be happy we move into their neighborhood?"

The argument was about me telling City Council to make our separate equal. The argument was about how are we to live in this land. The argument started long before me and maybe will never end.

"You really think they're going to let us do all that if we wall ourselves off from them?"

When our shackles broke, we had to decide how we will live in these United States. Integrated or separated or something in between? Wasn't our choice alone to make – although the law made it look so. Our choice was what we'd fight for. Early on came the idea we had to prove we are equal and when we did acceptance would follow. Made sense, in a way. Slavery made us poor, from centuries of wages stolen. Slavery made us ignorant, from centuries of education being forbidden. So, after a brief effort at restitution was aborted mid-birth, we ourselves were expected to make good these deficits. We could not become monied on our own, but we could become educated. The need for proper education became enmeshed with the need for proper deportment and the bourgeois blues fell on us. Respectability – meaning behaving white –

was going to lead us to the freedom. Must show ourselves civilized by doing, believing, acting as they do, and then waiting until they we had done it all well enough for them to bestow humanity upon us.

Other side was separatists wanting to get away from a government they didn't trust and stand on our own. Garvey saying people should go to Liberia was nothing new – the nation began as a colony where the U.S. would send us. Slavers wanted freemen gone to there so they couldn't rile up the slaves. Abolitionists, despairing at how terribly we were treated in "free" states, thought it would be better for us there. Such strange and terrible allies for an idea to have. Even so, some of us signed on. After the Civil War, the white supremacists thought it a grand idea and this is what cost Garvey in the end. Blinded by his dream he didn't see the Klan's love of the idea as the mark of the beast and proclaimed them his new friends.

But there were other ways to be separate, ones that didn't end in playing along with those bastards.

One almost worked. Fleeing the South, we joined the great rush West and started towns. Most in Oklahoma, when it was still the Indian Territory. Then we lived alongside Native Americans who didn't have to be told that we, too, were people. Then it became a state and the first law passed said we were definitely not people and got worse from there.

Be separate because it's what we want, that's what I was thinking.

"Do the math," said Mrs. Terry. "There's more of them than there are of us. They are here just as we are here. We cannot live apart."

"Not totally, no, but why not make it we're having as little to do with them as possible?" I asked. "I don't like them, and I don't trust them."

"Desmond nearly swindled you out of everything in the world," she said. "That's what comes from letting skin color tell you who to trust."

Point.

"They're people just the same as we're people," she said. "Good ones, bad ones."

"Thing is they've had laws and power for centuries telling them we're not human and they've profited off it," I said. "Warped their thinking so much I don't believe most of them can change or want to."

"Exactly why we need laws that do not separate us. We have to force them to live up to 'all men are created equal' and with John Henry, we can."

Didn't have a comeback which probably meant I started pouting. Very grownup.

"How long you think you're going to live?" Mrs. Terry asked. "Just because no one's found anything will hurt you doesn't make you immortal. Time will take you down just like it does everything. What do *we* do then? If we're all living in our separate little towns and places when you die, where does that leave us? We will still be 'them.' Y'know what happens to 'them'? Ask the Jews. 'They' always get the blame. Harder to be them when you're the neighbor, the guy you work with, the teacher, the doctor. Then you're just another person. Won't be easy to get there, even with John Henry, but it can be done."

"It won't be easy? It won't happen. As long as we look different from what they think 'people' look like we're gonna be separate. We gotta be together and be ready. Our strength is all of us together."

"You're the reason that argument doesn't make sense," she said. "Now we have John Henry, and they have to listen to us. They must treat us as the equals we are. Without him, without you, what would we have done? Kept on the way we were by trying to shame them into equality through our suffering. Now, instead of hoping their consciences will make them give us our rights, they don't get a say about it.

"Without John Henry how long would all this have taken? How many more people would have died waiting for justice? Maybe, to make themselves feel good, they'd eventually make discrimination illegal. They'd do it because they'd still be safe from equality. Sitting on top of all the wealth we made for them they'd say it's our fault for being poor. Our fault for not catching up with them when they started so far ahead and tore up the road behind them. With John Henry they can't do that. Not just moral force on our side. Without him? Hard to imagine."

Nodded. What I do when I don't agree but don't want to say it.

30

WE UNDERSTOOD HOW I'D changed things before they did. Long before. Course we did. Waiting for it before we were born.

Change does what it wants, then keeps going.

Jet was first of us to figure it and she saw it all.

"You're more than you, you're a new power in the land."

"I'm a what now?"

"OK, think about law. What is it? It is an unassailable power. It can be corrupted, made good or bad, or twisted until no one believes in it anymore. What it cannot be is destroyed. That is because it is made by the people who run a society to keep them running it. If they are smart, they know there has to be some give and take in the law. Not enough to change anything but enough so when the people are riled there is a valve to let out the steam."

"Losing me again."

"See, the ones in charge give up something to keep the rest of us happy. An example: At first you had to be white, a man, and a landowner to vote. Then voting was extended to all white men, not merely landowners. Then there was the Civil War and the law changed to say black men could vote, too. At least they could in any place the white men did not object to it. Now women may vote. This looks like progress, but it is not. Who votes may change, but who runs the nation does not. What happens is more voters may pick from among the same group of people as was available to the smaller groups of voters.

"Or consider the enacting of social security and the rest of Mr. Roosevelt's New Deal. He said it is to help the economy and those who are suffering and while that is a byproduct, the first reason for it was to appease the people away from a revolution."

Went into history lesson off of that, which she was always on the edge of doing any time. Said this is an old, old game. Romans called it bread and circuses. Keep poor folks fed enough and entertained enough so as to not be rioting. More than that, too. Got them going along with things didn't make sense to go along with. Rome goes republic to empire and the folks are screaming Julius has to be emperor. Said he'd protect sacred, ancient rights whole time he's taking them away.

"Make it look good and fair," Jet said. "Let the great unwashed win a couple of times and they will believe it is justice."

"So, the law is a numbers game?" I asked. "Pays out just often enough for you to believe it's not rigged. More you believe that more you'll keep playing and never see the pay outs are part of it being rigged."

Looked at me like I was a star student for that. Didn't get that too often.

Then she went for a long talk:

"Rich whites rig the game with the law, it is their power. Poor whites, as long as law keeps us below them, believe in the law even as it is taking their land, their money, and anything else. But their belief is so strong they will shout hallelujah as this is happening and damn as a Communist anyone who tries to tell them otherwise. Cannot fool a Negro that way. We truly see how the society operates because we are the ones it operates on. We are free of all the cant and illusions about America's 'noble principles.' We look at America and see it for the rich man's con game it has always been. Our existence is a rebuke to all the claims about the nation's greatness. That is why they have done everything possible to silence us.

"And they could until John Henry made it impossible. You, Moses Crawford are a miracle. There is no other explanation. However, a miracle was not enough for us. We added to it our hopes and needs and created John Henry, who is the strength of all of us made into one. We have always known that all of us cannot be stopped, all of us cannot be killed, but one or ten or a thousand of us could. No more. John Henry is indivisible. All our strength, our invincibility combined.

"The difference between you and John Henry is that you cannot be everywhere and with everyone, but he can. We can carry John Henry with the same certainty the white man carries the support of the law and the society. And, like them, it does not matter if we ever use it or need it. His existence gives us confidence that we can demand to be treated as people and that anyone persecuting or murdering us for doing so will be held to count.

"John Henry is invincible. He cannot be killed. He cannot be stopped. He is unassailable. And he is for us. From Los Angeles to New York – people who will never meet you – they know they have a power they never have had before. They know the people who run the things have to take you into consideration, take *them* into consideration. That means we do not have to ask any more. We do not have to hope moral appeals will change white hearts. We can say this is what we are due, and they must listen and treat with us because if they do not then they will face John Henry – whether he comes as you or as hundreds of us. They have something to be afraid of, something no law will protect them from."

"All this, from believing I'm gonna show up and bust things?"

"This is not about belief, it is about knowing. Knowing John Henry is real. The headline in the Defender after Scottsboro said exactly that."

"This John Henry sounds like he's really something."

"Personally, I prefer Mo Crawford. He keeps me warm."

31

Scottsboro was September, so an election coming up. Usually didn't mean a damn for us. This time, though. Whites didn't see it. Likely most of the thought was on me and not on us. Jet was one with the idea, again.

How to prove John Henry's power wasn't only with or for me? By regular people taking power. What Jet saw was to succeed it had to be done not somewhere, had to be done everywhere.

Began in odd way. Erlissa and me and the truck going on a slow tour of every burg, village, city, town of Alabama. Every one. Some places no more than a gas station and a wish but we went. Walked every Main Street – whether or not that's the name.

Every place was lined the up and out to see me, hug, cheer, have us to lunch, dinner, wash the truck, try give us things but all we'd take was kids' drawings and some gas because we couldn't stop that. And some pies. All right, lot of pies. And cakes. Be a fool said no to them. Always want me to speak at the start, but Erlissa always said he will say hi to all y'all one to five at a time but not more. Eventually word moved ahead, and that particular asking stopped.

Did tricks like the circus show I said I'd never do. Bend old rail track, pick a surprised cow overhead with one hand, that sort. Had a big finale. Go get that Confederate soldier statue, one every town, city, or collection of outhouses has, crush it, throw it high and catch, higher and catch, highest – which was damn high – and not catch, smash right into the plinth it'd been on and then let it sit there in the center of a damn good size crater.

Whites didn't believe it. Could not be happening. Almost froth coming from most all their mouths. Couple places someone shot me. One, a man had a bunch of pistols and a shotgun and wasn't going nowhere until he got to shoot me with all of them. Should've charged him by the bullet like a carnival game. He was most not-noticeable person I've ever seen. Aside his guns only thing stood out about him was nothing standing out about him. On a small side but not enough so it'd draw comment, not too skinny, wore little round glasses, white button-down short-sleeve, khaki pants, shoes, belt, and suspenders. Look on his face, though. An angry to melt steel. Eyes fixed on me and not blinking but likely seeing every wrong done to him. Picked him up by that shirt while he's still shooting. Held him up, my arm straight up over my head. He'd shoot me with something then drop it to the ground, take out another, and get going with it. Counted seven pistols dropped. Couldn't figure where he kept them all. Walked over to the police station once he ran out. Cops actually looked at me apologetic, a bit. I shrugged, easy for me not to take it personal. Said, this guy needs to go away.

Each place I'd be at least a couple days, a large discouragement to any of them doing anything after my leaving was my hope. Wasn't just them upset at me. Some of us didn't like it, said I was riling for no good reason and things go better when it's quiet. Didn't argue because it wasn't as they were wrong. Lot of different ways in to be in the world.

NIGHT BEFORE WE GO into Birmingham, we're sitting on a porch playing Spades with Mr. and Mrs. Everett, who'd invited us for the night. Nice old folks, looking like grandparents anyone would want to have. Want to have if they don't mind getting scorched at cards.

State police man with a prettiest uniform – gold stars and stripes like a Christmas present – pulls up in a car. Says the governor would like to talk and would I go somewhere for it.

Can't remember if it's the mountain or Muhammed, but whichever, I'm not the going one. Governor can't be seen talking to you, he said.

"Bid three," Erlissa said.

Love seeing a cop look so miserable, which he does while we ignore him long enough to get the message and leave.

Comes back with man says he's a lieutenant governor and now *he's* asking can I come with him to see the governor.

"A what governor?" I ask Erlissa.

"Don't know," she said. "Sounds like a job you give to the stupid kid so doesn't feel bad."

"You think?"

"Well just look at him."

All four of us turn and give him an eye. Erlissa, put down her cards and lit up a cigar.

"You're likely right," I said.

Those two drove away faster than they arrived.

"That one was gone before he left," said Mrs. Everett. We were playing for matchsticks, and she already had most of them.

"Been on the wrong end of the things for centuries and think we don't know the game," said Mr. Everett. Nodded and wondered at how I can have so many useless cards in one hand.

Cop came back again minutes later with another man.

"Didn't take long," I said.

"Must keep 'em stashed nearby," Erlissa said and looked slow at the newest visitor. "You a real governor or pretending like the last one?"

Smart man, like that Tommy the Cork, knows to roll with it. Knows going along with getting laughed at can be a strong set up. However, I didn't know if a smart man would let himself get stuck as governor of Alabama. This one's skinny and looking so average the second time I looked almost didn't recognize him. Pinch face, like there's a skinned lemon in his ass. Too old to look young was most standout thing about him except his suit was same color daddy was wearing when he died. Face getting redder with every word he heard. Ap-po-plec-tic. Jet said that's how I looked one time and too angry to ask a meaning. Now I knew.

I was wondering if his heart was going to attack him like that police chief when the governor took a long slow breath and his face went back to being ugly pale.

"Mr. Henry, I'm Bibb Graves," he said, pinch face now a smile and his hand out as enthusiastic as if I was a Kiwanis president. "I am so pleased to meet you at last."

Politics is a skill, like any skill not a lot are really good at it. Bibb Graves, he's damn good. "Mr. Everett, Mrs. Everett, how have you been? Dixie does as best she can with the peach cobbler recipe but it's still not as good as yours."

The Everett's smiles weren't a yes or no on the governor but did say he was likely telling the truth about the cobbler.

"Dixie the maid?" asked Erlissa.

"Dixie is Mrs. Graves. Very nice lady," said Mr. Everett *almost* hiding his disappointment in Erlissa's manners and she noticed.

Governor pulled up a chair next me and had out his own cigar, offered me one. "Playing the Everetts' at Spades?" he said, eyebrows gone way up his forehead.

"Didn't know," I said, trying not to whine. "Thought I was good."

"I did too," said Graves with seemed genuine sympathy. Damn near great at politics.

Put down the cards, should've done a while before, and Mrs. Everett got lemonade for the governor. All sat a bit, watching lightning bugs and cigar smoke.

"Running for governor, Mr. Henry?"

"Not I know of," I said. "Someone said so?"

"No, sir," said Graves. "But your tour of the state looks exactly like what someone would do for that. Senator?"

"Not either," I said, warming to him against my own instinct. So damn good.

"Secretary of state and highway commissioner both said you've gone places where they didn't even know there were places."

"Getting me followed?"

"Yeah, put my nephew Claude on you," Graves said. "He's a hard case."

"His asthma getting any better?" asked Mrs. Everett.

"No, ma'am."

"Then I wouldn't worry too much about him, Mr. Henry," Mrs. Everett said. "He's partial to licorice. I've some you can have to keep on hand if he's making you nervous."

Erlissa laughing so hard started to cough on her cigar smoke.

"Not exactly a top-secret effort going on here," said Graves. "Claude said he said hello to you in four different towns. Usually follows right behind you so he doesn't get lost. That's what he tells me."

Erlissa and me looking embarrassed about our great powers of observation.

"Oh, yeah," she said. "Green car, right?"

"Bright red," said Graves as the Everetts took to laughing.

"Next pie we get, I'll ask if he'd like some," I said. "Feeling like I've been rude."

"He'd be tickled," Graves said. "He's kind of star struck about you. Said you're like someone out of the comic magazines he reads. Good boy but a little strange. Smarter than any I've met. He says a rooster can pull a train, buy a ticket and get on board. Most things he reads are written in some sort of science code – all numbers and things look like letters been used for a taffy pull. Even so, loves those comic books. Go figure."

Really could've sat there listening to him talk the night through and all without trusting him a damn.

"What are you up to Mr. Henry?"

"Just out for a ride, governor. Very pretty state we got here."

"I believe Mr. and Mrs. Everett will say I do my best for the Negro," he said and the Everetts' showed agreeing.

"Weren't you in the Klan?" Erlissa said. Wouldn't even know the governor's name she hadn't told me.

"Never said I didn't make mistakes," he said. "I truly have done my best to make amends for that."

The Everetts nodded and we all let that sit in the air for a moment.

"You give much thought to what you'll do if Alabama has a 'race riot'?" I asked.

"A lot more since you showed up," said the governor. "Stayed up plenty late trying to figure what we do if you get involved. Don't suppose you have any thoughts on the topic?"

"Y'know, you shouldn't have waited so long to ask me that," I said. "What you do is make sure I don't have to be involved. Have the police do their job protecting *everyone*. Have firemen do it too. Sending in the militia? Then no murdering us. No looking the other way. Do their job. Do what they should've been doing without me here. Do that and I'll still come by, but that's all I'll do. Don't do it and I'll do to your city what all y'all did in Tulsa."

Not many thinking about us living in Oklahoma, not now. Once a time we did and did well even with law as much against us as it could be. Towns there that were all black got started after the Civil War when it was still Indian territory and a lot of them did OK. Couldn't let the people alone being self-sufficient, could they? Became a state and in the constitution put all the rules saying we didn't get to be people. So, we left for Mexico, Canada, anywhere. Still neighborhood of Tulsa called Greenwood did better than hang on, it got along fine. Negro Wall Street because people there were making money, more than a lot of the people in the rest of town. They were until Memorial Day 1921 when two teenagers got to yelling at each other. Her, she's white, and him is one of us. She was running an elevator. He slipped getting out of it, grabbed her hand, and she screamed. Next, he's arrested for that old, threadbare lie. Need to say what was next? A difference was people gathered to protect him because who else was for it? First it was just the locals, then militia got in on it with machine guns and giving out pistols and rifles to any whites who wanted. Airplanes used to drop turpentine balls and cans of gasoline. More than three hundred dead, more than thirty-five square blocks burned to the ground. Wasn't a race riot, it was a race massacre.

The Everetts looked hard at the governor now. Manners said be polite, didn't say never show your steel.

"You know what he said is right, governor," said Mrs. Everett. "Shouldn't be you need someone to tell you, either. Known each other since we were small, Bibb. Grew up together with my momma bringing us over when she was cooking and looking after you. Why I know you're a good man. That's why it hurts to say what I'm about to say. If John Henry wasn't around, you wouldn't be worrying about what happens when the whites come after us."

Governor started to try to speak but then a look from her shut it.

"Oh, you'd have tried to do the right thing, alright. But you wouldn't have thought how to stop it before it happens. Lynchings are just a fact of life so what can you do? That's what people say. White people. No one's asking why. That's left to us to do, and no one cares what we think anyway. Try and tell me I'm wrong.

"I know standing up for us can't gain you votes. Still, you go doing what you can to get us some jobs, money for our schools. We always say thank you but then we're back the next day asking for more. Never satisfied. And don't try to tell me that's not what you think, Bibb Graves. You come from good people. I know your parents did right by us and stories are your grandparents did too. Y'all did it because it's right to help the less fortunate. But here's what I know, you never did it because you thought we were people. You think everyone should be treated with manners, *even us*. In Alabama that makes you a damn good man. In Alabama."

Silence followed. What can you add to that?

Governor knew it would be rude if he left right after so all set until his cigar was done. Wished us all a good night and walked back to his car. Gave a look over his shoulder right to me, honest one, all pinched and sour like when he arrived.

The silence kept until after even I couldn't see the taillights anymore.

"Thank you, John Henry," Mrs. Everett said. "He should have been told that years and years ago. You gave me strength to said it."

"Moses," I said. "Now you really got to call me Moses."

Erlissa let out a long sigh.

"Thought he was on to it when he asked if you were running," she said.

"Me too," I said. "I don't think any of them are, though."

Was right, too. Not until a week before election day. That's when flyers were posted around Tuskegee saying Mrs. Terry was running for city council as a write-in candidate. Nothing was said about us voting anywhere else in the state, though. All the attention was on Tuskegee.

Some of them didn't understand her running and our voting was a sky-blue fixed fact. Some still thought they got a say in it. Packed themselves into cars one night, went over Mrs. Terry's. Always an advantage when they think you're as stupid as they are. Pulled on to the street but then two trucks made it so they couldn't pull out. A talk with bunch of Haley Earle Jr.'s boys left them with fewer teeth and cars that couldn't move. Police come by later, cited them for disturbing the peace while they're lying on street and illegal dumping because of the cars. No out loud noise about her running after that. They were all still pissed though, no doubting.

Governor was anything but stupid and only one figured it wasn't just going to be Tuskegee. Two days before election called up all the National Guard that Alabama had. Kept some in Birmingham, split the rest in four parts and sent them toward the corners of the state.

In our trip around the state, while I was giving a hard eye to some and entertaining the rest, Erlissa was out telling. Someone else of us would have come through saying it before we got there and after another would be by to say it again. Damn smart organizing I had nothing to do with except following orders.

What was told? This was going to be our Election Day and here's how we're going to make it so. Get groups together with guns and go down to a polling place and vote. Pay no mind to registering, walk right by anyone say there's a tax or a test. Say John Henry's name if they haven't figured out already. Say it again and again if it helps. Have a bunch stay there and see vote counted and called in. Be smart, expect a fight, shoot first if you think shooting's gonna come. Don't count on John Henry. If he can, he will but there's a lot of 'bama and only one of him. Always have another group ready and gunned up to catch them from behind if they catch you somewhere. Don't have the numbers? Stay home. Head down and eyes out. Don't get caught alone. Not that day, not days to follow. Be smart. Not a protest, it's a fight. Time to ask is past. People gonna die, make it them, not you.

Election day came and it surprised them alright. Most wouldn't believe it could happen and some still didn't after it did. Surprise wasn't all enough, though. There were plenty of fights in a lot of places. Eight died but only one was ours.

Funny was I didn't vote. Spent the day in Birmingham with the secretary of state, keeping him company until and after the votes came in. When a town called in, they'd say how many registered voted and how many unregistered voted and who they voted for. Made sure the unregistered number was about right and that it was added to the vote properly for the certification. For all that it was mostly the same people got elected as was expected. Alabama had some Republicans around somewhere, but in the South it'd been mostly all Democrats since Reconstruction ended. A couple of places where Republicans found someone to run they won. Not it mattered much, a Southern Republican then was just someone pissed because Democrats were in charge and not them. Wasn't the point. This time was proving the point.

Day after the election didn't have any violence to speak of but so much rage in the air you could almost taste it. Old Franklin D. called up Bibb and offered to send Regular Army and Guard from other states. Right then is when the governor started doing what'd get him into the White House a few years later. Said no, out-of-state soldiers – Federal or not – would make it worse.

Went on radio that night, starting out full of anger and outrage about the Negroes voting then slowly switching it, talking about the shame that the Negroes had to show us how wrong it was that every man (meaning white), every man could not vote in our great state. Huey Long had been killed a couple of months before and that night was like Bibb had stolen his spirit. Talking straight to the poor whites, who the money in charge of the state mostly pretended didn't exist. Said about how they're kept out of voting by taxes and literacy tests kept us out. Governor went on about how wrong it was Negroes got to vote while there were Alabamians who didn't.

That was the trick right there.

Change the argument, start talking about our vote as showing up the whites who still couldn't. If those damn niggers can vote than every white man better be able to as well, is what he made it out to be. And now more than ever, with all those Negroes voting, we needed every white vote we could get. Called a rally in Birmingham two days later for the "little folk" telling the legislature about whites got to get the vote too.

Good at his job? Nah, Bibb may be among a best ever.

Next day whites still angry at "them," but them wasn't us of a sudden. Now it's politicians, money, and laws they all made for keeping the working man down. White folks from all over came to rally and yell and demand and a lot of that pressure was building from our voting got let out.

Lot of the radio and newspapers went along with him. Knew it was a hoodwink. Also knew other choice was a lot of dead and cities burning. Also, probably remembered after Scottsboro and what the powers in the land besides me were wanting.

Don't think the governor's not liking me had changed, but the feeling wasn't mutual. I was all the way to admiring him right then.

Mrs. Terry won with votes all from the unregistered.

Time came for her to be sworn in she had Haley Earle Jr. at her side and escorting her to her seat in the council room. He called out to mayor and three councilors all by first name and they called back without thinking. Dr. Stuart, the fourth councilor, knew who Haley Earle Jr. was. There was no damn reason any of them should have met, what with him being from Birmingham and not even a regular visitor to Tuskegee. That was the point he made, and it was a good point. All were very careful to treat her with respect and take seriously when she spoke. Dr. Stuart even made it a point to invite her to his tea parties.

32

Erlissa said she was having a Christmas dinner and we should be there, which was her way of an invitation.

Christmas dinner was a big to do. A gathering of family from far and from wide and hosting it was an honor much chased after. Lot of indirect negotiating where you have someone else put your name out. Once that happens there's the talking and your suitableness is figured out based on who of your relatives hosted last, the dishes you'd brought before, what you'd been like as a child, what your spouse is like, how well behaved the children are, and more. Then another name would be put forward and they'd get the talking and repeat until all the names gone over. Following all that a decision was made by the oldest folks and you had to be one of them to know how.

Sometimes host was someone who hadn't asked for it. Then it was always someone going through a hard time. When it was over the family would have left behind all sorts of food, fire wood, clothes, and what else might be needed. No way of knowing who'd given what. Done that way so there was no feeling they owed anyone. Erlissa's family hosted the year her daddy killed himself.

How she got to host this time was a mystery she wouldn't say a word on. She'd lived by herself in her parents' house and had since a few years ago when her mom went to take care of her grandparents. She was doing all right for herself, so it was clear she'd asked for it but why? Erlissa not a home-keeping type of gal, making it all even stranger.

Day came and shut my mouth because the house was as done up as anyone could ask for. New curtains, flowers, couple new carpets, polish and shine everywhere. Had to not let my jaw hang down.

Packed and packed with people, more than I could recall ever seeing turn out. So, crowded I didn't get to see Erlissa until everyone took seats to eat. Tradition was right then is when the host spoke – not for too long – and then got to lead us all in grace.

Erlissa stood up at the head of the table and I almost gasped. Wearing a dress, holiday dress, hair done smart and makeup, too. My cousin, not in dungarees. I always knew she was pretty but never crossed my mind she was beautiful.

And nervous.

Stood quiet for a long moment even after everyone quieted down.

"Thank you all for being here tonight," she said. "I know there's some here I haven't seen in quite some time and I am so grateful you came. Family means everything."

She looked down at the table for another long moment, then raised her head back up.

"Someone I'd like to introduce to you," she said, working her way up to something. "You'll be glad to know she did our share of the cooking."

Laughter at that, as no one had ever seen Erlissa make more than a sandwich before tonight.

She held out her hand and another woman walked over and held it.

"This is my special friend Sally McDaniel and she's, uh, going to be living here."

A noise like everyone inhaling at once, then maybe the longest pause I've ever been part of, and someone started to say something involving the word 'abomination' when Auntie Rachel's voice cracked over it.

"You any relation to the McDaniels over in Wilmot?" she asked. Then, not waiting on answer, she said to momma, "Which one of them was it you knew?"

"Tessa McDaniel. We went to grade school together."

At full height Auntie would've normal sized but her back was bad and she walked bent over at a right angle. Used two hickory canes, one for walking and the other to hit anyone out of her way. How old? No one could say with a certain as she'd outlived her brothers and sisters, two husbands, and all her children. Even meaner than she was old. On her third husband, Harold, who's back was bent just like hers. Only used one cane and everyone called him grandpa like you did with old men related to you, but you didn't know how. But she was always Auntie, capitalized. Not sure how you get to be matriarch, but she was it and had been since before momma was born. Law giver, high court, Opinion That Counted.

And what did The Great Determiner want to know?

"You know Tessa?" Auntie asked, saying the name almost like it was a bad smell.

"Um, yes. That'd be my Aunt Tessa."

"You'd be Eugene's girl," Auntie said. "Pearl, you remember Gene McDaniel, I know you do because you were hanging on him all that summer your daddy was so drunk he almost drowned trying to bare hand catch a catfish."

Aunt Pearl tried to say none of that was true but several other older women started talking at the same time, arguing over if it was Pearl's father or someone else who'd almost drowned. Went on until Auntie interrupted again.

"Said she looked familiar," she said. "Didn't I say that, Bill?"

From far down the table someone shouted, "Yes, you did!"

"Last I saw her she was about four or five," Auntie said. Couldn't miss that now she was talking about Sally and not to her. "It was a picnic over to her daddy's house."

"The bullfrog picnic?" asked Grandpa Harold, sitting next to Auntie. "The bullfrog girl! She's the bullfrog girl!"

Sally looked confused and a smile the opposite of nice came on Auntie's face.

"Bet she doesn't know she met Erlissa then," Auntie said. "Erlissa been about two."

Harold screeched, "She don't remember about the bullfrog, do you girl? Tell about the bullfrog!"

"She'd gone off to some pond somewhere and come back covered in muck with a big, big, ugly bullfrog and you'd a thought was a puppy from how she was holding it."

"Big around as a pie plate," said Harold.

"Had a stupid name for it," said Auntie. "Anyone remember that name?"

"Mr. Ribbles," said a woman down the table. "Lordy, I will never forget that name."

Erlissa and Sally still holding hands. One looking nervous moving toward scared, the other staring hard at Auntie like a momma bear getting ready to protect a cub.

"She brought it round and introduced it to everyone," said Auntie. "Made all the grownups say hi and all the time talking all about how sweet this Mr. Ribbles is. All that and she didn't look after him, because later on he run off."

"Here it comes," said Harold.

"Over and over, 'WHERE'S MR. RIBBLES! I WANT MR. RIBBLES!'" She said it in a horrible, whiny way. "WHERE'S MR. RIBBLES! I WANT MR. RIBBLES!"

"Musta been a thousand times," said the woman from down the table. "Why I remember the name."

"And no one could quiet her, so every man there started running around looking for that ugly frog," said Auntie.

"'Cept me," said Harold.

"Because you'd been at the shine all afternoon."

"Damn right."

All attention on Auntie – exactly as she wanted – with everyone waiting on what comes next.

"Didn't stop screaming until those men got all these bullfrogs put down in front of her," said Auntie with a sneer then paused and looked Sally right in the eyes. "You looked 'em all over, real slow. When you were positive none were your Mr. Ribbles you shrugged your shoulders and went off to bed."

Confused looks around the table as Auntie wasn't one for telling subtle stories.

"Remember what I did then, Harold?"

The old man shook his head.

"I laughed and laughed at how a little child got all those stupid men do her bidding. Then what did I say? What did I say, Harold?"

"How'm I supposed to remember after spending all day drinking?"

"I said, 'Got all those big men to get her a bullfrog so she didn't have to go back to the swamp. That's a girl knows what she's about.'"

A surprised silence as that wasn't how anyone thought the story was gonna go. Auntie and her mean smile, sitting there waiting for the shouting to start.

Bill is first in and goes at the top of his lungs: "Auntie you know, YOU KNOW, the Bible says it's wrong! An insult to God!"

Auntie's head turn toward him slow, like a battleship turret taking aim.

"What's the Bible say about showing up to Sunday services right from the whorehouse and still Saturday night drunk, Bill?"

Bill and Bill's wife start yelling at that, saying Auntie is lying but we all know she never does because she knows so many secrets. Other people get in on the shouting. When I hear someone say "dyke" is when I speak, using what Jet calls The Voice. Not terribly loud but deep as death and with a force can't be ignored.

"You *will* watch your language."

Family being family no here ever treats me special because of John Henry. I'm just me, someone known since I was in diapers and seen me do stupid things or grew up hearing stories about the stupid things. Right then, though, they needed reminding about me and how Erlissa's my best friend.

Auntie not pleased though because apparently, I should've known she was about to speak.

"Just because you think you're somebody doesn't mean you get to interrupt your elders," she said, giving me an evil eye. No one ever looked back when Auntie did this until right then when I did.

Likely it only lasted a second or three and certainly I looked foolish, giant me having a stare down with an old, old lady, but wanted to prove a point to her and the rest of the family. Somehow both of us knew exactly how long it should go on and gave a little nod to each other at the same time.

"Yes, Auntie," I said but she's talking right over me.

"Anybody not respecting the cook shouldn't be here helping themselves to all she made," said Auntie. Of the 30 or so people there 10 started to get up from the table. "Auntie got lots of stories to tell when you're gone."

Let out a laugh that had nothing to do with funny.

While they were on the way out, Erlissa's mother shooed someone out of the chair next to her, saying, "I want Sally sitting here so we can talk."

That was all Erlissa could take. She walked into the kitchen and when I looked in I saw she was crying and Jet was hugging her, which wasn't something she did a lot.

"If I had to, I couldn't have done that," I said. "Never in my life been that brave. Never in my life."

Erlissa nodded and kept on crying a bit more. Then told us that Sally had been cast out by her entire family, even her parents and brothers and sisters. None would speak to her.

"So, when mom said Sally should sit with her ... I couldn't even..." said Erlissa.

Now I'm crying and Jet is looking even more uncomfortable but then someone shouts impatiently from the dining room, "Because we can't eat until Erlissa says grace is why!"

Erlissa walks over, gives me a hug, and whispers, "Ever mention me wearing a dress and I will kill you dead. Understand?"

Gotta love her.

33

That year was sixteen years since Red Summer, when we were murdered all across the nation.

Then it was whites home from war wanting back jobs they'd had before. Saying we took them. Took, like thieves, because what else? Took, like someone didn't hire us. Like weren't recruiters and ads all the South over pitching hard on, "Want work? C'mon up here." From South and we're foreigners some way. Peoples' families going back here 300, 400 years, before Bohunks, Polacks, Eyeties, Krauts, Micks, Norskies, all, and we're foreigners. No mind on Negroes living right in these cities since they were built. Foreigners. And we're doing the jobs for less pay, so now even they get them back gonna be hired at nigger wages. Our fault, too. Like didn't want as much money, like they would ever stomach us getting paid much as them.

Race war.

Race riot.

What all newspapers scream. Never White war or White riot. That's a right name because not whites and us going in on each other, only them coming after us. Invade our homes, our neighborhoods, burn them down, kill us. Arizona to D.C., thirty places and more we got killed. Some of those places though we had the spirit and fought back. Weren't just whites back from the war. We're back from it, too. Fought, killed, died in all ways they did. What those vets decided was doing that means it's our country and fuck them who said other. Why, in some cities, they come to our streets and we're up on the roofs with rifles and South Side Cocktails – bottle with gas and rag for a cork and to set burning before throwing. Know the terrain. Take high ground. Flank them! Get in behind and close and using long, long knives like learned hand to hand in the trenches. Make a clear fire field for them to get across while we're shooting all the time behind hard barricades. They're mobs and mobs are stupid, so don't be them. Those cities as many or more of them die as us. We learned from that. We remember.

Now it's 1935 and coming around again.

What set it going? Voting in the South, money in the North.

In the South what we did in Alabama, that got a lot of them terrified – even more than always. They know we're not stopping with one state. Know, too, we outnumber them in a lot of places down here. A lot. Cities and towns. How are they going to keep their feet on our necks now? Only know one way. It's killing time.

For the North, money. For maybe a half year or so the Depression got a little better. Some hiring going on. Hope's powerful and dangerous in people desperate for so long. What little hope they had got them through days of no food, got them on a road or stealing a ride on rails going north, east, or west, because a rumor of a job somewhere that's always far away. Things only need to be a little better for their hopes to go sailing up and faster than a rocket. But that little better didn't last, and that rocket exploded into shit and fell all over those people. Had to get someone for this, had to know who's fault. Money usually means it's the Jews but in America wasn't Jews enough to go around. So that meant going after us, the ones who don't have the same jobs they don't have, one always hired after them anyways. But when it's find a victim time, what difference is sense going to make?

First is in Milwaukee because someone's gotta go first and Milwaukee hates us hard.

Starts with tire going flat on a truck late to the afternoon and a man who'd been delivering beer to bars all day walks into one through a front door looking for a pay phone. Later it's said he said something about a white woman or to a white woman but no heart in the claim. Felt obligatory.

Truck driver dead and whites figure kill one why not all? Mob gets together. No one gives a thought on some giant lives way far away South. Mob gets bigger and where's the police, the mayor? All gone to nowhere to be found.

Required move, like pawn to king four, knight to bishop three. Old, familiar opening everyone knows. Mobs find us now trapped in the neighborhoods where an hour before we could go as long as someone paid us to be there. Beaten, raped, killed.

Geographically Milwaukee is almost cliché: Whites in the south, us in the north, Menomonee River Valley in between. Sounds pretty but it's factories and shit. Over and above it all is three bridges. Longest in the world locals call them because they go from Poland to Africa. Night's come down as mobs coming across and soon after fire's in the sky and news is on the wind.

For me it was supposed to be a plowing day but instead I'm on a train for several hours by time dawn shows up. Before I go down to the station and after a nod from Jet, I use the White House phone. First time. Answered before a second ring and put through to the president like lightning. Not on long, just enough to tell him what I told Bibb Graves: No machine guns, tanks, or anything of the like gets used or even threatened to use on us. Militia, police, fire will be about keeping *us* safe and killers out.

Got to Milwaukee couple hours after sun did. The sky filled with smoke from fires still going.

What to do. What to do. Question my only company on the train. Could see name and face of John Henry doing something. Had a power of attention now. Show up and so do all those news boys, coming along behind is politicians like flies to lamp in a night. Gotta be careful where I step. Gotta not be stupid.

Aside that, not sure what to *do*. Could face down a mob and beat as many as don't run away but might just get back together somewhere else. Or there's a bunch of mobs. Block a street, block bullets, tear down things, put a pile of rubble anywhere needed and fast. One place at a time though. You can do anything, is what people said. Maybe in one way of looking. Problem, though. What about when everything needs doing?

Train pulls in and seems like all of a circus except the elephants waiting on me. Got the cameras, men in suits, men in uniform, more than any clown car would fit. Thought of piling them on top of each other came and went. Almost smiled.

Before I'm even off the train: MR. HENRY! JOHN HENRY! MR. HENRY! JOHN HENRY! MR. HENRY! JOHN HENRY! MR. HENRY! JOHN HENRY! MR. HENRY! JOHN HENRY! MR. HENRY! JOHN HENRY! MR. HENRY! JOHN

HENRY! MR. HENRY! JOHN HENRY! HENRY! JOHN HENRY! MR. HENRY! JOHN HENRY! All over and over like everyone else wasn't shouting the same damn thing.

Quiets some when I come out. Been told seeing me in person is quite the thing. So, there is me, standing up and it's clear I'd put a hand on top of a train car easy. Makes other things look wrong, Jet said. No horse or truck or house supposed to be small as it is with me on a side of it. In the pause of all this looking at me, three men come forward.

"Mr. Henry, I'm General Carmody," said a uniform with stars on its shoulders. "This is Governor La Folette ..."

"Call me Phil!" said one suit.

"... and this," the uniform said, clear it didn't want to, "is Mayor Carter."

"Pleased to meet you!" the other suit said like asking for my vote.

Did what I do best and nodded to all. Uniform kept talking and other uniforms cleared a way out. Uniform said they'd like to take me to city hall. Three cars lined up for the job and not one to fit me. Mayor sees what's what first and gives a laugh.

"Mind walking?" one of them asked.

"No, but I'm going to where the fire is, not city hall."

Set out at a clip and the three are running but can't keep up. Finally, a car comes, and they follow me in it.

Come to a place I can see those bridges and stop. Middle of one bridge there's a truck and cars all crashed together. Those three come over to me and I ask which way's north, where we live. Where they point there are buildings burned but look south and I see the same.

The general starts shouting up to me what he calls a situation report. He and the National Guard arrived maybe an hour before me. And in numbers. Can see them holding the bridges, patrolling. Looked to be more of them to in the white neighborhoods than in ours. Uniform said the orders are to break up any groups of more than three, so mobs don't form again. Give them more nods. Always play to my strength.

No word on why it started – wouldn't find out about the truck driver for days. What happened was serious, serious fighting. No one of us forgot 1919.

"Fucking looks like a civil war out there," said the uniform. "Once you people got organized, some went across that near bridge and got fires going in the white neighborhoods. No killings though. Just lit 'em up and left. A few got caught and are down at the jail."

"Let them go."

"We can't do that!" went the mayor.

"I can."

"Look here," said the governor. "We're working hard for equal justice. What kind of message does it send if we let them out?"

"Equal? Got a long, long way to go before you get to say anything about equal. Now they're coming out, that's decided. Only choice you've got is if the jail is still standing."

General looks like there's other, bigger problems need addressing while Phil and the mayor shoot looks at each other but then one nods and other, too.

"Alright," I said. "Now what we're gonna do is get a few of those press boys with cameras and have 'em come with us for a long walk on the white side of the bridges. Let everyone get a view of me and all y'all being with me. Next is we go see the folks on the north side and you can let 'em know what you'll be doing to make everything right by them. Got it?"

During my walk around our side of the city lots of people were talking about someone named Robby Bex. Guy got everyone organized fast soon as he got first word of fighting. Got barricades across streets, positioned folks up in buildings for crossfire shooting, even was one of the people went and started that fire on in the white neighborhood. Guessed he was a vet from all he did but met him and damn if he wasn't my age. About 6 foot 3, skinny, damn, damn smart. Cool. Probably coolest I ever met. No screaming and shouting, probably why he got listened to. Powerful voice and attitude of 'I know my stuff.'

Didn't so much as to raise an eyebrow when he sees me a first time. Can't think of anyone else pulled that off.

Gave me a nod, like a man does to show respect and show he expects the same. I felt good getting it, like, 'I'm cool because he said I'm cool.' Takes a lot of presence, doing that.

Offers me a cigarette, then looks at size of my hands. "Probably get lost in those. Have to have your own special size cigar you want to smoke."

Nodded.

"Never really got interested in it," I said. "I ask you a question?"

"You're the man I'd be glad to give an answer."

"How did you know? To do all you did, you had to learn all that somewhere."

He went 'yeah' with a shake of his head, pulled a cigarette from behind one ear, and had it in his mouth and lit so fast I never saw the match he used.

"I don't really know," he said. "I just looked at the bridges and thought on men coming across them and a best way to counter it. Knew they'd be running and blind angry so it would be easy to set a trap and cut them down. It was just what made sense."

"Well, you got that right."

All I did in Milwaukee was get there late and stick around a few more days, mostly to hang with Robby. Still papers wanted me to do have done something, except the ones that didn't. Stories were either John Henry put an end to the war or the governor or the mayor or whomever else that paper favored had stopped the John Henry monster from destroying the city. Everyone except Robby Bex got their name in print saying they'd been a hero, but he didn't mind. People knew it was him and his being cool about it? That right there was the start of him being *known,* which maybe what he wanted. Maybe, because he'd never said.

Milwaukee just a first.

A week later on a train to Hartford, in Connecticut. Fucked reason for seeing all those United States. Really. Get to Atlanta and there's telegrams saying need for me even less than was for Wisconsin. Went anyway and saw it was true.

People in Hartford saw Milwaukee and got organized. Neighborhood watch, armed patrols and not only in our parts of town – keep an eye on our own going and coming from work. Put together our militia of folks armed and ready if the bell gets rung. Got the police up on their toes and doing what should've been done right along. Only us getting killed the cops show up late and not particularly interested. Now it might be everybody's bodies? They're out in force, stepping extra careful as they'd be the middle if things got noisy.

Wasn't only people in Hartford got on the case. L.A., Boston, Kansas City, Charlotte, Washington, Chicago, Louisville, Cleveland, and a lot of some other places. KC and DC the police tried going in with the whites in coming at us. On both I put a call to my good friend Mr. President and said someone's going to handle this and you don't want it being me. Didn't have to call twice.

People didn't only take care of this at home. In St. Louis caravans went out when trouble started in Ferguson, Webster, Black Jack, even cruised through sundown towns like Bella Villa and Creve Couer to make a point to the residents.

Why doing this now and not previous?

Jet puts it all on John Henry. Says people have something won't let them be crushed for standing their ground. "John Henry is in the wind and the world. People are making him into what they need." Hate it when she goes poetry, but Mrs. Terry agrees so no arguing. Besides pretty soon saw the proof to that poetry. Each time after Hartford it was easy telling there's nothing needed from me, so old Moses Crawford stuck to farming at his home. John Henry? He was seen at each and every. White and black alike told they saw him. News people took to reporting it, too. Said likely he was there but behind scenes and quiet. Be a damn big scene to have me behind it and not seen.

34

TUSKEGEE CITY COUNCIL WASTED it's time worrying about where to get money. It came on its own. Federal to start and they don't know about spending just a little. Bucketsful for our schools, roads, electric, sewers. Got fire station, little police station, and library, with us working in them. Lot of jobs got made, so much that you'd have had to work not to get one.

So much money no one notices poison coming in with it.

Before the Great Depression, before the Great War, there was a Great Migration going on. The people heading North, wanting jobs, voting, place to live that's not about worrying if you're next to die. Kept going strong until everywhere falls apart and there's no jobs for all. It's not as many going North but still some are. Now, of a sudden, there's a new place to go. So, people are coming to Tuskegee as word gets around it's a safe place for us. Maybe even better than safe, maybe where things are fair.

Bring with them a lot of smart that never got a chance to be used before. Got to starting businesses, some on money from family, some who can on money from a brand-new bank. Man got it going said we each don't have a lot but put together we'll have more and can loan it out to our own. The 1st Family Bank of Tuskegee founded on a lot of little money. Loaning to our own didn't mean being stupid. Want 1st Family to back you? Got to get an OK from Mrs. Terry who they hired to be lock certain on those loans paying back. Charge higher interest because they could – who else you can go to? The people all over the state wanting 1st Family for their bank and no way to get to it. Smart is sending armored cars as banks on wheels and hiring Haley Earle Jr.'s boys to be protection. Altogether turns out everyone puts in what was hiding under a mattress adds up into a serious cash.

Businesses keep starting up with ways to make things better, faster, for less. All those good ideas never got listened to before because what could one of us know, right? Color of money won over the color of skin and these things selling even in time when selling wasn't easy. As more sold, more people getting jobs, more tax money, and city doing better. Magazine called Fortune put it on a cover calling it Tuskegee Miracle. Mrs. Terry spit at that. "Sad times when good business practices have to be called a miracle."

Money and jobs weren't only going to us but even with that not all whites liking it. Can't be on top unless there's an underneath. Still, even they found something in their wallets that made it OK to work for us.

35

The people also come to Tuskegee wanting a look at me. OK if I'm in to town but come out to the farm? No.

Farm is a bit of a ways out from Tuskegee, but not too far. Road right to it is hard to find. Not hard enough. Go down a dirt road that's off another dirt road that's off a street don't look like going nowhere. Both dirt roads almost hidden by trees and don't clear scrub out of the way until it can't be driven through. Doesn't do any good. There's always someone coming.

A problem without the neighbors. Want to get to our place means going by three farms, the Tanner's, Gram Simmons', and January Concho. Road goes along right by in front of them and then turns at January's. A serious gate where the road turns and on other side is a big stand of trees. January said he's got all sorts of things in the woods. Saying nothing there to do a real hurt on anyone but get them turning around in a hurry.

Believe the second part. A Marine who fought in the Belleau Wood in the war. Lives by himself. Sometime him and Jet shoot cans on a fence. Other times, only him and me and his smoking cigarettes. Between us maybe four or five sentences the whole time. War isn't really gone past for him. If a quiet is long enough and the day right, he'll tell a story. God damn, war is wrong.

Not a farmer, lets Gram Simmons and hers use the land. Big, strong lady with big, strong sons none by the same father. Doesn't ask questions or bother with too much polite unless you're someone she doesn't like. Walking into her farm house means getting told to work – could be washing or telling her a story but it's something. Work and you get a plate at the table and somewhere to sleep if you need. She keeps January fed.

Four extensions on her house, for each son who moved back after trying out a larger world. All returned married and only kids they ever had were with their wives. Gram raised them not to be acting like her. Grandchildren and a couple great grandchildren moving about in one big, noisy, dirty pile any day they weren't to school. Always clean and something like quieter when dinner comes.

The Tanners are a bit us and a lot Tuskegee Indians. Means they're here since before anyone. Mee Maw at least a great, great grandmother and likes to act in charge. Looks old enough to have fought Confederates. Never been in a good mood, so if she fought, she enjoyed it. Never seen or heard of her kids, but must have had some because there's grandkids. It's them, Willie Rae and Mace, running the farm. Odell is their oldest and then comes the twins, Bess June and Billie May, then is a few more girls all having names like that. The Tuskegee in the family gives them straight hair and Roman noses. Those Tanners will throw a party. A "c'mon over" will go three days and something important, like a wedding? Might as well move in.

Good and different having people look out for me. Protecting what's a real value: My privacy.

Get by all that and there's the dogs. Jet found them on a farm somewhere outside of nowhere one day. Says they are Cane Corso, a breed Romans used at war. Take her word because never heard of or seen before. She came home with six pups. Holds one up to me and is all, 'Don't you think this one looks like an Arusianus?' Didn't even know what she said was a name. Other names every part as bad. Took weeks learning to say right and she let me know loud if it was wrong. Giant is what they definitely are. Got steam shovel jaws with more teeth than seems possible. I train them with Cat teaching the house is only for her and get out the way if Cat wants to lie down. Guess the dogs would tear up anyone they didn't know came over our fence. Guess because no one yet stupid enough to try.

All that is to say, not easy to drop by without being known.

Mostly who tried weren't quite right.

Usually ignore them but this one day I listen in.

"Ma'am, I told you there's no one home," said January. He's got a patience and kindness when he's out at the gate that makes it OK with most folks when he says no.

"I don't care. I have to see him!"

"Well, here's what we can do. Why don't you leave a note with your name and I'll see he gets it."

Woman got louder.

"But he won't remember my name! It was just once. That's why I have to see him, so he'll know who I am!"

She sounded close to going over whatever edge she had.

"I'm really sorry ma'am but he's not here today."

"You don't understand! I came down to see him and then I have to leave! Please!"

Seems no end of folks with strange ideas wanting to see me. Think I'm Jesus and can cure them. I should come away with them or they must live with me. Some said there were fortunes to be made, one went on about a trip to the people living at the center of the Earth.

I got it.

John Henry and me, we're larger than Life. Everyone sees in John Henry whatever they want. If you have the trouble of mind then want becomes a path to places no one else can know or see.

Honest, don't have the patience I should and never have. Now nearly everyone – strange or not – seems to want something from me. Add how I get nervous around strangers, no matter what their mind is like, and that's why I need the farm protected even when I can't be hurt.

Anyone with enough upset can sound crazy. Mix together any or all of despair, desire, desperation, outrage, terror, or righteousness and it's there. Lady was right at that but ... something familiar, so I headed over.

"Ma'am, would you like to set and have a glass of water? Maybe we can figure something out..."

"No, no, no," she said, then saw me coming. "It's you, it's you! I told him it was you and it's you!"

She was right about me not recognizing. At first. Last I saw she was altogether someone else, worn away from hard work, being poor, and never enough to eat. When that's your case, all you do is worry about food and the simple things you don't have, change of clothes, socks without holes, somewhere safe to spend a night. This woman here was none of that. Healthy, dressed in a pretty good Sunday best, and bright eyes comes of knowing tomorrow won't be another hell.

Ruth.

January got out of her way, and she fired straight to me, hitting me hard and solid then wrapping her arms around me like never letting go. Put my hand on her head while she sobbed and said "I knew" over and over.

Finally stopped, wipe tears off her eyes, and stepped back for a look.

"We saw that Scottsboro film and I told Willie straight off it was you. He said it wasn't but only because he likes disagreeing. We went back and sought some more and finally he said maybe, which is a yes coming from him. I didn't come sooner but honestly, I was afraid. You're someone now!"

Ruth.

"I thought you were dead. I thought I killed you, too."

Look of sorrow and anger came to her. Grabbed me and I let her pull me down until we're eye to eye and she put a hand on each side of my face.

"You didn't kill anyone," she said, slow and careful. "You saved us. All you did was set an innocent man free. They did it, all the killing and burning, all of it. They wanted to do that. Must have wanted it for a long time. You were just an excuse."

When I started crying.

Something I didn't know had been in me, a giant shard of glass causing a pain I'd forgotten because of always being there, slipped out and away. Stood there, suddenly relieved of sins I shouldn't have been carrying.

"You saved us. Me and Willie got out on the last train before…"

Her voice faded and we stood there in quiet, filling in the words she might have said.

They'd gone to Chicago and made it. Willie was working in the stock yards which he hated but no more than any one with sense would. On weekends they go to the clubs in Bronzeville and dance to kill the devil. Said it was one thing he never complained about.

"I'd ask about you, but I read everything in the papers," she said.

"Maybe half of that's right," I said. "But it's all about John Henry, not me."

I took her around the farm which was doing alright despite me being away so much. Jet came out and said I was awful for not letting her know we had a guest.

"Jet, this is Ruth, Ruth ...," I laughed. "Ruth, I don't even know your last name."

"Williams!"

"Willie Williams? That's his name? No wonder he's got a temper."

"Yeah, and that's as good as his parents ever did by him," she said, looking sad.

Go in the house for coffee and Jet gets Ruth laughing telling her how I do all the work of the home.

"Cooking, cleaning, laundry," Jet said. "All. Of. It."

"How's that possible?" Going by her face, Ruth likely more impressed by this than me tearing up a tank.

"I made it very clear before we got married," Jet said. "These are not things that a scholar concerns herself with."

"And she can't cook," I said.

"I am perfectly capable of making my own tea," Jet said.

Took a lot of work but Jet finally got Ruth to talk about herself. She was working as a secretary and going to night school.

"No, that is not all," said Jet. "There is more to you, Ruth. You are not a shy person but there is something you are not telling."

"Might as well tell her," I said. "Once she's on something she never turns away."

Ruth squirmed a little, looked around the room, then said in a real quiet voice, "I'm a poet."

"WHAT?" said Jet. "That's wonderful!"

Ruth looked a little confused and a bit abashed by the enthusiasm but nodded her head.

"I've been published," she said, a bit louder but still not comfortable. "In magazines. Ummm, a lot of magazines and there's this, I brought it to give to you." She reached in her pocketbook, took out a slim, tan book, and put it on the table.

What Ever Comes After

Poems

Ruth Williams

Jet picked it up and looked over the outside like it was a priceless vase.

Jet started reading and I didn't know what to say. Ruth stared into her coffee cup, looking like she wanted to be somewhere else. Then Jet sucked in her breath hard and read out loud.

They Shouldn't Have

Given a look.
Made that sound.
Kneeled.
Stood up.
Stood still.
Run.
An attitude.
Took so long.
Shown me up.
Stayed home.
Gone to church,
Tried to vote,
Been
     Lazy.
     Stupid.
     Smart.
     Uppity.
     Disrespectful.
     In the way.
Education.
A job.
Money.
Good clothes.
Nice home.
Shiny car.
Smiled.
Frowned.
Talked back.
Kept quiet.
Shown their face.

Been

    There.

    Asking.

    Telling.

    Reading.

    Singing.

    Whistling.

    Praying.

    Crying.

Saying what Jesus said.

Not known what I'd do.

What's rightfully mine.

Been with the black girl I want.

Said no.

Begged me not to.

Earned silence after that. Then Jet's turn to look shy for maybe the only time.

"Would you, would you," she stuttered, another first and only. "Would you mind terribly...that is... Could I ask you ... to sign the book? It would be such an honor."

Ruth, looking happy, nodded, and nodded and then nodded some more.

January offered Ruth a ride to town to get her train so later, after dinner and coffee, I walked her over to his place.

"Before I left Willie said it wasn't you and even if it was, I wouldn't get to see you," she said. "But then he told me, if I did see you, to tell you he was sorry. Almost soon as you and Roscoe were gone, he started feeling terrible about how he acted. Eaten at him ever since. I know it's why he didn't come."

Struck me how two of us had spent all that time regretting with no reason for it.

"Oh, he's so wrong. Please, please tell him in all this time it never crossed my mind to be angry at him. Not once. Not Roscoe either. He said Willie wasn't 'being no fool.' That's praise from Roscoe."

"Told him he was being an idiot."

"Let him know we got that in common."

36

The New York Age
Institute Professor Elected Mayor of Tuskegee

The New York Times
Tuskegee's Little Woman Mayor
Is First Negro Elected in the South Since Reconstruction

Austin Statesman
Midget Negro Lady Plays Mayor

37

JOHN HENRY DIDN'T NEED much of me. He got bigger and bigger in the world while I stayed home and farmed.

Jet had gotten all she could from the Institute – it was an ag school so why it even had a classics department? – which was all stuff folks who got to go to school before college learn. Election or not, Jet's got things to do and do not get in her way. Why she went to Spelman and got the rest of her degree there. In a year.

Hard not having her around but no other way for it. She came home for semester breaks and all because no way John Henry can come to town incognito for some quiet time together.

So, we wrote to each other. A lot. For a while her letters would include my last letter – with all the punctuation and grammar mistakes corrected. Don't know what got her to stop. Maybe someone said something to her or maybe she got tired of hearing me rolling my eyes every time.

Her letters though...

She let free in them. Saying what she never has anytime else.

I was imagining what it might be like to truly have skin that defined you. It would need to change as I would prefer translucent on some days and opaque on others.

I want to be translucent on days I want to be seen and have strangers know me. They could see me as I am, composite all my parts and experiences. They could see as much or as little as they are capable of. I would not be their preconception of a "race." I would not be turned into whatever amount of mela-nin I happen to possess. I would not even have to be "woman," which is usually even less than a color. A woman is defined as what she is not allowed to be – intelligent, bold, angry, loud. I am those and many believe there is something wrong with me because I do. Especially women.

"How could you do that?" Said as if I have betrayed not merely my gender or my "race" but my entire species. This is because I have been poor and am black. If I were a rich white lady, I would be called eccentric.

That is one reason I keep Mr. Colt. Knowing he is there, even when buried at the bottom of my purse, reminds me that it is other people, not me, who should take heed. I always remember what you told me, that you thought the gun super-fluous because being shot is the easy way out in an argument with me. I know you were teasing or perhaps complaining but I think of that regularly. You know what is important to me, Mr. Crawford!

On the days I was not translucent, my skin would be shining and irides-cent like mother of pearl and impenetrable like yours. Let no one know me then. Instead let them be astonished by the fact of me. Or maybe I would just be a force, a great, pure force. That would be joy.

She "would be a force"? I do wonder what she thinks she is now.

After Spelman only one place she's willing to go: Catholic University in D.C. Had her mind set to it since not long after Scottsboro when we got a visit from a Bishop Toolen, who's the state's top dog Catholic. Jet knew all about him because she knows all about everything. Came out to intro-duce himself and ask if there's anything he could do for us or anything we thought he should be doing. Only reason that didn't have me get my jaw back up from the floor was Jet told me whites called him the Negro Bishop, only not saying negro.

I don't know what a Catholic bishop is supposed to be like but this one was pretty nice. Even brought a cake. Once he found out about Jet and the Latin and such? Well, after a little I excused myself because even when they were talking English, I couldn't follow the conversation. He'd told her Catholic was *the* university for Latin and classics and that's what she wanted.

So, she wrote them, asking if she could go there and had a couple nice let-ters from teachers at Spelman to go with it. They said no and it almost wrecked her. Back home then and when she read that letter, she went and curled up in bed and tried to hide her crying from me. Stayed like that for two days, wouldn't take more than broth and water. I understood.

What it took for her even to get to be someone who would even think of college, never mind more than that. Beyond imagining of her entire family and likely anyone she'd ever met. She imagines it anyway. Coming out of culture where having a couple of pigs might be the best you ever do. You're that poor *and* black? How big is your horizon allowed to be? Maybe a steady factory job. Nothing wrong with that work. But if you want to do more than that and don't know anyone who has, one of the big things is not knowing where to start or even who to ask about what to start.

'No' hits extra hard then. It's everyone's opinion coming down on you and if this place says no then that's it.

Never occurred to Jet it was because she was black and a woman. Sound strange, given all her life, but it's true. That's why it cut so bad. Also, why I had to work and work at her to let me call our bishop friend. She was embarrassed to let him know she failed. Just as I got to "screw this I'm letting him know anyway," she said OK. Made me promise to see if he could find out what was wrong with her studies that kept her out.

Her application never had a chance. University hadn't let any of us in since who knows, so couldn't conceive any of us matter enough that they should. Jet's name should've told them different, but they didn't get it. Say Crawford and Tuskegee to any of us anywhere and you'll get asked, "Related to?" But whites only knew John Henry's name, so how those fools going to know anyway?

Phone call didn't last long enough for me to ask. Felt like I could hear the bishop getting angry as I told him. Said to give him a day.

Final story: He brought the holy fire and then the Vatican did – a surprise to me. I'd forgotten John Henry was international but that didn't mean international had forgotten about him. Seems a lot of countries wanted to be getting on my good side.

You'd think it was all settled now, but no.

Jet got it in her mind that she was only getting in because of being Mrs. Me. Convinced everyone at the school would be thinking that and now she couldn't go. Conquered all of college in the years since getting out of the cotton field and my name is why they're letting her in.

Gave up and called in the biggest gun. Mrs. Terry came by, gave her a "poor thing" look, and explained how the world worked. Not a gentle, tea-and-sympathy type talk either. She doesn't work that way. Worked, of course. I'd argue with Jet before taking on Mrs. Terry.

Year and a half later she's done and it's Dr. Jet Crawford, if you please. Her circumstances were now living up to who she was and damn that made me happy. Also got her back to being her old *force majeure* self. Had a sit down with The Institute's president and mentioned it would be acceptable with her to teach there.

Being Mrs. Crawford only gets you so far and last anyone at that school had seen her she was a great student and that's all. Still president needs to be diplomatic so it's "I need a day to think about it." Calls Spelman and Catholic to find out they already offered her a job. Later she got a letter from professor at Princeton saying he cried when school wouldn't let him make an offer because Negroes were only hired as maintenance staff. Said he almost quit on account. Why'd he think someone care what he almost did? Hope it made him feel better. Almost.

Tuskegee president invites her back and all he says is how grateful the entire college was she would be joining them. Never asked anyone else in the school about it, which ticked off a Professor Wilkins who thought he was running the Classics department. Got worse over time as Jet was publishing articles and other schools inviting her to come talk. She let Wilkins go on about it for a couple years when she dropped a hammer. Never mentioned it at home so I only found out when she sent a letter while she was away to Oxford for a conference.

Professor Wilkins invited me to a small gathering last week for a visiting professor from Yale. She wears the look of someone determined to help whether or not it is needed. I am uncertain who she wants to help. Is it those of us at The Institute? (There is a move afoot to change us into a college. Colleges are common. The Institute is singular.) Possibly. That would explain why she went to great lengths to say how much she admired our school. How insulting. Can you imagine saying the same about Yale? There is no need to say this. Do you compliment Mt. Everest on being tall?

The gathering was a high tea, which I appreciated, but was otherwise just the usual useless types of talk: inquiries about family, complaints about how warm it is, etc. At one point Prof. Yale and I and several others were standing around (this is wrong for high tea. It should involve sitting and a much better selection of small cakes!) when she asked if we preferred black or Negro or colored.

My colleagues were silent, likely embarrassed for her, so I spoke.

"I'm sorry, we teach classics, not anthropology."

She pursed her lips, like you do when you whistle, and breathed in and out very slowly. Someone else said something and broke the long awkward moment I was enjoying very much. In response, Professor Yale started to cry. I offered her my handkerchief, which she refused, had some more tea, and left.

Wilkins, with self-righteous anger, came immediately to see me. He went on at length about how I had embarrassed him and The Institute. As he went on, he lay more charges against me, saying I had permanently damaged our relations with all the Ivy League and thus with significant donors who were graduates thereof. I was a bit disappointed he failed to hold me responsible for the stock market crash and the kidnapping of baby Lindbergh. I do enjoy hearing a good, incoherent rant and this one was no exception until he said, "Being John Henry's wife won't help you out of this!"

This time I said all.

"If you did not want what happened to happen you would not have invited me. As you well know I am almost never brought forth to meet the visiting dignitaries even though my work, my articles, and books, are trumpeted whenever The Institute wishes to boast its way into getting funds. I have no problem with that. It saves me from tedious time convincing dignitaries I care about what he or she has to say. You invited me in hopes that this person would 'put me in my place.' Or, failing that, that you would have a grievance to take up with the president and an excuse to attempt to intimidate me.

"You are a passable teacher, Robert, but I am afraid you have no understanding of 'how things work.' So, I will explain. We have twice the faculty and three times the students as when I arrived here. In our rarified field we are now considered a prominent institution. Do you believe Professor Yale would be here otherwise? As far as the administration is concerned this is my department, not yours. You have been maintained as chair because you are quite good at paperwork none of the other faculty want to do. If you have any doubts about this then yes, please do bring your complaint to the president.

"You may leave now Robert. I'm sure you have work to do."

See? Why bother with a .45?

38

Next election go round Mrs. Terry won for mayor. Part of why was a lot of us had moved to Tuskegee, other part was man going against her being a fool. Lester Mann been mayor about 10 years back and for this campaign spent all his time talking on Mrs. Terry in ways no one would've minded even a year or two ago. Likely not everyone minded now, but those as did were ones with money and running businesses and not shy with their opinion that a vote for Mann was a vote for being out of work.

Now whites were working beside and for us and even those in charge who agreed with Mann personally knew this wasn't the time for him. Workers and owners had to choose between hating and earning. Didn't have to go too far past the city limits to see The Depression still raging tough across the country. Fighting and arguing? No money for it, at least not then.

Didn't mean feelings changed or we forgot our past. People just set it to the side. Result was us and them being a nervous type of very polite around each other, like dancing in a minefield. All calling each other by mister, missus, or miss, and last name unless the two people knew each other a lot. Understood one person uses a first name then the one they're talking to gets to do the same. Only time you hear 'boy' or 'girl' was to a small child and it was learned fast putting 'little' in front would avoid a bit of trouble. Please, thank you, pardon me, and sorry were thick in the air like at high tea with a bishop. Mostly us and them dealt with our own if they got out of line. Progress, such as it was, was us and them having a word together with the incorrect party. Not much of that but not none either.

Mrs. Terry didn't run as Republican or Democrat. New party had formed informally in the couple years since her first election. Start in Tuskegee before going statewide. Wasn't a real name for it for a while, just "our party." Damn easy to tell who was in and who wasn't. But then the people who'd organized for protection in Milwaukee and those other places decided they should all stay organized together. They reached out to our party and like that we were nationwide. Have a national convention for it here in Tuskegee and a name was needed.

"It's called John Henry Party," Erlissa said to me. She'd been hired as staff, executive secretary – which she said meant she did all the work – still it was way better than plumbing.

"What?"

"You heard me," she said. "Everyone knew that was the name. No one even suggested another one, which means it only took two hours of talking for us to come to agreement on something we all already agreed about. The fastest we got anything done all day."

"Don't you have to ask me?" I was sounding pretend upset about it because ... well, it's me and Erlissa.

"No," she said, like I was a complete fool. "Anyway, you don't even like that name."

"Not true. It's useful for going out in public. Like wearing a nice suit of clothes."

"As if you'd know anything about nice clothes"

"I wore a tuxedo to my wedding."

"Because your bride is the only one on the planet could kill you and would've if you hadn't."

"Fair enough," I said. "But if it's all decided, what are you here about, other than stealing sweet potato pie?"

"Not stealing if the owner watches you do it."

"You're not saying something."

"Yeah," she said. "Me and Mrs. Terry flipped for this, and I lost. Got a request for you."

"OK."

"From the delegates."

"And it is..."

"They want you lead the party."

My laugh is normally too loud, like scaring birds out of trees loud. Do my best to remember to cover my mouth when I do but not this time. This was so loud Erlissa put hands to ears and ran from the room. Came back when I calmed.

"You owe me a whole pie for that," she said.

"They're serious?"

"Yessir. John Henry's Party should have John Henry running it is what they think."

"You tell them I can't talk to a crowd of more than three?"

"Yep."

"You tell them they couldn't find anyone worse for the job?"

"I was going to tell them nearly every damn stupid thing I know about you but convention's only a week long. I just hit the highlights."

"And what they say to it?"

"Now, here's why me and Mrs. Terry flipped the coin," she said. "They said you could be – and here's their exact words – 'a figurehead.' There'd be someone else do the work and tell you what to do."

Gave a quiet laugh and shook my head just like Erlissa was doing.

"Told them they'd have better luck with a Missouri mule. Even offered to sell them one. But still, they wanted me to ask. Some of them wanted to come over and do it themselves, thinking you'd be flattered and all. Took Mrs. Terry and me doing a lot of talking to get that out of their minds."

"Cousin, I do so appreciate you looking out for me like this. I'll make you two pies."

"But we still got a problem, Mo. How can there be a John Henry Party without John Henry?"

A too good question. Everyone would look on what I did no matter how I felt. Me not being on board could kill the damn thing, make people think John Henry's against it when it's just that Mo Crawford doesn't want the bother.

"All right," I said. "I'll be a plain old party member. Take a picture of me signing up and getting a membership card. Not the first one to sign up, either. Like after all the delegates and you do."

Erlissa looked at me, shook her head, and said, "Damn, I'm gonna have to go tell the delegates I was wrong. You're not a *total* idiot after all."

"That cost you a pie."

MAN NAMED SYLVESTER "SLY" Pennington, out of Atlanta, elected head of the party. Came out to see me when the convention was done, wanting to know what I thought. Should've told him not to pay attention to my thinking but it was an anniversary of daddy's death, and I was in a sour mood, one that got worse when he showed up.

Could see he thought too much of me. All filled with awe and worshipful, which pissed me off more. So, I unloaded all the irritation I was feeling, thinking to show how low and stupid his hero could be, how I didn't deserve any pedestal. Or maybe I just wanted to be mean. Can't teach fools, though, not him or me.

Start in with how I don't like whites, how there's no trusting them unless you sure you got something can force them to keep their word. On and on about staying away from them is what should be done. How you gotta take because there's no giving in them.

Then on to how we're better standing on our own. Got to maintain our identity and be proud of it. Be ready to fight the world if we have to. Be ready to die for the cause, said the man no one could hurt.

Words came out of my mouth, but I wasn't listening.

39

Ask anyone at that convention what John Henry Party was about they'd say politics. Not Democrat or Republican but partner up with them sometimes. Cut the best deal, get the most for people. Amazing what some politicians will agree to for a reliable percentage of the vote. And reliable is what our voters are. No one ever seen anything like it before. We'll fight and scrape with each other. We'll argue all night long just because. But on Election Day? John Henry Party comes out in size, like it's about more than politics.

That gets you a big seat at the table and it's not like all we do is getting others elected.

Our candidates won a lot right out the gate. Partly it was because so many politicians in both the other parties thought we were idiots. Child savages with our fingers up our noses who couldn't add one and one is what they believed. Know what Napoleon said? "Never interrupt your enemy when he's making a mistake." So, we let them keep thinking it until the truth hit them when they're un-elected. For some even that's not enough, and they're still out there. Can't help it. Keep giving them books and giving them books and all they do is chew on the covers.

Also won a lot because the idiots couldn't figure how many of us there were. Down South they ignored what was in the census because they never believed we'd get to vote, even after we did! A lot of cities down here there's we're close to as many and sometimes more than they are. Took them a couple elections to catch on to that and by then we had mayors, city councilors, sheriffs, Congressmen, judges, and more. In the North we'd never turned out in huge numbers before John Henry Party. Now voting's almost a sacrament for a lot of people.

Not that getting elected was the end of it. Fought us once we're in office like they never fought each other. Some violence at first, dropped off fast. Now it's all law and politics. Gets ugly – real ugly – at times and that's alright because it's the way societies are supposed to work things out.

Problem was Sly Pennington. Didn't want a political party, wanted a movement. Wanted us standing apart and ready to get in peoples' faces. Wanted us to be a kettle kept just below boiling so it can go off in a minute's notice. Wonder where he got the idea.

First things he did were good. Programs to make sure kids got breakfast expanded to community centers where all sorts of good things got going. All sorts of good things get to going on: Dances, doctors, churches, art shows, free movies, help for drunks, shelters for women been beaten, classes for learning to read and write and math for all ages, and more. Put together a youth league and every center had a drum and bugle corps and who isn't for that?

Our people saw John Henry Party was serious about helping. White people saw the same and wanted to work with us. Gave money and goods. Sly was a good businessman and ran everything clean and aboveboard. Forward thinker, too. Didn't care if you were a man or a woman as long as you were good at the job. No one had a bad word about how he treated others – not then or after when there was good reason for plenty bad being said about him. Not a drinker, not fooling around on the side, good to his wife and children.

Problems started when Sly wanted John Henry Party going in another direction. He was done with compromising and political deals, got adamant that what we did should just be for us. Centers had been open to all were becoming blacks only. No white people helping as volunteers, although he was still OK with taking their money.

Surprise. Not everyone happy.

Let the fractures begin. Party supposed to be organized so each state's organization in charge of all local chapters. Now some cities are splitting from states and states splitting from national organization. At the start only a few places had two groups saying they're the party and running against each other. Mostly we stayed solid with state and city getting out the vote for JHP candidates whether they were with Pennington or against. But no one expected it to last.

40

Then came the bad year. The plague year. Funerals, intrigue, cowards, blame, dissolution, death, terror, and hopelessness.

Strange things started in January. At the time looked like just that: Strange but no more than other stuff that happens and never think of it again. Now? The first breeze of a hurricane.

New Year's Day break-in at the Tuskegee party offices. No one could find anything been stolen. Window busted for someone to come in, open the filing cabinets and dump the papers all out. Nuisance. See it now, though, and maybe it's covering up a person takes pictures of some files. Want to do that, why trash the place? No sense to it.

Executive director Erlissa is in Tuskegee with most of the national party staff while Pennington's office is in Atlanta so he can stay on top of his other business. Erlissa's doing her best to not take sides in the split. Pennington, a decent man, likes that. He isn't saying "my way or no way" about things. He argues for it, twists arms, gives money here and holds it back there – trying to get what he wants without breaking the party altogether.

Week or so later after the break in, Erlissa gets a letter said Big Boy Pratchett, running the party in Kansas City and set against Pennington, is meeting with city police, and hiding it. Not unusual for a letter or call to arrive accusing someone of something. Was happening before the split because that's how people are. Different about this one was a week later there's another letter with a picture of Big Boy talking to a cop in a diner. Letter said where they were is over in Missouri, long way from KC. Probably bullshit – why's he sitting in a diner with uniform police if he doesn't want it known? But then again, why's he sitting in a diner with uniform police at all? Then again, he's a political boss talking to cop and that happens all the time.

Executive director responsible for seeing to it party president doesn't have to deal with nonsense, so it's entirely right she decides how to handle it. Knows it might be something and it might be nothing. Also suspicious because this is a perfect way to make raise suspicion and set people against each other. Finally, mailed it all off to Big Boy, saying someone's trying to do you wrong and now Big Boy has it in his mind to wonder if he's still trusted.

After that lot of letters arriving at every part of the party. Most are nonsense, not all. One said Harry Spector, Chicago alderman and in charge of party finance there, was skimming money. That is something national party can look into. So, Pennington calls Mrs. Terry who sends a protégé of hers to check the books. He finds Harry has been using funds to cover the cost of keeping a woman in style in an apartment in Bronzeville. Handled it all quietly, he quit fast to spend more time with his family.

Suddenly no one's certain about what's nonsense and what's not.

Call it all a storm warning.

41

Right after Valentine's Day, Robby Bex came down from Milwaukee for a talk.

Thought it was about the good problems he was having. Wanted to be a behind-the-scenes guy but the people wanted him out front. Had a voice and ideas that carried. No shouting or preaching, Robby's gift was talking straight. He said it, you know he meant it because he didn't care what you thought of it. Even you didn't agree with him you knew there's no bullshit in there.

Wasn't just us and the party listening either. Robby talked about everyone being used to keep the rich in style and racism being one of the ways they did it. Whites turning out to hear him, too. Didn't tell them "Love your fellow man" or "We are all brothers." Said, "Don't even have to like each other but if you want to stop getting fucked over you've got to fight together."

Used clear, every day words to tell people it was on them to make something better.

"If you dare to fight, you dare to win," he said. "If you don't, then go back home. You don't deserve it."

What got people wasn't only how Robby talked, it was how he listened, too. Gave all his attention to people then. Wanted people to know they were heard. Caring like that, that's what was behind his cool. He could be a hard, hard man. He'd be cutting with someone he thought should know better, but always patient, always going out of his way for the hurting and the needing. He might treat you like a damn fool, but he'd also show up when you needed. Why people had trouble staying angry with him.

Everyone, including Bobby, knew he was our future.

Party may have been run out of Tuskegee and Atlanta, but everything was run through Milwaukee. Anything big got checked with Robby because he thought about things and saw things no one else did. Also, he didn't get into fights. Never took an argument personally. Wasn't for or against what Pennington wanted to do. Saw parts he liked and went with those. Why Pennington was always saying good things about Bex. Lots of us, including me, counting on him getting John Henry Party back together.

All this got him the reputation he'd wanted, don't think he realized how big a profile would come with it, though. Big profile is a big target.

First was the whisper attack saying Robby was a Communist. Better people knew Robby more they laughed. "Fuck the Commies," he said, a lot. "No one taking what's mine or what's yours." Laughter went farther and faster than the whisper, with people saying, "Won't believe what someone tried to say about Bobby..." Next whisper was he was snitching to police. Try passing that along not only got you laughed at but marked *you* as one likely too friendly with the cops.

None of that's why he came to visit. Was a worried man arrived at our farm.

Alabama's beautiful but not in February, not that day. Sky and ground cold and gray, with a wind going hard enough to rattle windows and spinning dust devils all over. Stoked up the fire, making the room warm, but it was also making what Jet called a tread-snow sound, whistling like a kettle which meant snow coming.

"There are some subtle motherfuckers fucking with us," Robby said.

"Well, fuck that," Jet said, trying to get him to smile. He gave a little snicker but look of his face didn't go along with it.

"Unusual stuff going on down here, too," I said. "You think it's the same fuckery?"

Smiled at that and nodded, then told us a story which was more about what he didn't find than what he did. Robby was wired into everything in Milwaukee, mayor's office, villains, cops, churches, reporters, probably garbagemen, too. He'd been testing the wires to see which connections were good. Tell some people one thing then see who hears it and who they hear it from.

"Y'know people tried that shit on me – letters, rumors, all that. Expected it. Set things up so I'd be able to find out who's putting it out. I walked quiet about this, making sure no one knows it's me on the trail. Followed three cases as far as I could, and they all dead ended the same way. Someone comes to town a year or so ago, makes friends, gets established, gets known as reliable type. So, when he does say something, it gets listened to. Puts out a story, then a month later leaves town. One was a bartender, one an accountant, one a mechanic. All disappeared. Cost me a little but I found out none were who they claimed. No one by those names come from where they said they did. Also, the accountant, place that hired him checked his references, talked to people at two different companies."

"Going out on a limb," I said. "They don't exist?"

"Not the people or the companies."

Subtle motherfuckers, indeed.

Said he had a couple of hard boys he'd grown up with doing some digging in other cities where similar was happening, see what they find. Hoping for a bigger picture but not holding out hope.

"Got people you can trust?" I asked.

"Yeah, those boys I mentioned and my girlfriend Shawna."

"Is that all?"

"Uh-huh. Few months ago, would have said a lot more. But now? Caught myself wondering about my mom but then remembered she's dead. Be absolutely positive before you trust anybody. That's what I'm saying."

Couldn't bring myself to believe it all. Didn't doubt something was going on but figured he'd been working on all this so much he was seeing things worse than they really were.

"I hear what you're saying, but remember you got me and Pennington backing you. You'll be OK."

Shook his head.

"Pennington's got all sorts of stuff going on he doesn't want people to know about."

"You think he's involved in all this?"

That got a smile.

"Nah," Robby said. "Sly ain't that sly."

"Then what is it?" I asked. "Because Erlissa thinks he's alright and she's working with him all the time."

"That's because she's only seeing half of what he's up to," he said. "What he does isn't through the party. He's spreading money around, helping folks out of jams, paying off gambling debts. Know Johnny Clarke, runs the party in Boston? Know for a fact Pennington's paying for college for one of his kids. Likely doing the same for Lamont Hutchins in Dallas."

"He's got money, he spends it," I said, irritated. "That's what a rich man gets to do."

"I don't think he's got near as much money as he makes out he does. Not the way he's been spending. Don't know for certain yet, but I will. One other thing. Y'know those rifle corps he's got marching with the drum and bugles? Seems some of them might be getting real rifles soon."

Shook my head at that. Told Robby he was too far in it and maybe take a little rest so he could come back at it with clear thinking. Should've been listening to him more than talking. Really should've.

42

Once Mrs. Terry became mayor, Haley Earle Jr. got almost patriotic about Tuskegee. Wanted it a place to be proud of. Didn't mean no crime, meant no crime he didn't control. Muggers, house burglars, stick-up men? His boys let them know, 'Not here, you don't.' The knowing could be broken arms and legs or sometimes being dead. No hookers on the street, have to be working at a house. Bootleggers – because it's the South and we had them before and after Prohibition – could only sell shine that wouldn't kill you. Gambling didn't have to be up-and-up, but only bad thing allowed to happen was getting fleeced. And, of course, Mr. Earle Jr. got a cut of it all. Enlightened self-interest, just like the founding fathers.

Plenty of customers for him. Tuskegee was growing and growing crowded. Too many of us wanting to live here, thinking it's a promise land. A lot of them coming because they'd heard there were jobs. City doing better than a lot of places but not well enough to keep up with this. Got big enough now to have our own Skid Row.

Pains me to say anything good about Rev. Williams but here I have to. He'd taken to drinking which cost him the wife and the job at the church and landed him sleeping rough down on the Row. Looks to be what he needed because he put down the booze. Made over an empty store to a church and soup kitchen. Not nicer, for all that. Full-time rage. His "parishioners" didn't mind him raging at them because he was also raging for them. No meeting of city council, Rotary, Chamber of Commerce, PTA, or any others took place without him showing up and raining down hellfire about those in need. Even came to the farm and spit it to me. He still didn't scare a damn.

Worked, too. Got him food, blankets and what else people needed but after a while also got him ignored. Folks pick up a book or talk during his rants or give him stuff so he wouldn't start. They'd heard it before. Meant no one heard when he was saying something new, saying people were dying and drugs were doing the killing. Besides, it was winos and bums so even ones who heard it felt like it's not happening to real people and it was their own fault. Attitude let it get worse and worse and also why no one thought to ask the important question: Those bums and winos could barely stem enough for rock gut, how'd they pay for heroin?

Different world, too. Most nobody even heard of it or anything else stronger than whiskey. I knew about weed but only because Roscoe told me once. "Don't try it," he said. "Leave it all for your elders."

"Wouldn't matter if I took it all," I said. "Once drank a keg of shine because I was curious. Didn't do a thing. Poisons can't hurt me."

Roscoe looked genuinely sad for me.

Eventually and somehow what the reverend said got to only one it needed, Mayor Terry. Didn't bother her police department on it. Called her godson, Haley Earle Jr., who didn't know where it was coming from and pissed. Exactly as the mayor hoped.

43

One thing running through all these problems: Nothing in it for John Henry to do.

Can do anything, but he can't do everything. Steps hard and large. Can scare, can inspire. Need something big destroyed, like that piece of shit carving on Stone Mountain? Did it and happy to have. Fact is, not much needs me to do it. Maybe a rescue if a building collapse or burn. Stop a robber.

But nothing to do for someone who gets rolled, house burning down, tornado, any of it. Why it was Haley Earle, not John Henry, for dealing with a drug problem.

John Henry can be a motherfucker, but no subtle in him.

44

Next thing happened did it when I was out of town.

Jet at home, middle of a July day, hears something knocked off a shelf in another room, then Cat giving out a hiss. Goes looking and finds a man – well-dressed, white man – with a gun and Cat hanging by the claws to the arm holding the pistol. She shot him in the neck and with a .45 that knocked the man's head right off.

Neighbors, heard the shot, got to the house fast and ready.

"Y'know Mace Tanner own a Tommy gun?" Jet asked me later. Still upset is why she's talking like when she picked cotton. "Willie Rae have a sawed-off, two-barrel scatter-gun. Also got her a pistol in the belt. Odell? The oldest? A rifle has a bayonet at the end. *Bayonet?* Do what? Sweet of him, gotta say. Wanting to bring all he could. Two oldest girls with a .38 each. Think I'd like a Tommy?"

They got there and Jet's out on a porch chair, leg over one arm of it, swinging the Colt by her side, pipe in her mouth, and Cat on her lap. Asked Mace for a light. He looked over, said there's no tobacco in the pipe. "Explains a lot," she said.

Word got out and more types of law come by than you'd figure could fit in Alabama. Locals, states, state bureau of investigation, federal bureau of same, Secret Service, federal Marshalls. Jet said made her wonder what Coast Guard and postal inspectors were busy with. President called, too, asking after her health. Some of all that done for finding out about the crime and more of it so know they were taking this seriously, so for me not to be getting upset.

On a train while all happened. First I know of it is walking to home and seeing police cars. Jilly Sue, youngest and cutest of Mace and Willie Rae's, come running up.

"Who she shoot?" Hand to God, that's first I said.

"Only the one," Jilly Sue goes. Definition of nonchalant. At seven years could already tell she was going to be hell at Spades and on boys.

"Dead?"

She rolled eyes at me, rightly.

"Momma said the man's head come off and rolled under a sofa in your parlor." Said while picking dandelions and like nothing unusual.

When I figured man shot was in the house is when I got worried.

"Where's the dogs?"

Now Jilly Sue looked upset. "Momma tell you," she said, and ran off.

The dogs just one part of so much didn't make sense about any of it. Trained those dogs myself. Put steak down for them and they wouldn't move on it less me or Jet said to, but this man got them to eat something, and it killed them. Cat did good but nothing usual to how it did it. Never known Cat to hiss before, always right to attack, no announcing it first.

Man himself wasn't right in any sense of the word. Body in the house was a flash dude, suit and hat color of pistachio ice cream, slick back hair and rings on fingers. Inigo Gomez from a place not big enough to call a town in the way back of Oaxaca in Mexico. Folks there said not the smartest but always nice and helpful. Left a couple years back without giving a why or a where. Nobody, not the feds, not bunches of reporters, could find him after that until he's here. Clothes from New York City, rings from Mexico City, and pistol a Webley. In the war Brits gave thousands and thousands and thousands of those to soldiers, so no knowing where Gomez got it.

Attorney general and a toad of a man named Hoover took to coming down regular from Washington to tell us how they're working at it and what they're finding. Hoover runs FBI, not saying much, and not ever seeming he wants to be here. When they get out of clues to follow, they start talking about who want this done and why because not for a minute anyone think this Gomez was on this alone.

"Maybe a foreign nation," said the AG, old, tall, and a face not to remember the moment you look away. "Germans, Soviets…"

"Commies," said Hoover. Croaked that word out any time he could.

"No Americans come to mind?" Jet asked, voice back to its full-on deep and regal. Whenever these two come by, she made sure to have Mr. Colt in one hand and that smoking pipe in the other. All that and herself being herself, which in this case was full fired anger, brought out the nervous in them.

"Well, we have commies here in the United States." Croak.

"That is a very good thing for you, now, is it not? Otherwise, who would you have to blame everything on?"

One toad, not happy.

She sent them away, saying to call if they found some *facts*.

All the different cops wanted to do the same thing, put guards around the farm.

"Jet'll shoot any and everyone she sees," I told them all. "On purpose."

All shook their heads, and all believed it. Neighbors felt horrible. Kept saying sorry for letting us down. Finally had to get angry about all the apologizing to get them to stop. Find out later Gram Simmons had the boys build a blind up a tree in woods out back of us and to this day if I'm not at the farm one of them is there day and night.

45

Haley Earle Jr. was getting frustrated. He told Mrs. Terry and she told us. Mayor had some concern because he wasn't a man to admit a problem had him bothered. Knowing that, what's a situation where he's willing to say "frustrated"?

Finding dealers wasn't a problem, finding the source was. He and his boys hurt the dealers they found, and it didn't do anything really. Said there was always more showing up, like what happens after you've been stomping roaches. Managed to lay hands on a few of the guys dealing to the dealers, but they didn't know shit either. Whoever was supplying them would work with someone a few times, then drop them and get someone else. Only thing Haley knew for sure was none of them talked like they were from Alabama.

After that he up and disappeared, him and three of his top boys. All was known was something about a meet up, but no one could say where. A week without a word of Haley was a long time. It was two weeks before he was found, hanging in an abandoned barn, his three guys swinging beside him. Bad, bad deaths. Slowly strangling, heads in nooses hands tied behind their backs.

News spread through the city and silence followed it because this wasn't something could happen, like looking up and part of the sky is missing.

All sorts came out for the funeral, and not just ones you'd expect. The working girls because he never beat them without reason, the hard boys with blood in their eyes, businessmen who'd paid him protection money, other bosses wanting to be sure he was dead. Even our Chief of Police in full dress uniform out of respect for the mayor and knowing his work was going to get worse now Junior wasn't there to keep the lid on.

Lots and lots sent flowers, biggest bunch was bigger than the casket with a card reading, "Deepest sympathies, Memphis Rod & Gun Club." That was Bucky Pilcher, boss of Memphis and north Alabama, doing what all agreed was a classy thing because he was white, and his gang and Haley's had spent more than a little time killing on one another.

Rev. Williams, still angrier then should be possible and stay alive, insisted on officiating, even bullied the elders at our old church to have the funeral there. To start he swept in from the back wearing black monk's robes with a hood up. A lean man, he'd gone so thin there seemed to be nothing between skin and skeleton. All he was missing was a scythe. No comfort in his service, just a rage that almost turned it into a scream. Only slowed a little for the sermon which was a thing unto itself. First, he railed at gambling, boozing, and prostitution – all Haley's favorites. Then he got quiet and looked almost to be arguing with himself as he talked about how Haley died trying to clean up the town and keep people alive. He must have won the argument because he closed by telling, not asking, God this made up for every bad Haley had ever done. Finished, came down out of the pulpit and walked by me, pausing to spit in front of my feet. Now as he was an honest man and not hiding anything, I was really coming to like him more and more.

Someone brought a chair up to the pulpit and Mrs. Terry stood on it giving the eulogy.

Started gentle, talking about holding Haley as a baby when he got baptized and what he was like as a boy running around in short pants, doing everything he could to get her to laugh. She didn't have illusions about him, knew he had done all that his father had done and likely a lot more. Still, she loved him as her own anyway. Even got me crying.

Then she showed what no one had ever seen of her before and filled the room with a voice to scare the prophets and put Rev. Williams to shame. Laid out a curse and a damnation as might have come from the burning face of God. Not just on who had killed Haley so horribly and without honor, also on any who knew or aided, and their families, too.

Always take Mrs. Terry at her word. Always.

✷ ✷ ✷

WASN'T TWO DAYS IN the ground before trouble started but nothing to do with Mrs. Terry's curse.

Cause was business as usual, people wanting to get a piece of something or everything that used to be Haley Earle's. Police weren't able or willing to do anything, so I moved to town for a few days, taking long walks and dropping the hammer on whatever looked bad or heading that way. Didn't stop the fighting, but that wasn't my intent. The trouble moved indoors and a lot more attention paid to not hurting civilians. What stopped that was arrival of a man named Slappy Jackson. He'd run Mobile and the coast for Haley, said to be number two in the organization. Hadn't shown for the funeral, though. Questions whispered about where he might have been when Haley got hit. Whispers died out once a few of the whisperers did too.

46

August burned into September.

Halfway into the month we heard about Robby not being heard from for a couple weeks, but by then it was long past too late.

Four state police raided his apartment, looking for a stash of guns, they said. Claimed they were returning fire when they shot into the bedroom 89 times. Eighty-nine bullets meant they did a lot of reloading. Twelve found Robby, seven his girlfriend – who was pregnant.

No one ever found this bullet they say was shot at them. Only found one gun. Belonged to Shawna who bought it legal and even had a permit. One bullet missing alright, but gun hadn't been fired in maybe weeks.

That right there was as close as anything about the murders came to making sense.

Raid was in the city, but no city cops involved. Milwaukee PD only found out about it because Staties called the city coroner to take the bodies. Once he's there and not seeing any city uniforms, radios city police HQ.

State cops couldn't produce an informant, a warrant, or even an order for what they'd done. Told a story about a meeting with a captain and a guy they didn't know giving them these orders. Clear they were expecting some higher-up to arrive and get them out. Chief of police calls that captain, and he doesn't know anything about a meeting and sure didn't give any orders.

So, no cover for these guys.

Clear set up, but that wasn't doing them any good. Didn't even know who Robby was. Figured out he wasn't just another negro when the mayor came upset to the scene. Was a coalition with John Henry Party got him elected.

Police chief was mad even before the mayor came and yelled at him, because he knows it's a shit show and why the hell are there state cops on his turf. Any hope those boys might have had ended about six hours later with a district attorney bringing murder charges. Whole history of Wisconsin doubt there were total of four cops ever charged with murder before. And bet my farm not a one was for killing one of us.

Someone who knew Robby must have been in on it. He and Shawna had gone to ground for two weeks before he died, and no one knew where. On his dresser were two tickets for early morning train with connections down to Tuskegee, so that's the only night he was there.

Long after, Milwaukee PD found a man in some woods with the bullet from Shawna's gun in his head. Was a man Robby was once tight with and from what cops could find out was Shawna shot him. Eventually came to light was another guy sold out Robby. That one got his, too.

47

Even a plague of a year can have a happy time.

Having people over for no particular reason but having them over. What we told them, even though there was a particular reason. A small pig pickin', only Erlissa and Sally, Mrs. and Mr. Terry, momma, and the neighbors – Tanner and Simmons families, and January Concho, makes it around 40 but probably more because there's always girlfriends, boyfriends, and children.

All the work is for me and none for the Professor.

"I'll make the ice tea, if you want," she said.

"All by yourself you'll heat the water, put the tea in, set it to cool, and add the sugar and lemon? You'd do that, all by yourself?"

"Now you explain it, I see how those jars could get awfully heavy. You better take care of it."

Knew that's how it was gonna work out as soon as she offered. Honest, with her cooking skill, she'd likely messed it up anyway.

Day before the party, Mee Maw Tanner has her rocking chair set up by where I'm gonna do the roasting and lets me know when the coals are ready, and I should put on the pigs – two on account I eat a lot. Quite clear she's in charge and everyone else is labor. First, she lets me know what's wrong with the pigs but says it'll have to do. Succession of Gram Simmons' grandkids do the turning and she tells them they're doing it too slow and too fast. She catches one making a face at her and that's good for an hour of how there's no respect anymore. I baste as it roasts, which Mee Maw says is wrong and there's plenty that agree on it. Do a South Carolina mustard-vinegar sauce which is no good she tells me along with secret ingredients I have to add – including tobacco *and* cigarette ash. I take it back in the house, come out a few minutes later telling her she was right even though it's the same sauce, she tastes and tells me she told me so. Mee Maw wasn't against everything I did. Made Alabama white sauce she said was passable and shoulda been on the pigs instead.

Mee Maw's main responsibility was to say when the pigs were cooked, which meant serving her little pieces from wherever on the animals she directed us. She knew how to play an audience. Kept everyone hungry and guessing for I'd guess about 15 minutes which got everyone laughing and a big shout when she gave the OK.

After everyone had their first helpings Jet stood up on a bench.

"Can I have your attention," she said as command not question. "I would like to make an announcement..."

"She's pregnant," Gram Simmons said loud enough. "Known about two weeks."

Mee Maw nodded agreement.

Nonplussed. Jet taught me that one and it's exactly how she looked. Total confusion as we hadn't told anyone and not sure what to do now. I knew exactly what to do, fell on the ground from laughing so hard. When I caught my breath, I saw Jet standing over me.

"So maybe I should have let you finish when you proposed to me," she said, which got me laughing all over again. Of course, a lot of laughing and shouting congratulations was going on everywhere and everyone had known me awhile so theydidn't pay much attention to the giant lying on the ground flopping like a fish and howling each time he thought of the look on his wife's face.

Momma, who was living with us now, came over.

"What is so funny?"

Tried to explain but kept talking over each other and giggling. Momma smiled and didn't seem to mind.

"Well, I'm so happy about the baby but I wish you'd told me about it sooner."

We'd told her two days previous. Had a nice, long talk about she didn't remember. Why she was living with us now. Hadn't really noticed her memory slipping because it got worse little at a time until a lot worse all at once. Hard to see and live with and would've been more so without neighbors. Even the little ones were always looking out for her. Mee Maw, who liked telling the same story a few times – "improving" it as she did, spent hours with momma every day. Some days worse than others, like today.

Still loved music and dancing, though, and both were going on.

January on squashbox accordion, Bessie Ann Tanner guitar, and Gram Simmons' current boyfriend and his brother both sawing away at fiddles. Me and Jet brought momma with us to and we all danced like the happy fools we were.

Spun and shimmied and everything else then took a breather. Sat down at a table and had ice tea with Mrs. and Mr. Terry.

They fit each other almost perfect. Mrs. Terry was Mrs. Terry to everyone but Mr. Terry was Phillip. A professor, like Mrs. Terry, had a relaxed way of being which balanced out her intensity. Smart man who tended toward quiet. In large gatherings he wouldn't say much but when he did it was funniest of anyone. Always good company. We're planning on asking them to be godparents.

"It's wonderful about being pregnant but I do wish they'd told me sooner," said momma, sitting next to Phillip. Eye contact made around the table by everyone but momma and I almost cry. Used to be one of smartest I know and way she was crushed my heart.

"The band really is something," said Mrs. Terry, knowing to change topic. "Do they play together often? We are planning a grand event for next 4ᵗʰ of July and I wonder if they would be willing to perform?"

"Well..." Jet started but momma talked right over her.

"You know my brother Roscoe has a band," she said. "They are called Catfish Brown and the Skinners." She paused and laughed at the name, as she did every time she said it. "My Lord, what a name." She looked around the table and we all did our best to smile like we hadn't heard it before, but it didn't seem to be coming easy for Philip. "They have even made a record. Imagine, my brother on a phonograph recording. Will wonders never cease? There are two songs on it. On one side is a song called Rabbit Foot Blues. That is so perfect for my brother. He has always gotten away with so much that he must have a rabbit foot in every pocket."

Again, she looked around the table and we all did our best to smile like we hadn't heard it before, except Philip with a stern, unhappy look now.

"And the other song is... the other song is ..."

"Papa Don't Tear Your Pants," I said as gentle as I could. "That's the other song on Roscoe's record."

Today was one of momma's really bad days and she started over

"You know my brother Roscoe has a band," she said. "They are called Catfish Brown and the Skinners." Paused and laughed. "My Lord, what a name. They have even made a record. Imagine, my brother on a phonograph recording. Will wonders never cease? There are two songs on it. On one side is a song called Rabbit Foot Blues. That is so perfect for my brother. He has always gotten away..."

Too much for Phillip.

"With so much that he must have a rabbit foot in every pocket," he said. "We know, we know."

Then stood up, looked all around and all agitated, and walked off toward where cars were parked.

Mrs. Terry upset as I ever saw her.

"I'm so, so sorry," she said. "I've no idea what's come over him."

Told her it was fine and not to worry. Momma was hard on your patience and know what Philip had said I'd wanted to plenty of times.

Mrs. Terry got up and started after her husband.

"Can we come visit tomorrow?" Jet shouted after her. "There is something we would like to ask."

"How about Monday?" Mrs. Terry shouted back. "Come by the office for lunch. I'm sure Philip will have calmed down by then."

A few months later, realized couldn't take care of momma anymore and got her into a hospital. She passed about a year later. Spent her last months mostly asking where daddy was.

48

Being horrified matters. Being able to feel the kind of upset that's never forgotten, that's difference between human and not.

Found out when January Concho told me a story. Probably only time he ever told it.

"In the war, in the trenches, are things that never make it into the history books, because no one – even us who were there – wants to know. Rats grown big as dogs from eating like kings on bodies of dead men. Protein, lots and lots of it. Keep a pistol with you when you sleep because the rats got so bold they'd go after anything wasn't moving a lot. Some of them you had to get them with two shots before they be put down. Two shots out of a .45.

"Mud, though, mud scared me most. More than flamethrowers, mustard gas, or being blown up. Seen guys take a wrong step into a hole and be gone before we could even try to grab at them. Reach in as far as you can and find nothing. It'd bury whole squads with a wall collapsing because of artillery or there'd been too much rain. Go along and where there should more trench there'd be dirt with hands and arms sticking up, guys trying to claw, hands feeling the last air they'd ever know.

"Rain made mud worse and everything else, too. Would wash away dirt, bringing out things no one should see, things no one should have had happen. All the time the war was washing away something, the thing that should be saying no, should make you run away from it all because that's only rational response. I didn't even notice because it was happening to all of us, most of us. Shit we'd laugh at. One of their guys dead, just past the wire, grabbed his crotch because getting his dick and his balls shot off is what killed him. We all had jokes about him. Finally, body got blown up by artillery and we spent days talking about what a shame it was he was gone. Guys hang up a jacket or gear on an arm or leg or who knows, sticking out of a trench wall. Get used to anything.

"Everyone wants a souvenir, right? Guys got real particular, too. Want a Luger, a flag, medals, or one of those helmets with a spike on it. One guy wanted a machine gun. Getting it's not the problem. Took a long time of talking to make him see they wouldn't let him take it home. So, nobody took notice when I started bringing in skulls. Don't think I even noticed. Not really. Skulls were easiest thing to get. Always around. Some with still with faces on them, some clean as old Yorick. At least I was getting clean ones. Made a place for them in the dugout we'd sleep in.

"One day I'm talking with a buddy and start in on about how I never looked at the teeth, how they gotta have gold in them and I get out my bayonet and start over to the skulls. My buddy nodded, like it made sense. Another guy, though, he started talking to me. 'Sarge,' he said, 'You certain you need to do that? This is definitely something to be sure about before you do it. Get a moment for yourself and give some thinking on it just to be certain. Because once it's done, I think you're on a road that'll be really hard to get off.' Says all of it soft and quiet, like trying to settle a horse. Worked. I sat back down and went to cleaning my rifle. Did bring a skull home. Still have it. It's got all its teeth."

That story. Think about it now and then, because a world of trouble for the world, and for me, if I ever get up to where was.

Now, the night after our party, an October night with a big Hunter's Moon, all gold and dark red, hanging near the top of the sky. Me and Jet walking across a farm field on the far side of the city from our place. We're here because of a call from Erlissa telling me to get there and hanging up before I could ask why. Out in the middle of the field, where there's no reason for it to be, there's a car. Mr. Terry's car. Get close to the driver's side and hard to make out what's inside because there's blood and bone and brains all over the window.

Jet ran around to the other side and lets out a cry sounding deeper, older than truth. A keening that hurts to hear, hurts in every chamber of my heart.

It's Mrs. Terry in the passenger seat, head fallen back in an impossible way because of the great, long cut across her throat. The knife is lying between her and Mr. Terry on top of an envelope holding a letter explaining everything and explaining nothing.

When Mrs. Terry became mayor, she gave up her job at the bank, and they hired Mr. Terry, respected professor of business, to say yes or no to every loan. Too smart a man, unfortunately. Saw chances and opportunities no one might else would have. One was how to get a payoff from people wanting loans and mortgages who shouldn't be getting them. At first it was just ones on the edge of maybe, but over time that edge got big enough to fit anyone who could pay. Also figured out a way to get a cut on the bank side. Don't know where the money went. Letter he left behind said everything but that. Bank was all hollowed out. Said he killed Mrs. Terry to spare her the shame.

Spare her the shame.

Horrified. No other word to put on it.

ALL THE TOWN – WHITE and black – and more showed for the funeral. Pennington and John Henry Party folks from all over the nation, both Alabama senators, Gov. Griggs, Bishop Tooney. They had to sit in back because we made sure family, locals, and Slappy Jackson and crew got up front. Many, many, many wound up waiting outside.

Not Rev. Williams this time. Got a famous preacher, one had known Mrs. Terry since she was an accountant, and he wasn't famous. Did alright. Could see he was hurting, too, and that's what matters.

I was the pallbearer. Carrying the casket in my arms, Jet walking at my side.

Been a long time since I thought of Mrs. Terry as small or little. Always seemed bigger than me. Wouldn't put up with nonsense from me any more than she would anyone else. Now, all of a sudden, she was in this small box. How could she fit in there? It didn't make sense for all of her to be in this tiny thing.

There are loved ones in the glory
Whose dear forms you often miss.
When you close your earthly story,
Will you join them in their bliss?

Outside the people lined all the streets out to the cemetery. The hymn spread like a ripple, loud and sad.

I was standing by my window,
On one cold and cloudy day
When I saw that hearse come rolling
For to carry my mother away

How do you do so much, change the world so much, and this is your end? Not right. Not how a great life ends. A pathetic man doing what he did, cutting her throat at night in a nowhere field, because of his very own shame? No, it wasn't right. Her death should have been something like leading a battle charge or at home, with ones who loved her all around, years and years from now. Years and years and years.

I said to that undertaker
Undertaker please drive slow
For this lady you are carrying
Lord, I hate to see here go

Cradled that box as gentle as my broken heart. She didn't weigh a thing, not to me. So, light I almost didn't believe anyone could be in it. Easy to believe because it still didn't seem real she was gone. I was thinking well of course she isn't in there because we're going to have lunch with her like we arranged at the party. Then remember we didn't get to ask her to be godmother. Let her know how much she mattered. Then started worrying she didn't know that, know we loved her and how much.

Then thinking not asking her to be godmother at least meant we didn't ask Mr. Terry to be godfather. Makes me ill to think we were going to. Makes me ill knowing I liked him. A horrible stain on so many memories with Mrs.

Terry, but most that last one. Must've known already what he was going to do. Want to think I saw something he did telling me how evil he was. Go back over all the times we were together, looking for any sign. Can't stop doing it. It's like her death is problem and if I solve it, she'll come back, what happened won't have happened. Grief is the price we pay for love. This hurts so much I can forget what I'm supposed to be doing while doing it. That's how it's supposed to be. Some comfort in that. Not enough.

Addition to asking her to be godmother had something special to tell her. How if the baby's a girl the name will be Ida Beth, which was Mrs. Terry's names. Her not knowing is a weight on my heart.

At the cemetery, got on my knees next to the grave and held the casket tight to me. Might be kneeling there still but Jet tapped at me, saying, "It's time."

Slipped it in to the hole gently as I could but not gentle enough to bring her back.

> *Will the circle be unbroken*
> *By and by, by and by?*
> *Is a better home a waiting*
> *In the sky, in the sky?*

49

Trouble never takes time off, especially when things are already wrong.

Middle of the night after the funeral the phone rings and Jett get it.

"Hey."

Long pause.

"I wish you were making this up, but nobody would make this up," she said, hands me the phone. "Erlissa has some news for you."

"Not gonna believe this one, Mo," my cousin said.

Up in Chicago some of the rifle boys from a drum and bugle corps got real rifles, just like Robby Bex had warned. They'd hit a National Guard armory to get more guns. To arm the people, they said. So, we could live separate and protect ourselves, they said. Doing it in honor of Mrs. Terry, they said.

Four dead – three soldiers and one of the rifle boys. Cops had the place surrounded and both sides waiting on what does John Henry think.

John Henry thinks those boys are idiots.

"Pennington got anything to do with this?" I asked.

"How am I supposed to know? Heard a rumor about him giving out guns but seemed too stupid to even ask him about. Do know he's been talking about all this separation shit for a long time."

At least part my fault then. I know what I'd said but hadn't thought how folks might have heard it.

"Take me some time but I'm on my way."

"Nah," said Erlissa. "They got a phone number into the armory for you to call."

"I'll call them," I said. "In case those fools don't do what I tell them need you to you let whoever's in charge of the cops up there know

I am OK with anything they might have to do."

"Anything?"

"Yep," I said. "When this is over let's get the word out, I want Pennington gone."

"Might not be that easy," she said, and was right.

I chose not to get involved so John Henry Party wasn't John Henry's party. It was what it should be – politics, alliances, and all the other things we needed our political party to be. Not like people took me for granted, only that they took me at my word about not being a leader. Still, enough listened to me to cause Pennington trouble but even a lot of them were like, "Where you been, Jack?" Seems once you step off a pedestal you can't step back on.

50

Next spring and it's a pretty day. First day felt that way since I don't know when and the phone rings.

"Mo, got some people wanting to see you," said January Concho, sounding nervous.

"Everything OK?"

"I think so, yeah, but there's two guys here and they're really scared and it's getting at me. Tried putting them off, have 'em go talk to Erlissa but one of them started crying when I did. Say they've got something only for you to see and you have to see."

"Send 'em."

Came in a beaten old pickup truck, tarp covering the back, D.C., plates on the front. Guys got out were past 60, one's hair all silver and the other's is all gone. Both wearing faded, green coveralls. Something about that got me to smile. Suggested they might have been using a special power of their own. That power, turning invisible, it's one we all have – except me, funny enough. All we need is coveralls or a housekeeper's dress, and add in a mop, bucket, broom, any of that, and no one sees us. Sounds better than it is. Doesn't work all of the time and even when it does it's not good for much, mostly. Now and then, though, it'll come through for you. Like if you've spent decades cleaning FBI offices.

Under that tarp was boxes and boxes of files they'd put into a big trash bin and rolled right out of the Washington headquarters, wishing a goodnight to each and every guard on duty because that's what they always did. Drove all night like hiding from the devil. Said they didn't think they could be safe until they got to me and right about that. Those files were J. Edgar's own.

Blow, winds, and crack your cheeks! rage! blow!

The toad was a subtle motherfucker, no doubt. Had an eye for the bank shot where one pool ball hits another in a direction that looks all wrong until it hits another, which hits another, and goes on until finally gets the down the ball he wants down.

First angle was setting up Tuskegee to get overrun with people. Wasn't just word of mouth claiming Tuskegee was a promised land. There were people around the country saying they're job recruiters, paying for railroad and bus tickets, and promising a job when you arrive. Even giving a little traveling cash for getting something to eat on the way. That news likely went nationwide in minutes and people who never met one of these recruiters were bumming down to Alabama.

That's a big operation, though, and it needs big money to do, money that doesn't come with a paper trail on it.

There's the second angle.

Toad got drug money to pay for it all. Heroin was another thing went nationwide when all this began. See there's a civil war going on in China and guy we're backing needs weapons, doesn't have much cash but opium? It's growing in the fields. Hoover cuts a deal with the War Department which was why the Chinese are getting machine guns before our Army does. This angle was even better than even J. Edgar could've guessed. Making enough off the drugs that he was turning a profit.

Let the FBI go really big. Had money to buy snitches, for blackmail to get more snitches, to get cops to look away or tip them for helping out, for letter writers, for whispers, for wrecking our bank. Lot of the money went into Tuskegee, but not much came out. Charged for dope in other cities but in Tuskegee? They'd give it away.

Paid for all the killing, too. Hoover didn't want his boys in on it unless there was no choice else. Most was done by local cops, the rest by The Mob and others, including Bucky Pilcher. Files showed he didn't kill Haley, that was some guys out of Philly. If there's honor among thieves, it's weird. Memphis Mafia stayed out of Alabama just like Pilcher said they would.

They murdered Robby alright. We weren't only ones saw him as the future. Fuckers saw it too. Robby was the leader, not me. He had the smarts, people who'd never, ever, ever listen to one of us listened to him. I could break things, but Robby could change them, and the bastards assassinated him because of it. More afraid of Robby than me when he was alive but now, he's gone.

Before I made a move the news and people went wild.

Not just us, either.

We had an advantage here. We didn't even know who was doing this all, but we all knew it was being done. When the news got out, we were angry, not surprised. Every one of us knows how the world works because we see it every day. Pay attention to what they do, not what they said. Lived by that for centuries, long enough it's in our blood. People who talk nice to you? They're the ones to worry about because you know right where you stand with the ones that spit on you.

So, no illusions for us, but white folks? That's all their world was. Talk about the nation being great, fair, and just. Where anyone can grow up to be president, everyone is free, and all are equal in the eye of the law. Such complete bullshit I can't even imagine how people fix their face to say it, but they didn't just say it, they have whole damn parades screaming it. Hell, they believe it so much our government goes around lecturing other nations about how terrible they are. Telling them to stop being evil and get righteous like us. Freedom is the way. Liberty. Christ help a politician won't say we're the greatest ever was or will be. Even his own family wouldn't give him a vote.

What is it they have between their eyes and the truth, I don't know. Whatever it is, Hoover managed to get past it. They saw how the game is really played and did not like it. Blew up those illusions, for a while. So bad even the ones who wanted all blacks in hell said, "Whatever they do, I don't blame them at all." Likely lost some of those when I dropped Washington's monument on to Jefferson's.

I'd be surprised we lost them all, though. See Hoover kept on being Hoover after the story broke. And why not? Nothing left for him to lose.

Day the news hit FDR had attorney general and a whole platoon of U.S. Marshalls to the White House and sent them off to arrest the toad. Got to the Justice Department building, the place with the attorney general's own office in it, but it was locked down and gunned up.

Hoover a subtle motherfucker, no doubt. So much so he forgot most people aren't. Most expect things to look a certain way, to follow the correct forms, and behaviors. Like having a trial before a hanging, even if the verdict is decided. That lets them believe in how wonderful our way of life is. Toad didn't do any of that. He disappointed people. Now the righteous indignation of a single disappointed white person is a powerful thing and he'd disappointed them by the millions. They were way past wanting to see the manager, the supervisor, or even the owner. Wanted to see heads rolling. Wanted their illusions back.

51

"I AM GOING!"

"You can't!"

Jet was sitting at the kitchen table cleaning her Colt, next to her the suitcase she'd packed.

"I have to go," she said. "They killed Mrs. Terry. I'll get Mace Tanner to give me his Tommy gun."

Her eyes wild from wanting to go with me to Washington all while knowing she shouldn't.

"What are you going to do there?"

"Kill me some motherfuckers."

"What about the shooting and bombs? What'll you do about that?"

"I'll hide and sneak. I can take care of myself."

So fierce she thought she could walk through it like I could.

"And what if they got something new for using against me, a gas or a new kind of bomb?"

"I'll deal with it!"

I didn't say anything to that. No point. She was having this argument with herself, not me. Her belly was huge with a baby right about come out. All the mother feelings come with pregnancy had hit her hard and unexpected. Not the nurturing type, our Jet. Until now. She'd gone from being a tiger always ready to fight to being a momma tiger who'd do anything for the baby she's carrying. At the same time Mrs. Terry had been the only mother Jet ever had.

She found out who was behind the murder and wanted them all dead.

Momma tiger won out. She started crying and I went over and held her.

"They killed her," she whispered through tears. "She was so good, and they killed her."

"I know, baby. I know. John Henry gonna make sure they pay."

Heard Erlissa's truck pull up, she'd come to take me to an airport where a plane was waiting for me. Then two truck doors slamming, then our back door did and...

"Tell her she can't go," Sally yelled. "It's too dangerous and you won't let her."

Came in first, her eyes red for tears, behind her Erlissa wearing a coverall and carrying her sawed-off. I raised an eyebrow at her and she raised one back.

"Mo, Jet, talk her to sense," said Sally. "There's going to be a war in Washington. Not her job to be there."

Learned decades ago, there's no talking Erlissa into or out of anything and not starting now. This was about saying something to Sally, though. Wasn't my place to be doing that either.

"Sally, she has to go," said Jet, walking over and putting an arm around her. "She has to go just like I have to go, but I cannot so she is going for both of us. We fight. It is what you do, what I do, what Erlissa does. We all do it in our own way. This is her way today. We are going to be scared about her, you, and me. That is what our fight is for now and you stay with me so we can go through it together because I am more frightened by this baby's arrival than what will happen in Washington. Besides, Erlissa will have some pretty big protection with her."

Sally looks at me but not what Jet was talking about. She hands her pistol to Erlissa.

"Mr. Colt has got a taste for blood but that does not mean you have to give him any," she said. "Bring him back with some stories to tell."

Jet looks me in the eyes for a long bit of time.

"Go. Best you are not here when the baby comes. You are not strong enough."

52

I'M FULL SIZE NOW, 10 feet tall and skin darker than black. A giant made of midnight, one song said.

Just like I figured, they didn't want me in D.C. Had the entire military out to get in my way. Army wanted to keep me out, but it couldn't get in the city either. Crowds, a lot of us and a lot of whites, too, were blocking every street in. People were coming to the city from all over and did not stop. No one organized it. Nobody told them. So many came the White House and Capital got surrounded.

Man in charge of the troops, name of MacArthur, didn't seem to care. Wanted to have tanks run people over, right until his number two guy, called Eisenhower, warned he wasn't sure soldiers would go for it. General might've given the order anyway, but then he got word Mrs. Roosevelt herself was out front of one crowd and talking nice to the boys in the tanks. Knew he was licked then.

Mrs. Roosevelt's super power was giving a damn. She took a deep interest in whoever she talked to, especially if they didn't come from money like she did. And she knew everyone. She'd ask one of those tankers where he was from and even if it was Nowhere, North Dakota, she'd know it. Would turn out she'd been talking to her third cousin twice removed who had a best friend said the cooterberry pie at Madge's Café in Nowhere was to die for. Soldier could be meanest man ever and he'd wind up promising to have his mom send a pie and the recipe, too. Mom would do it and Mrs. Roosevelt would reply with a long, hand-written note talking about what a sweet boy soldier was and how she got him to promise to dress warm in the winter time. Second time we ever met she did basically the same to me by asking after the principal at the school momma used to teach at.

First time we met was that day. Erlissa and I are standing on a hill, looking at all that army which I'm thinking I was going to have to go through it when a car pulled up and she got out.

Erlissa, scattergun on her shoulder and Colt in a holster, puts them both on the ground and walks over with her hand out. Looks a little starstruck. Any other day I might have been too.

"Mrs. Roosevelt, I'm Erlissa Davis. It's an honor to meet you."

"And the same with you Miss Davis. I'm very impressed with all you've done at John Henry Party. Executive directors do all the work for none of the credit. It's quite a feat keeping a party together when everyone is clawing at each other. If I thought it possible, I would hire you for the Democrats."

Know my cousin well enough to know head would be spinning from Mrs. Roosevelt knowing her name, the compliment too? But she's a pro and she'll savor it another day, work now.

"Mrs. Roosevelt, I'd like to introduce you to my cousin Moses Crawford."

I nod, put out my hand, and we shake.

"Mr. Henry," she said, "I have wanted to meet you for some time and truly wish it were happening under other circumstances."

Nothing to say to that so give a nod in return.

"I know this nation has done terrible, terrible things to black people. I know what Mr. Hoover and his men did is only the most recent of those. My husband has ordered the military not to attempt to prevent you from entering the city. No one will raise a hand to stop you from bringing the Justice Department building down with Mr. Hoover and his men inside it. Certainly, no one could blame you, if you did. Having said that, the president would like to ask you to let the government to capture these people."

"Pretty nervy."

"Yes. That's how you get to be president."

All the time with Jet got me a lot better at the politics and right off knew why he was asking. He wanted a makeup call. Wanted to show government could take care of things. Build that illusion back up.

Gave it a thought. Remembered Mrs. Terry, not her killing but what she'd done and taught me. Wanted revenge so much I could almost feel it in my hands. But then occurred to me my revenge wasn't only way for it. Came up with Mrs. Terry's way.

"Do it on one condition. Whatever replaces the FBI, James Gunner is in charge and gets a free hand in putting it together."

Mrs. Roosevelt smiled and then she laughed. Loud.

"Mr. Henry…"

"Call me Mo. Mo Crawford."

"Mr. Crawford … Mo … you have just made Franklin's day worse in the best possible way. I think Professor Gunner is an excellent choice."

Which is why I walked into D.C. alongside Erlissa, First Lady, and MacArthur, and a big bunch of army following. Went to where Hoover and his were at. Soon-to-be-former attorney general got on a loudspeaker and told them to surrender. One guy tried. Jumped out a window and started running but someone in the building shot him down. At that the army boys opened fire. At first it was FBI tommy guns against army machine guns which would've been a losing fight, but the toad's boys had some of those and a few grenades. What they didn't have was tanks. They blew some holes in the building, one being in the front door, then drove through, followed by lot of very angry soldiers. When everything got done the toad was found dead in the basement. Him and two others killed themselves on poison. Pissed me off.

That was Hoover's end but not the end of what happened. Mrs. Terry's curse had only begun.

53

Never realized what John Henry Party, meant to the people. Not a religion but more than politics. Maybe it's our illusion, what we need to believe in, saying we're more, bigger, greater. And the ones who betrayed it? Well, we don't bother with disappointment. Go right to full on rage.

Names in the files of snitches and worse all came out and so did the long knives. That's what The Four Days was: Mrs. Terry's curse being worked. Names belonged to cops, reporters, politicians, clergy, gangsters, and plain nobodies. People ran for their lives and lucky ones got beatings put them in hospitals. The mob boys did all their own killing, destroyed their own gangs – for a while. Snappy Jackson's name wasn't in there and for some reason I was glad for it. Most places cops were smart enough to not get in the way, not even protecting their own. Most places. Only heard of one pitched battle.

End of the first day and no signs of slowing. Calls, telegraphs, and visits from people wanting on me for doing or saying something might get it to stop. Even Mrs. Roosevelt called. Told her I had to talk it over with "my people."

Started to talk with Jet but she didn't have a word to say. Shrugged and set to cleaning her .45.

Maybe I should have been the better man. Maybe I should have called for peace, said violence wouldn't solve anything, talked of brotherhood and our common suffering. Maybe. Why do we always have to be the moral ones? Used to be said we needed to be sterling examples of decency to show we deserved to be treated like people.

Fuck that shit.

Doesn't equality mean we get to be assholes, too?

Didn't know the answer but I figured Rev. Williams would.

He was down at his same storefront church. Wondered if Jesus turned the man's blood to wine as I'd never seen anyone so drunk. Up and roaring, only audience a few folks passed out on folding chairs and the floor. Now and then push one, try to wake them up. None did and he didn't care. Went on about the room, damning them and himself for sinners racing to hell. No hypocrite here.

Saw me, paused long enough to ask me about what was happening. Went back to his shouting but a new topic.

"Son of a PERVERSE AND REBELLIOUS woman! DOOMED to eat your own dung and DRINK YOUR OWN URINE! Hear this, BREAKER OF THE COMMANDMENTS, for she trusted in you! MRS. TERRY TRUSTED IN YOU AND YOU FAILED! Remember her words. REMEMBER HER WORDS! Remember. She lay HER CURSE on you, THE ABOMINATION! You and all WHO SPILLED HER BLOOD must be put down AS FOUL SWINE MUST BE! CHRIST OUR LORD suffered on the cross for all mankind BUT NOT FOR YOU!"

Him, Jet, Erlissa. Only ones willing to rip into me. Difference between them is from the reverend I never took it personal. Sat there listening at least a half hour more, put five dollars in a collection box, walked on home.

Three days later all the trouble ended and with no word from me. Was it a right thing to do? Bloody times make bloody people. Know this, haven't had two thoughts on it since then.

54

DIFFERENT WORLD NOW, NOT only here in the states.

Last week news was about Italy invading Ethiopia. Should have been easy. Italians have a modern military and Ethiopians don't. To make it even easier the brave sons of Caesar had two armies, total 300,000 troops, going in from opposite sides of the country. Didn't get more than a little across the border when both ran into sandstorms, usual thing that happens there. Nothing usual about these ones. Blow so hard they tore off skin and shredded tires. Soldiers tried running away. Didn't help. Storms chased them. Say there aren't more than a thousand still alive.

Reports say there's a woman making it happen. Press call her the Desert Demon, Priestess of the Sands.

Whoever she is, she's not stopping. Once Italians out of the way the storms cut north, across Sudan, a place Britain said was theirs. The lady doesn't agree. Got all that sand making moves like Fred Astaire, tear apart anything is anything to do with the Brits and leaving folks who were originally there alone. Destroyed all of a building except where Sudanese people were. Next day British king is on the radio saying why'nt y'all take it and a bunch more back. That got folks in India and all around the world saying, "Yeah, about that," and not quietly either.

Now those storms moving right at Libya, another place claimed by Italians. Lot of boats leaving there at speed so they may be rethinking. There's a big international meeting going on right now with a bunch of countries racing to get out of the colony business. A lot but not all. There's always stupid around.

55

DIFFERENT WORLD NOW, BUT different enough?

Not like the day of jubilation came and now we all love each other. Laws changing don't change people. Still a lot of fights to have so we can get treated like people. There's no place for John Henry in those fights. He's too big, too powerful to do anything for real life.

What is he to poverty? Go in, knock down every building in a slum, even build new ones, doesn't change what made them happen in the first place. What's he to hunger, addiction, cancer, getting spit on, or never even being given a chance? Not a damn thing.

Maybe he can stop a war. He could damn well start one. No good to it.

John Henry's a hammer, sledge hammer, maybe biggest one ever. World needs scalpels and people can use them, needs lawyers, electricians, truck drivers, painters, singers, teachers, bakers, more than it needs John Henry. If it needs a hammer at all then it's got to be smaller, one that can knock open a door and not destroy everything comes with it.

Where's that leave us?

People still calling me and him a hero. Don't get it. So many risked and still risk so much, not me. No line for my life to be on. No one can stop me, so what's the overcome? Easy being brave when nothing can hurt you. Know what I did mattered, maybe made a lot of stuff possible. But wasn't me got it from possible to real. That's on everyone else. Ones speaking out, organizing, demanding. Ones facing the bullshit every day. I did but they're who's doing.

Tuskegee's become a Mecca and a damn tattered one. The people believe this is where change happened. That belief from a frayed and righteous people, makes the broken streets seem sacred, the whores holy, and the conmen's swindles blessed. No other reason why hundreds of thousands of visitors come – many again and again and again – to a place could just as well be anywhere. They see light and significance here, not understanding they brought it. Watts, Roxbury, Harlem, South Side, and thousands more places are all as important. They're where people are still getting hurt doing the hard work of making the world right.

Acknowledgements

STEVEN LOCKE, WHO LET me listen; Lisa Port White, who is a great writing group; Scott Klebe, who knew where it should start; my daughter Lizi, who really wanted to read it; Michon Neel, who is a great sensitivity editor; Dave Hutchinson, who was cheerleader supreme; Mary Evans, who told me to shake the world; my classmates and the faculty and staff at Viable Paradise XXI, who inspired and convinced me.

Selected Bibliography

Allen, James: *Without Sanctuary: Lynching Photography in America*, 2000, Twin Palms Publishers, Santa Fe, NM

Baldwin, James: *The Fire Next Time*, 1963, Dial Press, NY

Butler, Octavia E.: *Wild Seed*, 1980, Doubleday Books, NY

Parable of The Sower, 1993, Four Walls Eight Windows, NY

Cable, George: *The Grandissimes*, 1880, Scribner, NY

Coates, Ta-Nehisi, *The Case for Reparations;* The Atlantic Magazine, June 2014

Between the World and Me, 2015, Spiegel & Grau, NY

Dray, Phillip: *At the Hands of Persons Unknown: The Lynching of Black America*, 2002, Random House, NY

Ellison, Ralph: *Invisible Man*, 1952, Random House, NY

Fanon, Frantz: *Black Skin, White Masks*, 1994, Grove Press, NY

Jones, James Howard: *Bad Blood: The Tuskegee Syphilis Experiment*, 1981, Free Press, NY

McWhirter, Cameron: *Red Summer: The Summer of 1919 and the Awakening of Black America*, 2011, Henry Holt & Co., NY

Norrell, Robert J.: *Reaping the Whirlwind: The Civil Rights Movement in Tuskegee*, 1998, University of North Carolina Press, Chapel Hill, NC

O'Reilly, Kenneth: *Racial Matters: The FBI's Secret File on Black America, 1960-1972*, 1989, Free Press, NY

Palmer, Robert: *Deep Blues: A Musical and Cultural History of the Mississippi Delta,*1982, Penguin Books, NY

Phillips, Patrick: *Blood at the Root: A Racial Cleansing in America*, 2016, W. W. Norton & Co., NY

Rosengarten, Theodore: *All God's Dangers: The Life of Nate Shaw*, 1975, Alfred A. Knopf, NY

Rudwick, Elliott M.: *Race Riot at East St. Louis, July 2, 1917*, 1972, Atheneum, NY

Slim, Iceberg: *Trick Baby*, 2011, Cash Money Content, NY

Tisserand, Michael: *George Herriman: A Life in Black and White;* 2016, Harper, NY

Tuttle, William M.: *Race Riot: Chicago in the Red Summer of 1919*, 1970, Atheneum, NY

Umoja, Akinyele Omowale: *We Will Shoot Back: Armed Resistance in the Mississippi Freedom Movement*, 2013, New York University Press, NY

Whitaker, Robert: *On the Laps of Gods: The Red Summer of 1919 and the Struggle for Justice that Remade a Nation*, 2008, Crown Publishing, NY

Wilkerson, Isabel: *The Warmth of Other Suns: The Epic Story of America's Great Migration* 2010, Random House, NY

Woodward, C. Vann: *The Strange Career of Jim Crow;* 1957, Oxford University Press, Oxford, UK

About the author

Constantine von Hoffman was born in Chicago, raised in Rhode Island, and currently lives in Boston with his wife Jennifer and four dogs. A journalist for 25 years, he has written for *CBSNews.com, The Boston Herald, NPR, Harvard Business Review, Inc., Sierra Magazine, Brandweek, The Boston Globe*, and others. Con is a graduate of the Viable Paradise writing workshop, and his poetry has been published in *Elysian Fields Quarterly*, and the collections *Line Drives: 100 Contemporary Baseball Poems* (2002, Southern Illinois University Press) and *Cubbie Blues* (State Street Publishing, 2009).

For more about Con and his writing go to www.curseyoukhan.com

All proceeds from this book are donated to the Equal Justice Initiative: www.EJI.org